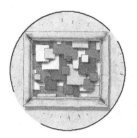

The RED BLAZER GIRLS

THE mistaken MasterPiece

Michael D. Beil

A Yearling Book

This is a work of fiction. Names, characters, places, and incidents either are the product of the author's imagination or are used fictitiously. Any resemblance to actual persons, living or dead, events, or locales is entirely coincidental.

Text copyright © 2011 by Michael D. Beil
Cover art and interior illustrations copyright © 2011 by Daniel Baxter

All rights reserved. Published in the United States by Yearling, an imprint of Random House Children's Books, a division of Random House, Inc., New York. Originally published in hardcover in the United States by Alfred A. Knopf, an imprint of Random House Children's Books, New York, in 2011.

Yearling and the jumping horse design are registered trademarks of Random House, Inc.

Visit us on the Web! randomhouse.com/kids

Educators and librarians, for a variety of teaching tools, visit us at randomhouse.com/teachers

The Library of Congress has cataloged the hardcover edition of this work as follows:
Beil, Michael D.
The Red Blazer Girls : the mistaken masterpiece \ by Michael D. Beil. — 1st ed.
    p. cm.
Summary: Sophie and her friends, who call themselves The Red Blazer Girls, embark on solving a case involving mistaken identities, switched paintings, and some priceless family heirlooms.
ISBN 978-0-375-86740-8 (trade) — ISBN 978-0-375-96740-5 (lib. bdg.) —
ISBN 978-0-375-89789-4 (ebook)
[1. Mystery and detective stories. 2. Puzzles—Fiction. 3. Art thefts—Fiction.
4. Mistaken identity—Fiction. 5. Catholic schools—Fiction. 6. Schools—Fiction.] I.
Title. II. Title: Mistaken masterpiece.
PZ7.B388234Ps5Rd 2011
[Fic]—dc22
2010030006

ISBN 978-0-375-86494-0 (pbk.)

Printed in the United States of America

10 9 8 7 6 5 4 3

First Yearling Edition 2012

Random House Children's Books supports the First Amendment and celebrates the right to read.

Don't worry, you aren't *mistaken*—
this is supposed to be this way.

For my students, past and present

Chapter 1

Trust me, I thought it was a non-contact sport, too

I glide through the water after a picture-perfect flip turn, the muscles in my arms and shoulders grateful for those two seconds of rest before my face bursts through the surface. With fifty meters to go and a comfortable lead, I could relax and cruise to the finish, but that's just not me. I'm not about to let a little discomfort get in the way of a personal best time in the 400 individual medley, so I come out of the turn and start the final lap with arms and legs churning. The last twenty meters feel like I'm swimming in oatmeal, and when I finally touch the wall, every molecule in my body is aching and I am struggling to get enough air in my lungs.

My swim coach, Michelle, is standing over me, smiling at the stopwatch in her hand. She bends down, holding it closer for me to see, but the chlorine in my eyes makes it hard for me to focus.

"Good?" I ask, squinting.

"Nope. *Grrr-eat.* You broke your own record by almost three seconds."

In the lane to my left, my teammate Olivia "Livvy" Klack touches the wall and lifts her perky, perfect nose to face Michelle.

"Nice job, Liv," I say, trying to be friendly. "Thought you were going to pass me in the backstroke." Of the four strokes in the 400 IM—butterfly, back, breast, and freestyle—the backstroke has always been my weakest, and it is Livvy's strongest.

Livvy doesn't even bother to look at me. She just kind of grunts and swims away, ducking under the lane markers to go talk to her friends, who are still finishing.

"What is with you two?" Michelle asks.

"Long story," I say.

And it is. For now, let me just say that while the Red Blazer Girls—that's me and my three best friends, Margaret Wrobel, Rebecca Chen, and Leigh Ann Jaimes—were busy solving the Mystery of the Vanishing Violin, we had a little run-in with Livvy and her friends. I know it sounds incredibly juvenile, but *she* started it. It's not my fault she picked a fight with four girls who are smart, stubborn, and not at all above a little revenge if the situation requires it. It did. So we did. And while she used to just ignore me, she now appears to be embracing an active hatred of me.

It's our last practice before our first meet, which is against a team from Westchester that has been together for years and is rumored to be really tough. We, on the other hand, have only been practicing at the pool at Asphalt Green, on the Upper East Side of Manhattan, for a month. When I was nine and ten, I was on another of Michelle's junior swim teams, but I took a year off from the sport to concentrate on school and the guitar. Funny thing, though. It turns out there *is* enough time in the day to swim, too, if you're willing to get up at five in the morning. Margaret is still amazed that I'm doing it; after all, I used to grumble and be grouchy all day whenever she decided we absolutely *needed* an early start on the mystery of the moment and called me at six o'clock. After a few weeks of getting up at five, six is a slice o' strudel.

Michelle gives the stragglers a minute to catch their breath and then turns us all loose for our final cooldown swim—800 meters, alternating between back- and breaststroke. She assigns the center lane to Livvy and me because we're usually fairly well matched, speedwise. The idea in sharing a lane is like driving a car— always stay to the right—which sounds simple, but nobody can backstroke in a straight line, so we're always running into each other.

When Michelle gives the signal, Livvy and I dive in from opposite ends of the pool. Even though I am definitely not slacking off, Livvy starts to creep up on me almost immediately. Each time we pass by each other, I get a whiff of pure intensity that overpowers the smell of the chlorine. I'll admit it—that all-out 400 took a lot out of me, and I am too tired to get into some weird grudge match with her in what is supposed to be a cooldown swim.

With two laps to go, she is still gaining on me, and Michelle shouts at me to hold her off over the last hundred meters. I groan to myself, but push hard off the wall before starting my breaststroke. When my face breaks through the surface, Livvy is right in front of me, backstroking like some kind of demented propeller-zombie.

"Livvy!" I shout, hoping to prevent a collision.

She veers right, arms still spinning madly, and the heel of her right hand karate-chops me right smack on the nose.

Direct hit. And instantly, the pool looks like a scene from *Jaws*—there is blood everywhere and Michelle is shouting at me to get out of the pool. Which I would be happy to do if only I could see something besides a gajillion stars. I feel someone's arms around me, dragging me to the side, where several more hands reach down and yank me out of the water.

Like most kids, I've taken a few direct hits to the noggin from soccer balls, but they were nothing compared to what is happening to my face as they lay me down on the pool deck and tilt my head back.

Michelle's first words: "Oh my God."

Not exactly encouraging.

"Sophie, we're going to have to take you to the emergency room. She really whacked you, and you probably need to be checked out for concussion. And . . . um . . . I think your nose is broken."

Not my nose! I *love* my nose. It's not perky like Livvy's; it's kind of a miniature version of my dad's classic French schnoz. Some people (small-nosed, small-minded people, most likely) might think it's too big. Personally, I prefer to think of it as having a little *character*.

I reach up to touch it. *Big* mistake.

"Owwwww!" I scream.

"Man, look at her *eyes*," says Carey Petrus, one of my teammates, who is leaning over me for a closer look.

"Wads wob wid by eyes?" I mumble. I know I'm not blind—my vision has come back enough for me to see the blood all over me and my swimsuit.

"Uh, nothing," Carey lies.

"Midchelle! Wads wob wid by eyes?" I shout. Yet another painful mistake.

"Nothing. Your eyes are fine. *Around* them is a different story. You're going to have a couple of good shiners for a few days." When Livvy, looking really sheepish, shows up with one of those blue ice packs, Michelle takes it from her and gently sets it on what's left of my nose.

"Ow, ow, ow."

"I know, I'm so sorry, honey, but you really need to do this. Try to hold it on your face for a few minutes, and then I'll get a taxi and take you to the hospital. We can call your parents from there."

I nod at her, wincing at the pain. "Okay, but huddy, 'cause I dink by face is gonna 'splode."

5

Michelle stands up and announces, "Okay, everybody, that's it for today. See you all tomorrow at five-fifteen. Don't be late!" Once a coach, always a coach, I guess. Even when your star is practically bleeding to death.

I try to sit up, but I'm dizzy and my head is wobbling around like one of those bobblehead dolls, and Michelle makes me lie back down.

"Whoa there, sport. You stay here with Carey. I'll get the taxi and come right back for you. Don't move."

I don't argue with her, because moving really hurts. I close my eyes for a few seconds and imagine that I'm curled up in my bed on a snowy Saturday morning with a favorite book, sipping hot chocolate and nibbling on Dad's freshly baked madeleines.

A very familiar voice cuts this little voyage to my happy place short.

"Sophie? Are you alive?"

I open my eyes, but all I can see is a vague shadow through the blue gel of the ice pack. "Mah-gid? Thad you?"

"Geez, you scared me to death, Sophie!" Margaret says. "I came by to see if you wanted to walk to school together since it's such a nice morning. Then I get here and see you stretched out, flat on the ground, with blood everywhere. What happened?"

"Libby."

"Libby? Who's Libby?"

"Dot Libby! Lib—by! Oww!"

"I think she's trying to say 'Livvy,'" Carey says. "They were, like, sharing a lane. Sophie's face sort of ran into Livvy's hand."

Margaret looks around me at all the blood and says with mock seriousness, "I always knew this feud with Livvy Klack would end in bloodshed."

I fight back the urge to laugh because my gut tells me that would really hurt right now.

When Michelle returns, the three of them help me to my feet and sort of half carry, half drag me out the door and into the waiting taxi. Michelle and Margaret talk to my parents on the way to the hospital, assuring them that I'll probably live.

Here's what I learn from my trip to the emergency room: if you're going to get your nose busted by your worst enemy, do it really early in the morning, because the place is basically deserted. With Michelle at my side, a nurse actually takes me directly into a treatment room; no waiting around for three hours while every other sick person in the city gets bumped ahead of me in line because they're sicker, or older, or younger, or, more likely (after all, this is New York I'm talking about), complaining louder than I am.

The doctor is much younger than I expect, and, well, let's just say she looks a little confused by the way I'm dressed at seven in the morning—I guess a clammy swimsuit and a bunch of bloodstained towels aren't part of the fashionable fall attire in the ER. The faces she makes as she pokes and prods aren't doing much for my confidence, either. Finally, she speaks.

"Yep. Broken nose. Did you run into the wall?"

"Another swimmer," Michelle says. "She gonna be okay?"

"Oh, she'll be fine—no sign of concussion or anything like that. It's a pretty good break, so you're going to have to be wrapped up for a few days, maybe a week."

A week with a bandage on my nose! Clearly, this is someone who either had the entire adolescent portion of her memory erased or skipped seventh grade completely. Why not just tattoo "Kick Me" on my forehead?

Just when I think it can't get any worse, my parents show up. When Mom sees me, her hand flies up to her mouth and she runs, crying, to hug me. "Sophie! I'm so sorry!" she sobs, like it's *her* fault I was practically decapitated by the Livvinator.

The doctor takes a stab at reassuring them that I'm not permanently damaged, but they both look so miserable that I figure it's time for me to take a look in the mirror to see why everybody is so wigged out.

Mystery solved. I am a *freak*. My hair, still wet, is so impossibly tangled that I'm afraid I'll have to just shave my head and start over. And that's the *good* part. Above the enormous bandage covering my nose, my eyes are circled by puffy purple and yellow rings.

"Ohhhh," I say, feeling sick to my stomach.

Mom hugs me again (gently!) and guarantees that

I'm going to be fine. "You're definitely staying home today, and maybe tomorrow, too. By then, the swelling should be gone at least. And the bruising will go away . . . in a few days. Now, let's get you home and into bed."

"Well, maybe a shower first," Dad says, squeezing my hand. "You still smell like the pool." He tries to straighten out my hair but quickly gives up. "And I'm afraid we will have to shave your head, too."

I give him a dirty look as Margaret, who is going to have to run to make it to school on time, promises to fill me in on everything that happens at St. Veronica's. And that's when it really sinks in: for the first time in my life, I am going to miss a day of school.

"Wait. I can't miss school."

But I can, and I do. And just like that, my seven-year perfect-attendance streak ends as I wave to Margaret, who bolts out the glass hospital doors.

My dad, who's the chef at a ritzy French restaurant, doesn't have to go into work until the afternoon, so Mom leaves me in his mostly capable hands. She objects at first, and is just about to call the music school and cancel all her lessons for the day, but I convince her that I'm fine. (Hey, I don't want to be responsible for a bunch of violinists wandering aimlessly around the city all day. After that whole Vanishing Violin thing, I'm *so* over the violin.)

On the taxi ride to our apartment building, Dad

promises to take good care of me—he'll fix me anything I want to eat. Now, under normal circumstances, that would be amazingly awesome. In fact, I have a whole list of his special treats that I keep handy for just such occasions. But there's a problem: I don't really feel like eating. My head feels like it is made of concrete, and even the thought of chewing makes me queasy. I just want to go back to bed.

When I get to my room, however, I make the mistake of checking my phone for messages. There's a new text from Margaret, sent right after she left me at the hospital. Like all of her texts and emails, it is properly punctuated and capitalized.

Sophie,
Call or text me after school's out.
And stop worrying about your nose. It will be as perfect
as ever.
I promise.
Margaret

And another, this one from Leigh Ann, sent at eleven last night.

big news ck ur voice mail

So I do, where I find three new messages—two from Raf, my not-quite-a-boyfriend-but-more-than-a-friend friend, even though I have told him that I never check my voice mail, and one from Leigh Ann. In one very excited breath, she says, "Sophieohmigoshyou'renotgonnabelievewhatIfoundoutIwasonmywaybackfromdanceclasstonightandtherewereallthesetrailersandsignsalloverthiplaceandguesswhatthey'refilmingthe*No-Reflections*movieintheparkcallmeassoonasyougetthiswehavetofigureeverythingoutbecauseIjusthavetomeetNateEtancallme."

Dad comes into my room just as I'm turning my phone off.

"Wait a minute. Is that a smile I see?"

I hold my thumb and index finger a mere millimeter apart. "It's Leigh Ann. She just left me a funny message. Oww. Smiling hurts."

"Into bed," Dad orders. When I'm safely under the covers, he asks, "Now tell me. What did your friend say to cause you so much pain?"

"They're filming a movie in the park tomorrow— you know that *No Reflections* book I've been babbling about for the past few weeks?"

"Ah, oui. Avec Monsieur Nathaniel Etan, n'est-ce pas?"

"How did *you* know that?" I say, a little too loudly for my own good. "Owwww."

"He was in the restaurant last night—"

"He *what*?" My head is spinning now. The combination of the morning's full-contact swimming workout and my dad's oh-so-casual mention that he was in the presence of *Nate Etan* less than twelve hours earlier is just too much for me. I mean, some of Nate Etan's molecules could be in the very air I'm breathing.

"This Monsieur Etan—he is someone you, how do you say, have a crash with?"

"It's a *crush,* which you have *on* someone, and, uh, *yeah*!" I shout, pointing to the bulletin board above my desk.

"Ah, oui," says Dad as he sees the sixty-three pictures of Nate Etan adorning it. "I'm sorry—I should have asked for an autograph for you."

"You *talked* to him?"

He shrugs apologetically. "He came in with a bunch of . . . big shots, I think you call them. Movie people. After dinner, they asked to talk to the chef. What can I do? *C'est moi.* I'm sorry, *mon petit chou-chou.* I didn't know. He seemed . . . very nice."

"Ohhhh," I groan. "Life is so unfair. I'm going to sleep. When I wake up, all this is going to be a bad dream. My nose didn't get smushed beyond recognition and my *father* definitely did *not* meet the most awesome guy in the galaxy."

"Or *forget* to ask him for an autograph for his beautiful but tragically disfigured daughter," adds my betrayer, who then bolts, laughing, from my room before I have a chance to hit him with a pillow.

Or something much, much heavier.

Chapter 2

Parents just don't understand.
(Hey, somebody ought to write a song)

I sleep away the rest of the morning and most of the afternoon, too. When I finally open my eyes and look at the clock, I am thoroughly confused, thinking it is three-thirty in the morning. And then I reach up to touch my face and it all comes back to me. The bandage is still there. It wasn't a dream.

Dragging myself to the bathroom, I check myself out in the mirror again. The swelling around my eyes has gone down quite a bit, but now the circles are darker. It's official: I am a raccoon.

I crawl back into my bed to pout some more about the general unfairness of life. A few moments later, Dad knocks on the door.

"I have to leave for the restaurant," he says, "but your friends are here to keep you company. They're helping themselves to some cookies in the kitchen—I wasn't sure if you were ready for visitors."

"They're going to see me sooner or later," I say. "Might as well get the abuse over with now."

"Oh, and this came for you." He sets a box on my bed.

"What is it?"

"It is a box."

"Thanks, Dad. Where did it come from?" There's no return address, just my name and apartment number.

"The lobby. The doorman—"

"No! I mean—oh, you know what I mean." I peel the tape off one end and open it. Inside, wrapped loosely in newspaper, is a shallow brass bowl, about a foot across and only a couple of inches deep. It definitely falls into the "used" category; it has its share of dings and dents and is badly in need of polishing. It's no thing of beauty.

"Huh," Dad says. "Let me see."

I dig through the newspaper again, looking for a card or a note, but find nothing. "I don't get it. Why would someone send me an old bowl?"

"This is maybe a good question for your friends. Do you need anything before I go?"

"Nope. All set. But, Dad?"

"Yes?"

"If Nate Etan comes in . . ."

"I know. Autograph. Picture."

"Riiiight."

Margaret, Becca, and Leigh Ann stick their heads into my room, and I can't help laughing at their different reactions as they see me in my damaged state.

Becca is her usual brutally honest self. "Holy crap, Soph. You look *terrible*."

"You should see the other girl," I say.

"Yeah, I hear Livvy's hand is really beat up," she says.

Leigh Ann, trying to be nice, lies to me, which I appreciate. "No, really, it's not that bad. The way Margaret described it, I was expecting worse. It *does* look like it hurts, though."

Margaret sees the glass as half full, or in this case, the nose as only half broken. "It looks a *lot* better than it did this morning. How does it feel?"

It? Not me, just my nose. Like it's a separate entity, with a life force of its own.

"Eh, *comme çi, comme ça*. Better. It kinda aches. And I really need to blow it, but I'm afraid to."

"Ye-ouch," Leigh Ann says, cringing at the thought.

"Oh, go on," Becca encourages. "No pain, no gain."

"What's the story with this bowl?" Margaret asks, holding it up and examining it.

"Oh, that," I say. "I was hoping you could tell me. It showed up here today in this box, with no card, no nothing."

Becca turns her nose up at it. "Dude, it's ugly. Looks like a used birdbath. Now come on, get your butt out of bed. We've got stuff to do."

"We do?"

"Didn't you get my message?" Leigh Ann asks. "We have to go over to the park. Nate Etan could be there right now."

"Well, you guys won't believe this, but my dad met him last night."

"What! Where?" Leigh Ann exclaims. "Did he get his autograph? A picture?"

"He came into the restaurant with a bunch of other people. And no, Dad just *talked* to him. He didn't know I liked him."

"Well, yeah, I mean, how would he?" Becca asks, looking around the room. "His pictures only completely cover one wall. Maybe when you run out of space in here and have to start sticking them up out in the hallway . . ."

"What did he say?" Leigh Ann asks. "What was he like?"

"I don't know," I admit. "Dad said he seemed nice."

"Nice? That's it?" Becca says. "Man, your dad really is kind of clueless, isn't he, Soph?"

"Tell me about it," I say.

Mom puts the kibosh on any thoughts I have of going with them to the park. I'm just about to pull on my favorite denim jacket when she strolls in the door carrying her violin and a couple of bags of groceries.

She almost cries—again—when she sees my face. "Oh, sweetie. How are you feeling? Are you in any pain? What can I get you?" Then she realizes I have my jacket on. "Sophie, you're not going out—not yet. You have to take it easy. You should be lying down."

"I just got up!" I protest, but Mom steers me to the couch, pulling my jacket off on the way.

"That's all right. It's probably too late, anyway," says Margaret. "By the time we get over there, it'll be dark and we wouldn't be able to see him."

"Who is this *him* you want to see?" Mom asks. "Raf?"

"Nope, her *other* boyfriend," Becca teases.

Mom raises an eyebrow at me. "Other boyfriend?"

"First of all, Raf is *not* my boyfriend. He's my . . . he's a . . . well, anyway, it's not Raf. Nate Etan is filming a movie in the park. And Leigh Ann is just as obsessed as I am. Maybe more."

"Well, at least that explains the crowd of girls," Mom says.

"What crowd of girls?" Leigh Ann asks nervously. "Oh no. We're too late."

"I walked through the park on my way home, and they were lined up by the boathouse. Hundreds of them."

"Well, it's not like you could expect it to stay a secret," Margaret says.

Leigh Ann sticks out her bottom lip. "A girl can *hope,* can't she?"

Indeed she can.

I'm having my breakfast, totally engrossed in reading the back of a box of Lucky Charms and enjoying every sickeningly sweet, marshmallowy bite, when my dad sits down across from me.

"Hey, Dad," I say, peeking around the cereal box. "Why are you up so early?"

He reaches over and pushes the box aside. Of course, he can't do it without a disdainful French grunt at its contents. He slides a large envelope across the table to me without a word.

"What's this?" I ask.

He shrugs as only a true Frenchman can. "Nothing big. You probably won't like it." He starts to pull it back.

I slap my hand down on the envelope, my mouth opening in disbelief. "You didn't."

Another shrug.

I peek inside the envelope. He did it. He really did it. "Ohmigosh. Dad. I *love* you." I pull out a glossy eight-by-ten photo of Nate Etan—and it's signed!

For Sophie—hope you're feeling better! XOXO, Nate Etan.

I jump up and hug my dad. "Thank you thank you thank you. You are the best. I'm sorry I ever doubted you."

"What's this all about?" Mom asks, walking in mid-hug.

"Your daughter has decided that I'm all right after all," Dad says. "And she hasn't even heard the good part yet."

"There's more?" I ask.

"*Oui*. Friday afternoon, you and your friends are going to spend the day with him."

My knees give out on me and I sit down right there on the kitchen floor. "Whachewtalkin'boutDad?"

He looks to Mom for a translation.

"Trust me, she's happy," Mom says.

"How?" I manage to ask.

"Apparently the young man spent his summers in France with his father, who is a diplomat of some kind. And my *poulet au vinaigre* reminds him of his childhood—he came back last night and ordered it again."

"And then you asked him for a picture?"

"In a way. First he made me an offer I couldn't refuse."

"That sounds ominous," Mom says. "What kind of offer?"

"He has to go on location to London for a week or two, and then he's coming back to New York for a few days of filming. He wants me to be his personal chef while he's in town. He offered me a ridiculous amount of money for the job, so I told him I would do it on one condition."

"Which is?" I ask breathlessly.

"That you and your friends get to meet him and spend a day on the set. There's no school on Friday, right? I checked your schedule and it's some kind of teachers' day or something. You four are going to be his guests for the whole day."

It's a good thing I'm already on the floor, because all the blood leaves my head.

"Sophie, are you all right?" Mom asks.

My head is spinning as I pull myself to my feet and

squeeze her and then Dad. The blood starts to return to my head, giving me a headache, and that's when it hits me. Friday is only two days away.

"Ohhh nooooo!" I cry.

Poor Dad is *very* confused. "What's wrong? I thought you were happy."

"My nose," I say, pointing at the mass of bandages holding my face together.

"What's the matter? Does it hurt?"

"No! It's fine. But he can't see me looking like this!"

Mom, who, like Margaret, always sees the glass as half full, tries to convince me that, one, it doesn't matter, that he'll be happy to meet someone who's obviously a real fan, regardless of how I look, and, two, by Friday I won't be quite so hideous. Okay, so those aren't her *exact* words, but they might as well be. I'm still going to have this stupid thing on my nose, but even if I take it off, everything under it and around my eyes is still going to be gnarly-looking.

"Livvy," I mutter. "This is all her fault. God, it's so humiliating."

Chapter 3

What if those fifty million Frenchmen are wrong? Has anyone even considered that possibility?

On the way to school, I wear a Yankees cap pulled down over my face as far as possible. I know I'll be able to remain incognito in the cafeteria until the first-period bell rings, but sooner or later I'm going to have to walk past Sister Eugenia's office. For somebody who, according to school legend, came to the New World on the *Santa Maria,* her eyesight is just fine, thank you very much; she can spot a uniform infraction from an ocean away. Make that two oceans.

"It doesn't look that bad, Soph," Leigh Ann says. "Let me put a little makeup on those circles—I'll bet I could make them almost invisible."

"How 'bout that big ol' bandage?" Becca says. "Can you make that disappear, too?"

"C'mon, Becca. We need to be supportive," lectures Margaret, who then turns to me. "Okay, Sophie, what is this big news you have? Some kind of secret plan for Friday, you said."

"All right, I'll tell you, but, guys, you have to promise: no screaming. I almost fainted when my dad told me, but I did *not* scream."

It's a self-improvement thing. Ever since that now-famous incident when I looked out the window in Mr. Eliot's room, saw that face staring back at me, and screamed bloody murder—right in the middle of English class—I've been working on keeping my emotions under control. How am I doing? For now, let's just say it's . . . a work in progress.

"Promise?"

"We promise. Get on with it," Becca nags.

So I tell them.

They scream. Like banshees—whatever those are.

I mean, jeez! Suddenly everyone in the cafeteria is looking right at us, and believe me, in my current condition, that is just about the last thing I want. I bury my head in my hands as the three of them work through the first stage (shock and disbelief) of Acute Celebrity Encounter Disorder (ACED) and progress directly into the second: eternal gratitude to yours truly for having a dad with the proper connections. When I finally lift my head to acknowledge their vows of lifelong devotion to me, however, I see a couple of eighth graders hovering over our table. *Not* a promising situation. As seventh graders, we know all too well that we rank only slightly above cockroaches in the upper-school hierarchy, but the occasional eighth grader loves to remind us of our lowly place in the world.

These two are not trying to bully us out of our table, though.

"Um, aren't you the girls who are, like, detectives or something?" the tall one asks, catching us off guard.

"Uh-huh," Becca growls. "What about it?"

Margaret elbows her. "Don't provoke the natives," she whispers.

I recognize the other one as the snooty, headset-wearing wannabe producer from the Dickens of a Banquet, which took place back when we were looking for the Ring of Rocamadour.

She looks right at me. "We were, like, wondering, um, if you, like, had a nose job. You know, the bandage. And, like, you used to have kind of a . . . well, you know."

"No, I *don't* know," I say, glaring at her. "*What* did I used to have?"

"Never mind," she says with an embarrassed giggle.

"I *told* you," her dim friend says, dragging her away. "Those stupid doctors won't touch you till you're sixteen at least. You're just gonna have to wait to get yours done."

I continue to give them the death-ray stare as they make their way across the cafeteria. "There's *nothing* wrong with my nose," I insist. "I mean, usually. Today doesn't count. I do *not* need a nose job." I look at Margaret. "Do I?"

"Of course not," Margaret replies. "Don't listen to those idiots. You have a classic Gallic profile. And what is it they say? Fifty million Frenchmen can't be wrong, right? Plenty of people would kill for your nose."

"Speaking of your nose, there goes its worst enemy," says Leigh Ann.

It's Livvy Klack and the rest of the Clique de Klack strutting in like they own the joint. Beth Aronson, who is Livvy's first lieutenant, spots me and points right at my nose. She practically falls on the floor laughing. The lower-ranking minions all do the same, but Livvy, oddly enough, does not join in these reindeer games.

"Could you *be* bigger losers?" she says—to her disciples, not to us.

Which leaves everyone involved speechless, at least for a few seconds.

"What just happened?" I finally ask as they move on to their usual table across the cafeteria.

"Make a note of the time," Margaret says. "I think we have just seen the first evidence that Livvy Klack has human DNA after all."

"Shoot. There goes my hyena theory," says Becca.

"You don't think she actually feels bad about yesterday, do you?" I ask. "She didn't exactly apologize after she whacked me."

Leigh Ann laughs. "Hey, anything's possible. Since I started hanging out with you guys, I've seen all *kinds* of stuff that I wouldn't have believed."

It does make me wonder. Call me naive if you must, but I don't *think* Livvy crashed into me on purpose.

Sure, she was annoyed that I'd beaten her in that 400 IM, and was trying to show me up, but for now, at least, I choose to believe it was an accident.

Friday, 6:30 a.m. I'm standing in front of the mirror in my bedroom, waiting for Margaret. We're supposed to meet Becca and Leigh Ann in an hour near the carousel in Central Park, which is where the day's filming is scheduled to take place. As excited as I am to be spending the day with an honest-to-God movie star, I'm feeling a little guilty, broken nose and all. At this very moment, all my teammates are in the midst of whatever torture Michelle has conjured up for the morning practice. And here I am, putting on makeup and debating whether to take off the bandage. I start peeling up around the edges of the tape, trying to see how it looks underneath. So far, so good. I'm about to give it a good yank when Mom stops just outside my door.

"Oh, good—I was making sure you were up. I should have known you'd be dressed and ready to go. I'm so excited for you girls!"

"Um, Mom? I know the doctor said to keep it on till Monday, but do you think I could take this thing off? I'll put a new one on tonight, I promise."

She gives me a look of pure pity and nods. "Go ahead. Just take it easy, okay? No soccer. Or fistfights."

I hug her. "Can you help me get it off? I think that doctor used superglue or something."

When the bandage is finally off, I get my first look at my nose in what seems like weeks. It's not too bad; the swelling has gone down, and it doesn't look any more crooked than before. The exact spot where Livvy clocked me with that big ol' paw of hers is clearly visible as a purple line across the middle.

Mom cringes as she wipes away the bits of glue and schmutz with her thumb and a little spit. "I'm not hurting you, am I? There—good as new. Well, almost."

The doorbell rings, and Mom lets Margaret in.

"Hey, the nose looks pretty good. And your black eyes are fading, too."

"Well, I got a little, um, artificial help."

"Makeup? You? Why, Sophie St. Pierre!" She spins me around in the light to get the full effect and to check out the chic-but-not-trying-too-hard-to-look-chic look I put together (with a little help from a late-night consultation with Leigh Ann, my fashion guru).

"Are you going to be warm enough in that?" Mom asks, eyeing my denim jacket. "It's not going to get much above forty today."

"Ah, but I have a secret," I say. "Layers. I have my long underwear on under everything. That way, I can stay warm while still looking cool. Leigh Ann is a genius when it comes to fashion."

"Humph," says Mom. "We'll see if you change your tune when you have pneumonia."

"That is *such* a mom thing to say," I retort. "Tell Dad I said thanks again. I'll call you later, from the . . . *set.*"

Oh yeah, I am *quite* full of myself.

Leigh Ann and Becca are right on time, which is a clear indication of how psyched we all are. I mean, it's seven-thirty in the morning on a day off from school. Living in New York, we've all walked past miles and miles of those "movie star" trailers and trucks full of lighting and camera equipment, but this time it's something special— *we're* something special, or at least it feels that way. We're about to cross over to the other side. To become part of the club. People will see us and wonder who we are. That and, well, *hate* us for being there when they're not.

The police have set up barriers in a big circle around the ball field next to the carousel, and a crowd of (mostly) girls is already four or five deep all the way around. When we get to the entrance, there's a big, dangerous-looking guy with a headset and a clipboard blocking our way.

"Sorry, ladies. You have to stay behind the barriers," he snarls.

"We're invited," I say. "We're Nate Etan's guests— we should be on the list. St. Pierre?"

He stares at me for a full second before consulting his clipboard, running his index finger down the long list of names. "St. Pierre?"

"Sophie," I say, trying to be helpful.

He grunts, then turns to Margaret. "And the rest of you?"

"Wrobel, Chen, and Jaimes," Margaret replies. "And that's Jaimes with a *J,* not an *H.*"

He checks their names off his list and then hands us laminated guest passes on bright orange lanyards. A little clashy with my outfit, but that's okay—perfect, even. I *want* people to see it. He steps aside to let us through the opening.

"Go straight back to that yellow and white tent—one of the assistants will be able to help you find Mr. Etan."

We can't stop grinning as we thank him. Behind us, I hear the chatter of the girls who are standing outside the barrier, and it is beautiful music to my ears.

"Hey, who are *they?*" one of them asks. "How did they get in?"

"They don't look like anybody," another answers. "They're just kids."

"Well, they got in, so they must be somebody," a third says.

"Did you hear that, guys?" I whisper. "We're *somebody*!"

Starting across the field, we all freeze when sixty pounds of black dog bolts out of the tent we've been told to go to. The beast is coming straight for me, and barking in a not-so-friendly way. I'm already visualizing the next day's tabloid headline: "Mad Movie Mutt Mauls Girl Detectives."

Instead of leaping at our throats, though, the killer canine stops suddenly right in front of me, wagging her tail so hard that her whole body is wriggling. Relieved that I'm not going to become just another tragic headline, I kneel down to rub her behind the ears, something that I know all dogs love, even though I don't have one of my own. Yet.

And then a miracle happens. I'm so busy petting the dog that I don't notice *him*. Nate Etan, mere inches away.

"Tillie!" he scolds. "Bad girl. Thank you for catching her—she usually doesn't run off like that."

From my point of view—kneeling—he seems ten feet tall. He's looking down on me and smiling that same gazillion-gigawatt smile that's plastered all over my bedroom. Okay, I know nobody has used this word in like a hundred years, but I'm pretty sure I *swoon*. My vocal cords, along with my legs, are paralyzed.

"This is Tillie," he says, clipping a leash onto her collar. He holds out his hand for me to shake. "Hi, I'm Nate Etan."

Well, of course you are. And I'm . . . I'm . . . Jeez, snap out of it, Sophie!

"H-hi, I'm So—So—Sophie. St. Pierre."

"Well, hello there, So-So Sophie." A nickname is born, I fear. "Oh, wait—you're Guy's daughter!" He even pronounces Dad's name right. "Excellent! Here, let me help you up." He takes my hand in his (deep breaths, Sophie!) and lifts me with astonishing ease. He is taller, thinner, stronger, and better-looking than I expected—and my expectations were high, believe me.

Seeing him in the flesh makes it obvious why he was cast in the role of James Blancpain, the impossibly handsome vampire in *No Reflections,* the book that Leigh Ann and I have recently become obsessed with. His pictures don't do him justice at all. Suddenly I'm feeling really small and extremely self-conscious about my nose.

I introduce the rest of the gang, and maybe he's acting, but he *seems* to be really pleased that we're there. He hands me Tillie's leash and starts leading us toward the tent. "I have one little favor to ask. Since Tillie seems to have bonded with you, can you hold on to her for a while? If she gets to be too much of a pain, I can put her in my trailer, but she likes to be outside. You're not allergic or anything, are you?"

"No, I love dogs," I say. "I want one so bad, but I haven't convinced my parents yet."

"Great! Let's go get something to eat, and then I'll show you around. My scene won't be ready to shoot for a little while. First time on a set for everybody?"

We all nod. Becca, Leigh Ann, and Margaret continue to stare openmouthed at him.

"Tell me, So-So Sophie—do your friends talk?" he says, laughing.

"Uh, definitely. Especially this one," I say, pointing at Becca. "We usually can't get her to shut up."

She sticks her tongue out at me.

And then I realize that he's staring at me—at my

nose, to be precise. When he realizes what he's doing, he laughs and apologizes. "I'm sorry, but I just *have* to ask. What happened to your nose? And do you have two black eyes? Are you, like, a boxer or something?"

"A swimmer," I say.

"No kidding. I didn't realize swimming was such a violent sport," he says, nodding earnestly. "I may have to pay more attention in the future."

"It was an accident."

Becca scoffs. "Ha!"

"It was. I swam right into another girl's hand. Broke my nose."

"Ouch," he says. "Well, I'll try to keep flying objects away from you today—except for Tillie. I guess it's a little late for her. She's kind of a self-propelled missile."

Finally, Leigh Ann speaks. "Um, Mr. Etan—"

"Nate. Please. Mr. Etan is my dad."

Her face lights up. "Right. Nate. I have a *lot* of questions for you, about acting and agents and stuff. I hope that's okay."

"I'd be disappointed if you didn't," he says. "I suppose you're all big fans of the book, right? Every girl in America is obsessed with it."

"Huge," Leigh Ann gushes. "I've read it twice—I just started the third time."

"Yeah, Margaret's the only one who's really not crazy about it," I reveal. "She's read it, but she's used to more—"

"Boring stuff?" offers Becca.

"I was going to say more *serious* things."

"Have *you* read the book?" Margaret asks him.

Nate grimaces and puts his arms around all of us, pulling us in close. "This is top-secret, okay? I don't want this out there in the gossip magazines—the producers would kill me. Officially, yes, I have read *No Reflections*. And officially, I *love* it. Between us, though?" He shakes his head and holds his index finger to his lips. "Couldn't get through it. I tried, but I have to be honest. I've never been much of a reader."

A little warning bell goes off in my brain. Nate Etan not a reader? That can't be right. He's perfect, isn't he? And if he's perfect, he must love books the way I do. It's only logical. Right?

He leads us into a tent that has a table covered with an amazing selection of breakfast foods—doughnuts, lox and bagels, pastries of every size and shape, a colossal fruit tray, every kind of juice imaginable, and those adorable miniature boxes of cereal, which are completely irresistible to me.

"Help yourselves to anything you want," he announces as I zero in on the Lucky Charms. "I'm going to have to head over to makeup, but I'll be back in twenty minutes. Is that okay?"

We assure him we'll be fine. I mean, what are we going to do—say no to a big star?

A few minutes later, we're digging into the breakfast buffet, but just when I take a big spoonful of cereal, with milk dripping down my chin, in walks the *other* star of the movie, Cam Peterson, who is only a year older than me. I have to be honest here; even though he has been in a few movies, I didn't even know who he was until I started checking out all the websites about the movie. He plays James Blancpain's archenemy, the young vampire hunter Hector Kreech.

Right now, though, it's not a wooden stake or an antique pistol loaded with silver bullets he's scaring me with—it's his cell phone. He is yelling into it, using the kind of language that I *never* use. Someone, somewhere, is getting an earful of profanity and abuse—all because Cam's email isn't working on his phone.

When he spots us sitting there stuffing our faces, he stops screaming for a few seconds and stares at us with a puzzled look on his face.

"Are you supposed to be in here?" he whines. Instead of waiting for us to answer, though, he picks up right where he left off—wireless network this, incompetence that, and on and on.

I lean over to Margaret. "Should we leave? He doesn't seem pleased that we're in here."

Margaret digs in her heels. "No way. We're Nate Etan's guests and this is where he told us to wait for him. *That* guy's the one who should leave. He's acting like a jerk."

If she wasn't my best friend, I would be tackling Margaret and stuffing a pair of dirty old socks in her mouth. "Shhh! Do you know who he is? That's Cam Peterson."

"So? Being *almost* famous is no excuse for bad manners," Margaret says. "I can't believe he's talking like that in front of us. He's just being rude."

I don't know if he heard her or not, but he turns to face us once more; this time he glares. And then he leaves, still yapping into his phone.

Oh yeah. Our first day among the beautiful people, and we're off to a great start.

Chapter 4

In which Becca walks in on a make-believe artist and I step into a minefield

The rest of the day is just about perfect. Nate shows us all around the set and introduces us to everyone, even the director, Kim Faraday. She is super-nice, if a bit intense. I guess when you're spending a kajillion dollars of other people's money to make a movie based on an insanely popular book with completely unreasonable, rabid fans who won't settle for anything less than a perfect adaptation, you have an excuse to be a little stressed out.

Because it's a story about vampires, most of it takes place in the dark, but the scene we get to see filmed is where James Blancpain is trapped—after sunrise!—in Central Park by his nemesis, Kreech. He's hiding in the carousel and has to make a run for one of the vampires-only secret tunnels before Kreech has a chance to take a shot at him—this time with a wicked-looking crossbow that is armed with silver-tipped arrows.

The scene has taken hours to set up, but finally everything and everyone is in place. We're sitting in folding chairs just behind the director and her assistants, one of whom is petting Tillie.

"Action!"

Even though I'm a mere spectator, my heart is doing the old *ka-whump ka-whump* in my chest when James Blancpain—he's no longer Nate Etan—races out from behind the carousel horses, knocking an off-guard Kreech to the ground. After the way Cam acted earlier, we especially enjoy that part; Blancpain hits his enemy at a full run, lifting him off his feet and sending the crossbow flying. Kreech recovers quickly, though, pulling Blancpain to the ground. The vampire and the hunter are then supposed to wrestle for a few seconds before Blancpain makes his escape to the tunnel.

Tillie, however, decides to rewrite the scene at the last moment. When she sees Cam pull Nate to the ground, she breaks away from the assistant director in order to rescue her human, grabbing Cam's pant leg in her teeth and trying to pull him away from Nate.

"Cut!" cries the director. "Nate! I thought we talked about this."

"Sorry," he says, taking Tillie by the collar. "She *never* does stuff like this. She's just not the protective kind."

"Well, can you get someone to hold her before she decides to tear my leg off?" whines Cam. "Look, she tore my pants."

Nate brings Tillie to me. "Sophie, can you do me a big favor and hold Tillie for me again?"

"Sure," I say, my head swelling with pride. Nate Etan asked me—me!—to watch his dog for him, and he did it in front of other people.

"Super," he says. "I totally owe you."

So I've got *that* going for me. Which is nice.

While I hold tightly to Tillie, they do fourteen more takes of the same scene. I'm not sure I have what it takes to be a director, because they all looked pretty much the same to me. However, we *are* all secretly enjoying the sight of Cam Peterson getting more and more annoyed; after the fifteenth take, he suggests having his stand-in take the hit from Nate, but the director promises him "just one more take," and he agrees, still grumbling under his breath.

The director guessed right; the sixteenth take is just perfect, she says, and then everyone cheers as an assistant director announces that they are "wrapped" for the day. After Nate changes out of his wardrobe clothes and removes all his makeup, he joins us back in the catering tent for a celebratory soda. We thank him over and over for his hospitality and pose for lots of pictures, individual and group shots, so we can show the whole world how we spent our Friday.

And then, as we're packing up all our goodies and getting ready to go, he hits me with the big one.

"Uh, Sophie . . . remember earlier when I asked you for that favor? Well, I have one more, and this one is really huge. And, I mean, you can totally say no to this, and if you need to call your parents first, that's cool, too, but I was wondering if you could take care of Tillie for a few days. I'll pay you fifty dollars a day. You see, I have to go to London for a few days, and I would usually have my girlfriend take care of her, but we just kind of broke up, so . . ."

"I'll do it!" I say without thinking.

"Really?" he says.

"Really?" Margaret says.

"Really," I say. "My parents are cool. When do you want me to start?"

"Um, today. Like, right now?"

"Oh. Wow. Right now. Okay. I mean, sure, why not?"

"Great! C'mon, I'll walk you guys out, and we can stop at my trailer so I can get her food and toys and stuff. And I'll give you money for a taxi home."

"Are you sure you don't want to call your parents first?" Leigh Ann asks.

"I think that's a *really* good idea," says Margaret, giving me her you-seriously-need-to-listen-to-me look.

"They *love* dogs," I reason. "It's no problem."

"It's your funeral," Becca says. "I know what my mom would do if I came home with a dog."

I turn to Nate. "Don't worry. It'll be fine. She's a good dog. I mean, she's house-trained and everything, right?"

A question, perhaps, that I should have asked *before* agreeing to watch her.

"Oh yeah. Of course. And she's quiet. She never barks. It's easy. Feed her twice a day. Take her for a walk when you wake up, another in the afternoon, and one more before you go to bed. Maybe bring her over here to the park every once in a while so she can run around a little. Nothing to it. You'll be ready for your own dog by tomorrow."

There you have it—Dogs 101, taught by Professor Nate Etan.

"She *has* been acting a little weird the past few days," the professor adds. (This information, too, might have been more useful a minute or two earlier.) "You know, like running off to greet you, and trying to protect me. And she doesn't seem interested in any of her old favorite toys. It's probably just the excitement of being in New York. She's used to California."

"Maybe it's jet lag," Rebecca says.

We reach the gate, where Nate says his good-bye to Tillie and thanks us for coming, and—here's the best part—he gives me his cell phone number and email address in case I need to reach him about Tillie.

"But you have to *promise* not to give them to anyone else, okay?" he says, opening the door of the taxi. Tillie hops right in and makes herself comfortable.

"Cross my heart and hope to die," I say.

"Good enough for me," he says. Then he kisses us

all *very* dramatically on both cheeks and shouts "Ciao!" as we drive off.

Becca snickers. "Please tell me he didn't just say 'Ciao!'"

"I'm afraid so," says Leigh Ann. "But he kissed us first. That has to count for *something*."

Oh, it counts. It counts.

Okay, confession time: my parents are considerably less than thrilled when I walk in the door with Tillie, who promptly sweeps a picture frame off the coffee table with her tail. Nor are they impressed when I tell them *whose* dog she is. Sheesh. Some people are just hard to please.

"How long did you agree to do this for, exactly?" Mom asks.

"I don't know *exactly* how many days," I admit. "But I'm getting fifty bucks a day, so I hope it's five or six at least. Christmas is just around the corner, and I need some shopping money. You want a nice present, don't you? I'll do everything—walk her and feed her—and she can sleep in my room."

I should just shut up right there, but something compels me to add these fateful words: "You won't even know she's here."

Saturday morning, four-fifteen. My parents know. I know. The neighbors know. I'm reasonably certain that Connecticut knows. Ladies and gentlemen, Tillie is in the house.

I think my head bounces off the ceiling at her first howl. It takes me a full five seconds to realize what's going on—there really is a dog in my room howling at the moon, which is shining straight through the window. I mean, we're talking *Hound of the Baskervilles* stuff here.

"Owwwowwwowwwowooooooooooooooooooooooooooo-ooooooooo. Owww—owwwowwwooooooooooooooooooooo-oooooooooooooooooooooooooooooooo."

Seconds later, my parents are at my door with panicked looks.

"Oh thank God," Mom says, holding a hand over her heart. "I thought that crazy dog was killing you."

"I thought you said she doesn't bark," says Dad.

"That's what Nate told me. And technically, I don't think that was barking. That was howling." I point at the nearly full moon. "I think she might be a werewolf."

"Maybe we close the blinds," Mom suggests.

Tillie jumps up on the bed and stretches out across my feet as Mom and Dad look on, shaking their heads in disbelief at the latest plot twist of the soap opera that is my life.

The doctor told me to stay out of the pool at least until Monday, so I actually have some unscheduled time on Saturday morning. After I take Tillie for a good walk and convince my mom that I'm fine, my nose is fine, and Tillie is fine, I head for Chinatown to meet Becca for some bubble tea and some of those steamed buns I love.

Ever since Elizabeth Harriman discovered her incredible artistic talent, Becca has been part of a special program for gifted young artists at a gallery in Chelsea that's owned by Elizabeth's friend Alessandra. So, when we slurp up the last of the tapioca "bubbles," we mosey on over to Twenty-second Street in Chelsea.

We're early, so we wander up the block, peeking in the windows of the still-closed shops. As we're walking past a gallery a few doors up from Alessandra's, I notice that the front door is open just a crack and one light is on. Three large canvases take up most of the back wall, each one a thick, swirling, angry storm of paint. Along the other walls, double rows of identically sized paintings stretch from corner to corner, and these immediately get my attention. When it comes to art, I'm a little old-fashioned. Sure, I like some of the modern stuff that Elizabeth has, but give me a nice still life any day. These thirty or so small canvases—each about twelve by fifteen inches—look like they belong in the Louvre.

"Hey, do you want to go in for a few minutes?" I ask. "The cold is making my nose hurt."

Becca says, "I don't know. It doesn't really look like they're open." She stops, smiling mischievously at me. "But that's never stopped us before, has it? The paintings look pretty cool, and there must be a bathroom, which I *really* need after that huge thing of tea you made me drink."

She gently pushes the door open and sticks her head inside. "Hello?" She looks at me with a shrug, and as we both go in, a bell at the top of the door jingles softly. We stand there for a few seconds, waiting for someone to greet us, but no one appears.

"Maybe they're out getting coffee," I say, choosing to believe that I'm not doing something illegal, and using the opportunity to get a closer look at the art.

"Probably. You stay here; I'm going to look for a bathroom."

I watch her walk down the hallway, opening and then closing doors on the way. As she opens the third door, she freezes, then says, "Oh! I'm sorry! I was just looking for—"

"Did you bring me my tea?" It is a young man's voice—gentle, but insistent. "Is it nice and hot? When they bring it, it's always cold. I do like my tea piping hot, don't you? With lots of milk. But the milk has to be *hot*. And honey. And for heaven's sake, in a china cup. Tea in a paper cup is a travesty. *They* bring me paper cups. Can you imagine?"

"Uh, yeah, er, no," Becca says, slowly backing up.

"Won't you join me for tea?"

"Um, actually, I was just looking for—"

From behind me, a voice booms, *"How did you get in here? What are you doing?"*

I try to talk, but my vocal cords are paralyzed again. I'm too scared to even get a good look at the guy; all I really notice about him is that his face is as red as a St. Veronica's school blazer.

"Get out! Both of you! Now! Or I'll . . ."

I don't need to hear the rest of that, so I turn and run.

Becca is one step behind me, and we don't stop running until we are two blocks away, around a corner, and positive that nobody's following us.

"What . . . who . . . ," I say, trying to catch my breath, "was that you were talking to?"

She shakes her head. "Some guy, never seen him before."

"What was he doing? And *pleeease* don't tell me he was in the bathroom."

"No, it's just a regular room. He had a couple of easels set up, and he was painting when I opened the door."

"Two easels? Could you see what he was painting?"

"One was like the big paintings hanging in the gallery. Dark and swirly. Like the sky in a Van Gogh. The other one was a still life, just like all the others on the wall. Hard to believe he does both—the styles are so different. But that's not the weird part—you've just *got* to see the room. On the wall behind him, there are two windows with curtains and everything—except that one of them isn't."

"Isn't *what*?"

"A window. It's just a section of the wall painted to *look* like the other window. You look at it, and you will swear you are looking at another building that's across the alley. It took me a second to realize that the curtains were just paint, too. It's freaky, it's so real. I didn't have time to check it all out, but the whole room is painted like that—the walls, the floor, even the ceiling."

"That does sound cool. But why did that other guy get so mad? What's the big deal? I mean, so you walk in on a guy painting in an art gallery. I'm shocked—*shocked,* I tell you!"

"Well, artists don't usually work in galleries. They have their own studios, and if they're *lucky,* they find somebody who likes their stuff enough to try to sell it. Did you happen to get a look at the name of any of the artists in the gallery?" Becca asks. "I wonder who he is."

I shake my head. "I didn't see a sign or anything, but it shouldn't be too hard to find out."

"Well, it's all very suspicious, if you ask me. There's definitely something going on in there."

When Becca's art class starts, I head back uptown to my favorite bookstore, where I spend most of the afternoon (and all of my money). Even though I have yet to see a single dime from Nate for my dog-sitting gig, the antici-pation of that fifty dollars a day makes me feel like I'm *rich.*

After the bookstore comes my guitar lesson on the West Side with Gerry, who is pushing me to get to work writing more songs, and then pizza with Raf.

He's waiting outside Gerry's studio, leaning against the wall and just being his usual too-cute-for-his-own-good self, as I come downstairs.

I give him a little wave, trying not to act *too* excited to see him. "What? No scooter this time?" I ask.

He smiles even though he's *still* paying for that little adventure. "Maybe next time."

"No! I want you to be able to stay out past eight-thirty before you turn sixteen. You're like the opposite of a vampire; I can only see you in the daylight hours."

He moves in closer to me to get his first good look at my nose; I haven't seen him since Livvy did her guillotine imitation on my face. "Hey, it's not too bad. The way you described it the other day made it sound like you were some kind of hideous creature."

"Oh, it's a *lot* better now. You should have seen it when it was all swollen and the bruises around my eyes were bright purple. I was stunning-looking, really. Luckily, Leigh Ann showed me how to cover up some of it with makeup. Nate still noticed it, though—he even teased me about it. He was really funny, by the way. It's too bad you couldn't come with us. We had *so* much fun."

"Yeah, I'll bet," he says, looking a little disgusted at the very idea of spending the day following Nate Etan around.

"We did, really! Nate was super-nice, and funny, and we got to see them shoot this scene—over and over, actually. Oh! And we got yelled at by Cam Peterson. Do you know who he is?"

Raf shrugs. "No. He *yelled* at you?"

"Sort of. He's really bratty. He didn't know we were, you know, friends of Nate's."

"Oh brother," Raf says. "Listen to you. Hanging out with your movie star friends. What, are you guys going to follow him around from movie to movie now, just because he talked to you?"

"Maybe we are," I say, taking Raf's hand. "Now that I'm taking care of his dog—"

"You're *what*?"

"Oh yeah, I forgot to mention that, huh? Nate had his dog with him on the set all day, and he asked me to hold her because she tried to kill Cam while they were filming. And then, at the end of the day, he asked me if I could watch her for a few days. And he's paying me *fifty* dollars a day."

"Humph."

He lets go of my hand and changes the subject. "So, do you want pizza or something else?"

"Oh, come on, Raf—what's the matter? I'll stop talking about Nate right now, I promise." I take his hand again and squeeze. "I feel like tacos instead of pizza. But, um, I do have one teensy-tiny problem."

"Now what?"

"I kind of spent all my money at the bookstore," I say, waving my bag of new books in his face. "I'll pay you back, I promise. As soon as I get paid by Nate, er, I mean . . . as soon as Becca pays me back the ten dollars she owes me."

It's like a minefield, this world of relationships.

Post-tacos, I'm spending a quiet Saturday night at home with Mom and Tillie, watching a crummy movie on cable, when Becca calls with some interesting news.

"Guess what? I went back," she says.

"Back where?"

"To that gallery."

"Where the guy yelled at us?"

That gets Mom's attention. "*Who* yelled at you?"

I wave her off with a don't-worry-it's-all-cool smile. "It was no big deal." And it wasn't, but I move into my bedroom to continue the conversation anyway. I'd rather not have to explain what we were doing in a gallery that wasn't really open yet.

"So what happened? You didn't go back in, did you?"

"Yeah, I did, but not through the front. I went around back and found the alley and the window—the real one. I had to climb up on top of a Dumpster to see inside, but sure enough, he was still in there, painting away. So I went across the street, bought a cup of tea, and then knocked on the window. I started tapping really gently, 'cause I didn't want to scare him to death, but I almost did anyway. He ducks down on the floor, but when he sees that it's me, he smiles and comes over and opens the window."

"You're crazy, you know," I say.

"Trust me, this guy wouldn't hurt a fly. Literally. While I was there, he saw a little spider on the wall and he scooped it up and set it out on the windowsill."

"So what is he doing in there?"

"I didn't get the whole story yet, but I'm working on it. I'm inside, drinking my soda while he's having his tea, which he poured into a china cup, and we have a really great conversation about art—the people we really like, the ones we think are phonies, everything. I even tell him about the class I'm taking over at Alessandra's, and show him my sketchbook."

"Which he loved, I'm sure."

"He did seem to like the stuff I did in the park—we have to draw a bunch of statues for class and I did that one of Romeo and Juliet over by the theater. And Aragorn, of course. I love that guy."

"You mean King Jagiello," I say.

"I don't care who he really is—he looks like Aragorn to me. Oh, and all the painting on the walls—the fake window and everything—he did all that, too. I think he's *obsessed*. He doesn't paint because he wants to; it's like he *has* to. Anyway, we're yakking away like we're best friends, and someone knocks on the door—the same door that I opened this morning. It was a girl's voice, and she kept asking him if everything was okay, because she thought she heard voices. Gus—that's his name, by the way—tells her he's fine, but never opens the door. After she leaves, he tells me that whenever the gallery is open, he keeps the door locked, because he's afraid 'that nasty little man' will come looking for him."

"What nasty little man? The one that yelled at us?"

"I don't know for sure, but I don't think that's him. He wouldn't say anything else about it. But the more he thought about it, the more paranoid he got. He kept checking to make sure the door was locked. I figured that it was probably a good time to go. But he told me to come back anytime."

"Are you going to?"

"What do you think? Of course. Oh, and something else—he said he's *always* there. He lives upstairs! So, yeah, now that I got a taste of the story, I've just *got* to know what he's so afraid of."

Chapter 5

Black-and-white television? No cable? *Quelle horreur!*

On Monday morning, I make my return to swimming, where I get a hero's welcome from Michelle and some of my teammates. Livvy is Livvy—no more or less friendly than usual, which is fine by me. And considering what happened the last time I was within an arm's length of her, I'm happy to keep a little extra space between us. In the swim meet that I missed because of my nose, she really stepped up, winning two individual events and anchoring one winning relay. Our next meet is with Tallmadge, another girls' school in Manhattan, and I have only a week to make up for all those missed hours in the pool. Thank goodness I have Tillie to make sure I'm up every morning at five o'clock.

Oh, didn't I mention that she gets up every morning at five? Or that when she is up, *everyone* must be up? Must have slipped my mind.

There are no weekends in a dog's life.

• • •

At lunchtime, as we regale anyone who will listen with tales of our day on the *No Reflections* set, Sister Bernadette hands Rebecca an envelope with THE RED BLAZER GIRLS DETECTIVE AGENCY printed in neat letters.

"I was asked to deliver this," she says. "I hope and pray that this does not lead to another one of your little adventures. But if it does, girls, know this: I will be watching you. Understood?" She stomps away, glaring at a table of girls loudly singing—for who knows what reason—the theme song from *Gilligan's Island*.

"Jeez, who peed in her orange juice? Oops, sorry, Margaret. I know you hate when I say that," Rebecca says with a malevolent grin.

"Seriously," agrees Leigh Ann. "All we did last time was save the life of a guy locked in a room in the basement, solve an impossible crime, prevent an innocent man from going to jail, and recover a priceless violin. We're, like, heroes. She should be praying that it *is* a new case."

"Why, the very fate of the world might be in our hands," I say.

"Easy there, Sophie. She's still annoyed that we didn't tell her about Ben as soon as we knew," Margaret says.

In the Case of the Vanishing Violin, Sister Bernadette hired us to figure out who was doing unauthorized cleaning and remodeling in the school after hours. It didn't take us long to figure out who—Ben Brownlow, the new assistant at the violin shop—but when he became the key suspect in the theft of the violin, we kept that information to ourselves for a while. Like, until we solved the whole case.

Becca tears open the envelope and pulls out a note written on personalized stationery.

"It's from Father Julian."

Father Julian is the young, slightly-bigger-than-a-hobbit priest who saved our butts more than once during the Ring of Rocamadour case.

Dear Red Blazer Girls,
  If you have a free moment after school today, please stop by the rectory. I have a small favor to ask.
                                    Father Julian

"A favor. Hmmm. Maybe he's going to ask Sophie to take care of *his* dog, too," Rebecca says.

In the past, that kind of crack would have earned her a good punch on the arm, but the new, improved Sophie St. Pierre lets it go without a thought. Well, except for the one where I'm thinking about how I'm letting it go without a thought.

"Can everybody make it today?" Margaret asks. "We owe him at least one favor. Maybe two."

We all nod. We are *so* ready for our next case.

• • •

Father Julian greets us at the door, and after we assure him that we're in no hurry to get anywhere else, he invites us into a comfortable living room while he goes off to the kitchen to get us some sodas. All the furniture in the room looks like something from the set of a 1960s sitcom, but it's all still like new. I guess that's what you get when you don't have kids running around the place. The TV is my personal favorite; it's not just a TV—it looks like an actual piece of furniture with its real wood cabinet and carved legs. It even has one of those rabbit-ears antennas sitting on top of it. The thing should be in a museum.

"Ah, I see you're admiring our antique television," Father Julian remarks. "It's a classic. We're thinking we might upgrade next year to color."

Leigh Ann's head tilts slightly to the left, reminding me of the way Tillie looks when she's trying hard to understand something I'm saying. "What do you mean?"

Father Julian laughs out loud. "I forget how young you girls are. I'll bet you've never seen a black-and-white television, have you?"

Leigh Ann nods. "I didn't even know there was such a thing. You're serious—there's no color at all, like old movies?"

"Exactly. Everything looks like an old movie." He turns it on, and we wait. "It takes a while to warm up," he says, tapping his foot. "Like a few days. Okay, here we go. There's channel two. And channel four. See?

Black-and-white. And no remote control, but that's not so bad. We only get four stations, so there's not a lot of channel surfing going on anyway."

"No cable?" Becca says in disbelief.

"Not yet, but in April we're going for it, if only to be able to watch Yankees and Mets games. The priests here are split about evenly between the two teams—and then there's Father Danahey. He's from Boston."

'Nuff said.

After clicking the TV off, he sets a large cloth tote bag on the coffee table in front of us and starts to talk.

"Okay, I'll start with the basics, and then I can always add details later if you need them. But here's the bottom line: I have a case for you girls."

Margaret smiles at me, then nods at Father Julian. "I thought you might."

"Is it something good?" Becca asks. "Don't tell me someone's cleaning the church after hours. I want something *juicy.*"

"Hmmm. I think this qualifies. But before we get into all that, are you girls Yankees fans?"

"Not me!" says Leigh Ann. "Mets all the way."

"She's from Queens," I explain. "But the rest of us are. Why?"

"Well, you might be interested in this." He stops, reaches into the tote bag, and pulls out something wrapped in tissue paper. When he unwraps it, we see it's an old baseball in good shape—no scuff marks or dings—but the cover has definitely yellowed with age.

"Are those autographs?" Margaret asks, leaning over the table for a closer look.

"Yes, they are. The entire starting lineup for the 1928 Yankees. This one is Babe Ruth, and here's Lou Gehrig. They're all there." He hands the ball to Rebecca to admire. "There's just *one* little problem."

He takes another baseball from the bag and holds it up next to the first. It is the same dingy color and has the same signatures in exactly the same places.

"Wow!" I say. "Are they both real?"

Father Julian smiles. "I suppose that is a possibility, but as a reasonable man, I have to think that it is *highly* unlikely, to say the least."

"Where did they come from?" Margaret asks.

"Ah, now that's a good story. My great-uncle Phillip and his younger brother Oliver somehow managed to get two tickets for seats in the outfield for a World Series game. According to family legend, they sat just to the left of the foul pole in left field, but I can't be certain about that. The Yankees were batting in the bottom of the eighth inning and Lou Gehrig hit a long fly ball that curved foul—right into Phillip's glove."

"Cool," I say. I've been to the old Yankee Stadium a few times, but I've never even come *close* to catching a foul ball.

"After the game, Phillip and Oliver head over toward the Yankees' dugout, and with a little luck and some good old-fashioned begging, they managed to get every starter's autograph. Phillip takes the ball home and is, I'm sure, the envy of every kid in the Bronx."

Father Julian stops to take a swig of his soda. "But somehow, between 1928 and now, this second ball appeared, and we don't know which is which. To tell the truth, we'd forgotten about them until Dad came across them when he was cleaning out the garage."

Margaret takes a closer look at the two baseballs. "I'll bet we can figure out which is the original. There has to be a way to tell."

"Well, you're welcome to try," Father Julian says. "That would be a huge help. So I guess you now have two cases instead of one." From behind the couch where we're sitting, he retrieves a package, about two feet square and neatly wrapped in brown kraft paper.

"This is the real reason you're here," he says, carefully removing the paper. "And, Rebecca, I think you are going to find this *especially* interesting."

"Why her especially?" I ask.

"Because she is an artist, and this case involves a piece of art."

He holds up a painting—a very modern, abstract picture of rows of overlapping squares in bright blues, reds, yellows, and greens, surrounded by a simple wooden frame that is painted silver. It looks vaguely familiar, like something I've seen on a museum visit with my parents.

"Holy cr—er, cow!" exclaims Becca. "Is that a Pommeroy?"

"Elizabeth Harriman wasn't kidding—you *do* know your art," says Father Julian. "That's exactly right. How do you know about Pommeroy?"

"We studied some of his paintings in my class. He always uses those same primary and secondary colors, and there's always some repetition of a simple geometric pattern—sort of his trademark."

I look at Becca with a newfound sense of admiration. I had no idea she knew so much.

"Are you saying *this* is by a famous artist?" Leigh Ann says, sounding a bit—no, make that a *lot*—skeptical. "I mean, I guess it's pretty, but I could—"

"Stop! If you say you could paint something just as good, I'll slug you," Becca warns her.

"Jeez. You artists are so touchy!" Leigh Ann says, backing away from *l'artiste*.

"Well, Rebecca can correct me if I get any of the facts about the artist wrong, but let me tell you the story behind this painting," Father Julian says. "And it starts a generation earlier, with my great-grandfather. He was what they call a finish carpenter—one of the people who did all that fancy woodwork in old houses—and from what I hear, he was one of the best. Sometime in the late 1950s, he was hired by Leonard Pommeroy to put up some wooden ceiling molding in his house out on the North Shore of Long Island. It should have been a quick job, but once Pommeroy discovered how talented my great-grandfather was, he kept finding more and more things for him to do, until he had spent several weeks there. They were both artists of a kind, I suppose, and became friends. When it came time to settle the bill, the artist was short of cash, and offered *this* to him in exchange. Now, my great-grandfather didn't know the difference between a Picasso and a paint-by-number, but he was at least aware of Pommeroy's reputation and he liked the painting. So he made the deal."

"Ohmigosh, and now it's worth, like, a million dollars, right?" I say, getting excited.

"Hold on," Father Julian says. "It's not that simple. So when my great-grandfather died in the sixties, the painting passed to his oldest child, Alice—my grandmother. She died in 2002 and left it to my father. My brother and sister and I are all trying to convince him to sell it and enjoy the money—travel with Mom, whatever he wants. They've lived frugally all their lives; they deserve it. Besides, he has never liked the painting. Goodness knows my siblings don't need the money. My brother is a successful broker on Wall Street, and my sister is a partner in a big law firm in San Francisco. Which leaves me—and I certainly don't want or need it. Well, we finally talked Dad into letting me take the painting to an expert to find out its value before trying to sell it. I did a little research and found a gallery that specializes in artists from the fifties and sixties, run by three generations of the same family. I don't know if they were trying to keep my expectations low or just playing it cool in case they wanted to buy it, but they acted very blasé about it. There's more to the story—I'll tell you the rest in a minute—but the most important part they told me is that before we can sell it, we have to be able to *prove* it was painted before 1961."

"What's so special about 1961?" Margaret asks.

"That's the year Pommeroy was killed in a car accident," Becca, who has suddenly become a walking and talking Wikipedia entry, answers.

"But . . ." The gears in Margaret's brain are spinning so fast she makes a whirring sound when she opens her mouth. "But that doesn't make sense. If he died in 1961, how could it possibly have been painted *after* 1961?"

A perfectly reasonable question, *n'est-ce pas?*

"The not-so-reasonable answer to that question is that *he* couldn't have painted it, but someone in his family might have," Father Julian explains.

"Oh, right. I heard about that," says Becca. "After he died, his sleazy family swooped in like vultures and found every scrap of paper and canvas the poor guy ever made a mark on. He used to prepare dozens of canvases in advance, doing really simple underpaintings in light gray or light blue. He would set them up all over his studio, and after a while, if he liked the way the shapes were arranged, he would add the color, and if he didn't, he would just paint the whole thing over with white and start again. Because he always used the same colors, it wasn't too hard for them to keep the Pommeroy money train chugging down the track."

"They kept it up for years," adds Father Julian. "And since he always had rocky relationships with the galleries that sold his work, neither he nor anybody else had reliable records of what he painted or when he painted it. It has created quite a pickle for people who want to buy or sell his work today. So here's the bottom line, Sophie: it's not worth a million dollars, but it is worth quite a bit *if*—and that's a big if—we can prove it was painted before Pommeroy died."

"What's the rest of the story?" I ask. "You promised to tell us."

"Oh, right. Well, when I first arrived at the gallery, I spoke to a young woman, but when I showed her the painting, she immediately went into the back room and brought out someone else—a young man who looked like he might be her brother. His eyes lit up like a Christmas tree when he saw the painting. He tried to hide it, but I could tell there was something he wasn't telling me. Then they *both* went into the back for a few minutes. I wasn't *trying* to eavesdrop, mind you, but I did overhear a few snippets—there were some raised voices. Things like 'under wraps until we know for sure' and 'not according to that moron's notes' and 'make a lowball offer right now, just in case.' And . . . I'm not positive, but I am pretty sure I caught the word 'masterpiece' in there somewhere. They didn't exactly fill me with confidence that they were playing fairly."

"What do you think they could be hiding?" Leigh Ann asks. "In case *what?*"

Father Julian turns his palms upward. "I suppose in case I find the proof they say I need."

Margaret rubs her temples for a few seconds, deep in thought. "When the artist gave the painting to your great-grandfather, wouldn't there have been a receipt or a letter or *something* to show what it was and how he got it?"

"We've looked everywhere. Nothing. Except these," Father Julian says. He removes the lid from an old shoe box that is held together with generations of yellowed tape and scoops up a handful of old family snapshots from the hundreds (*thousands,* maybe) inside. A few are in color, but most are black and white, and smaller (about three inches square) than I'm used to seeing.

"These may be our only real hope of proving when the painting was done," he says. "A lot of these pictures were taken at my great-grandfather's house in the fifties and sixties. We know that he hung it on the wall above the fireplace right after Pommeroy gave it to him, so it must show up in the background occasionally."

"Ohhhh. Cool," Becca says. "So you just have to figure out when those pictures were taken. And hope it's before 1961."

"Once again, I think what you meant to say was, *you* need to figure out when those pictures were taken," Father Julian says with a smile.

"How are we supposed to do that?" Leigh Ann says. "I mean, unless one of them has a guy holding up a sign that says 'Happy New Year 1961,' how do you prove when a picture was taken? It's impossible."

"*Nothing* is impossible," Margaret says, flaunting

that determined look that I know so well. She taps the box full of pictures. "The answer is in here. We just have to find it. These pictures are just another kind of code for us to crack. And we're getting pretty good at that, if I do say so."

"I like what I'm hearing," says a cheerful Father Julian. "I had a feeling about you girls the first time I met you."

He then puts the two baseballs back in the tote bag along with the shoe box full of photographs and hands it to me. "Take good care of these things. They may be our only hope."

"You can trust me, Father," I announce confidently. "I never lose anything."

Tell me I didn't just say that.

Chapter 6

Whew! My computer and I both need a break after that last chapter

Tillie has another surprise for me when I get home. My favorite shoes—red Chuck Taylors—are in shreds. Bits of canvas and rubber are scattered around the room, and she seems *tremendously* proud of her work. She brings me a piece of shoelace, trying to get me to play tug-of-war.

It's not that bad, I tell myself; it's only one pair of shoes. Lesson learned: put shoes in the closet, Sophie.

And then I panic. Mom's shoes! I race into my parents' room, terrified of what I'm going to find. But the floor is clean; not a single chewed-up piece of leather in sight. Inside the closet, her prized collection is safe. Whew.

Back in my room, I place Father Julian's tote bag—the one with the baseballs and the shoe box of pictures—on the highest shelf of the bookcase, away from Tillie the Terrible.

"Tillie, we would *both* be living on the street if you had done anything to Mom's shoes."

"What about my shoes?"

I almost jump out of my skin. "Mom! When did you get home?"

"Just now." She spots the remains of the Chucks. "Oh, Sophie. Your new shoes."

"Oh, they weren't that new," I say. "I've had them a few months. And before you panic, *your* shoes are fine. I already checked. You want to come with me? I'm going to take her for a walk right now. Come on. She really is a good dog. She's just a little . . . um, she's still a puppy. I promise to keep all my shoes in my closet from now on. And I'll pay for my new shoes with the money I'm earning from dog-sitting. I mean, I've got to have a pair of Chucks. It's part of who I am."

"All right, I could use a good walk. Let me put on some comfortable shoes—and put these *away*. Not that I don't trust you, Tillie dear."

When we leave the building, Tillie starts pulling us west toward Central Park.

"I guess we're going to the park. That okay with you?" I say.

"Perfect. Do you mind going to the Conservatory Garden? I haven't been by in months. It's my favorite place."

A strange thing happens next. We're walking past a row of beautiful old brownstones on Ninety-fourth Street when I see Livvy—at least I think it's Livvy—helping a woman on crutches into the door of an apartment building in the middle of the block. I'm trying desperately to put the brakes on, but it's like Livvy is holding out a handful of raw hamburger for Tillie, who is doing her finest sled-dog imitation, whining and pulling me in Livvy's direction. It takes all my strength to hold her back.

"Well, that's weird," I say when I finally have the beast under control.

"What's that, honey?"

"Did you see those people who just went in that building up there—the one with the fence around it? I'm almost positive that was Livvy Klack."

"The girl from school—the one who broke your nose?"

"That's her. I must be wrong. It's probably just someone who looks like her."

"Does she live in the neighborhood?"

"No, she lives down by the school, like on Sixty-second or Sixty-third."

When we walk past the front of the building, I catch a glimpse of a curtain in a first-floor window move to the side, but I resist the urge to turn and stare. It's probably not her, but if it *is* Livvy, I certainly don't want her to catch me in the act of peeking into windows. I can only imagine how *that* would be interpreted and spread around St. Veronica's.

But I can't stop pondering the sheer improbability of

it all: Livvy doing something nice. Again. All right, so maybe *not* making fun of my nose wouldn't count as being nice for most people, but in Livvy's case, it's all relative. After all, I know what she's capable of.

"She seems like such a sad kid," Mom says when we get to the corner. "I don't think I've ever seen her smile. Is she like that all the time?"

"Kind of. I mean, I've seen her smile and laugh—usually *at* people—but you're right, most of the time she looks absolutely miserable. She acts like a snob, and I really don't know why, because she's not super-rich or anything. Some of her friends are, though, and I think she hates St. V's because she feels like she ought to be at a ritzy school with them."

"Well, just remember what our good friend Atticus said: before you criticize someone, walk a mile in her shoes," Mom reminds me. She introduced Margaret and me to *To Kill a Mockingbird* over the summer, and as part of our exclusive book club, we discussed what the lawyer Atticus Finch meant by those very words. "You don't know what is going on in her life, so don't be too hard on her."

"Don't be hard on *her*? Mom, this is the girl who sabotaged my English project, totally insulted all my friends, *and* then broke my nose."

"Accidentally."

"Humph. Maybe," I say, even though I have suspected all along that there was nothing intentional about what happened in the pool.

We enter the park near Ninety-sixth Street, and Mom takes a seat for a few minutes on a bench while I run around the ball fields with Tillie, trying to wear her out a little. (Mom warns me that all I'm doing is getting her into tip-top physical condition; there simply is no tiring her out.) There are a few other people with dogs, and I get into a conversation with the owner of two yellow Labs, who shares a valuable piece of information: before nine o'clock in the morning, dogs are allowed to be off-leash in the park. A good long run might be just the thing to burn off some of that extra energy, so I promise Tillie I'll bring her over on Saturday morning if she's still with me. Of course, I'll have to check with Nate, to make sure she won't take off or something. Losing a big movie star's beloved dog would probably not be a great career move for me. I shudder, imagining thousands of Nate's fangirls chasing me through Central Park with pitchforks and torches.

I'm brought back to reality by Tillie, who has stopped in her tracks with ears perked up and head tilted, first to one side, then to the other. Somewhere in the distance, something—something that my inferior human eyes and ears can't see or hear—has suddenly become *very* interesting to her, and she starts dragging me toward it.

"Whoa, Tillie!" I yell, but she has caught me off balance, and I find myself running with her to keep from falling flat on my face. Which, considering the still-tender state of my nose, is *not* a great option.

"What are you doing?" Mom shouts. "I thought we were going to the garden."

"I'm . . . Tillie heard . . . We'll be right back," I call over my shoulder at her.

Once I regain my balance, I know I could stop her—she's not that big or strong—but I'm intrigued. When we get to the far north end of the ball fields, she stops again, all her senses on high alert. Just when I'm starting to think that whatever she's chasing is a figment of her imagination, I faintly hear a girl's voice shouting, ". . . leeeee . . . leeeee . . ."

And then, out of the corner of my eye, I spot a flash of black, as a fugitive dog, dragging its leash, races through the trees and away from the voice as fast as its long legs can carry it.

"Woof!" says Tillie—the first non-howling sound I've heard from her. "Woof woof woof."

"Hey, girl. What's the matter?" I ask, kneeling down to pet her. "It's just another dog." I finally get her to calm down, and we walk back to where Mom is waiting for us.

"What was that all about?" she asks.

"I'm not really sure," I say. "There was a dog who had gotten away from his owner, and the girl was calling him. Tillie seemed very concerned; she actually barked a few times."

"She's an odd dog. I think maybe the life of an actor is not really suited to pet ownership. Speaking of which, have you heard from your actor friend? Do you know how much longer we're—*you're*—going to have Miss Tillie?"

"Not yet. I'll text him later to find out. I guess I should also ask if she has any other bad habits I should be aware of."

Like shopping online with Mom's credit cards. On the other hand, maybe *she* can help me with my Spanish homework.

Chapter 7

So, who wins in a fight between a crocodile and a unicorn?

Now that we've finished reading *Great Expectations* in Mr. Eliot's English class, he has us tackling a bunch of short stories. And I'll admit that at first I wasn't too sure how I felt about short stories. No offense to short-story writers and fans, but I'm a *book* person. I just love novels, and the longer the better. Novels that I can get totally *lost* in—know what I mean? There's nothing like that mixture of excitement and regret when I get to the end of a book and I *almost* can't bear to turn that last page, just knowing that it's actually going to be over.

But lately I'm starting to appreciate the art of the short story, too. Right after we officially opened the Red Blazer Girls Detective Agency, Margaret loaned me a collection of Sherlock Holmes stories—sort of a how-to book for wannabe detectives, if ever there was one. I've been plowing my way through it, solving the cases along with Holmes and Watson, and you know what? Some days a few pages are just right.

The stories Mr. Eliot is giving us are different, though. We spent a lot of time talking about the conflict and irony in classics like "The Most Dangerous Game" and "How Much Land Does a Man Need?" and today we're continuing with a *very* short story called "The Interlopers."

We've already had our discussion of the key elements of the story, so at the beginning of class, Mr. Eliot tells each of us to find a partner for an assignment related to the story—and warns us that we have to present our answer to the class before the end of the period. Rebecca's not in English with us, so Margaret, Leigh Ann, and I look at one another, trying to figure out how to divide three evenly by two.

Finally, Leigh Ann, the newest of the Red Blazer Girls, says, "Go ahead, you guys. You're used to working together. I'll work with someone else." She looks around the room, frowning. "Hmmm."

I turn around, and there is Livvy, staring off into space; actually, she seems to be zeroed in on the very window where I first saw Elizabeth Harriman's face—the time I screamed right in the middle of class. I'm guessing she hasn't heard a word Mr. Eliot has said.

"No, Leigh Ann," I say. "I always get to work with Margaret. It's your turn. I'm going to ask Livvy."

Whoa! Did I just say what I think I said? Out loud?

I guess so, because Margaret and Leigh Ann are staring at me as if I have a horn growing out of my forehead.

"Have you lost your mind?" Margaret whispers.

"I'll be fine," I say.

I will be fine, right?

"Everybody have a partner?" Mr. Eliot asks as he hands me an index card with a single task: create a graph that illustrates all the conflicting emotions going through Georg's head as he lies trapped beneath the fallen tree. "Miss St. Pierre? How about you?"

I spin around again to face Livvy, and this time she looks back at me.

"What?" she snarls. "Jeez, what did I do now?"

"Nothing. I, um, need a partner. For this assignment." I hand her the card, and for a second she looks like an animal trying desperately to avoid a trap. She eyes Margaret and Leigh Ann suspiciously, but they're already hard at work.

She sighs dramatically. "Fine."

"Excellent," says Mr. Eliot, who gives me a strange nod before retreating to his own desk.

"So, any ideas?" I ask cheerfully.

She just glares across the table at me. After a long, uncomfortable silence, she says, "Why?"

"Because we need to get this done before the end of the period, and I just wondered if you had any ideas on how to get started."

"No, I mean, why me? I thought you and your friends hated me. You're smart—lots of kids would be happy to be your partner."

"I don't hate you, Livvy. I mean, you haven't exactly made it easy for any of us to *like* you, but . . . come on, let's just do this one stupid assignment, all right?"

Another resigned sigh, this one not quite so dramatic. So she's not thrilled to be working with me—but at least she doesn't give me the eye roll of death.

And you know what? It's not the most fun I ever had—in fact, it wasn't fun at all—but our answer totally kicks butt. Together we create a bar graph showing all of Georg's various internal battles in shades of blue and his external conflicts in shades of red.

The colors were Livvy's idea, and she explains our choices to the class.

"Blue for internal conflict, because it all makes him, you know, sad inside, thinking about all the time he has wasted being enemies with Ulrich. And red because he's angry at his predicament—the cold, the storm, the tree, and, uh, you know, what happens at the end."

"Very impressive, girls," Mr. Eliot says as we wrap up our presentation. On the way back to our seats—for just a fraction of a micro-mini-second—I get the feeling that Livvy's going to high-five me, but the moment passes, and we sit without another look.

After the bell, though, she secretly drops a note on my desk before leaving to join the Klackettes for sandwiches, sodas, and sarcasm in the cafeteria. It reads: "Sorry about your nose."

And there you have it: the cornerstone laid in a foundation. A first step up an imposing mountain peak. The first chapter of an epic novel. A . . . well, go ahead—you choose an appropriate metaphor.

"What was *that* all about?" Margaret asks me as we're putting books away in our shared locker.

I examine my nose in the mirror we have taped inside the locker door. "Hey, it's looking better, don't you think? You can hardly see the bruises."

"Sophie Jeanette St. Pierre. Are you ignoring me?"

"What? Oh, you mean the thing with Livvy? No biggie. Just a little experiment."

"Well, you're lucky your little experiment didn't just blow up in your face. Was the scientific method involved at all?"

"Sure. I had a hypothesis."

"Which was?"

"That maybe Livvy's not so bad."

Leigh Ann, who's down the hall at her own locker, hears me and slams her locker door shut. "Compared to *what*? A crocodile that eats its own babies? This is the same girl who totally stabbed us in the back on our last English project. And the girl who called us a bunch of losers, remember?"

"I didn't say she's a saint," I say. "I just think there might be more to her than we think."

"Yeah, well, I think there might be *less,*" Leigh Ann says with a snort.

"I have to hand it to you, Soph," Margaret says. "You're like the Gandhi of St. Veronica's—a peacemaker. I'll admit it—I couldn't do what you did. No way."

Leigh Ann's curiosity gets the best of her. "So, did she say anything, you know, about *us*?"

I smile coyly. "You're just dying to know, aren't you? Well, the answer is no. Not a word. She was all business. I'd forgotten how smart she is. And she's really pretty, too. You know, when she's not scowling or being super-sarcastic."

Leigh Ann scoffs. "In other words, about eight seconds a year."

"I'm not surprised you think she's pretty," Margaret says. "Except for your noses, you two could almost pass for twins. You're the same size, same cheekbones, same hair."

"Our cheekbones? You're crazy," I say.

Leigh Ann nods. " 'Fraid so, Soph. The other day, Livvy was walking down the hall away from me and I came *this* close to calling her Sophie."

"*That* would have been good," Margaret says.

"I know. My heart was pounding afterward," Leigh Ann admits. "I even had a nightmare about it."

Okay, let's stop and think about this for a moment, shall we? My best friends are afraid of how Livvy would respond to being mistaken for me.

I think I've been insulted. Again.

Harrumph.

Chapter 8

A visit with old friends, er, good friends who are old-ish

On Tuesday afternoon, we have a date with our old friends Malcolm Chance and Elizabeth Harriman at Elizabeth's townhouse, which is just up the street from the school. These two have quite a history. Married. Divorced. And, thanks to the Red Blazer Girls and the search for a certain ring, reconnected many years later. Current relationship status: unknown—at least to us. (Yes, I'm aware that it's a total cliché, but "It's complicated" seems to sum it up.) Malcolm seems to be spending more and more time with his ex-wife, but he still has an apartment on the Upper West Side, near Columbia University, where he is a professor of archaeology.

We're really hoping to pick Malcolm's brain about the pictures in Father Julian's shoe box, but first we need to spend some girls-only time with Elizabeth. So, after a pot of our favorite Flower Power tea, a plate or two of cookies (sadly, store-bought), and 237 questions (give or take a few) about our families, school, and every other

aspect of our lives, she leans back on the couch, satisfied.

"Okay, Malcolm. Your turn."

Malcolm returns from the kitchen with a dish towel
in his hands. "Are you quite certain, precious?" he asks
with a wink in my direction, his eyes twinkling mischievously.

"Don't you 'precious' me," Elizabeth says. "I'm merely
trying to stay abreast of our young friends' busy lives."

"Yes, dear," he says. "And I'd say you're doing
a fine job of it, too. That was quite a thorough cross-
examination."

Elizabeth squints at him. "If these lovely girls
weren't here, *sweetness,* I think I would conk you on
the head with this teapot."

"Well then, it's a good thing you girls are here. All
right, let's get down to work. You mentioned that you're
working on a case. For Father Julian, is that right? He's
a nice young man."

"Yep," I say. "Kind of an archaeology project. You
know how scientists can look at things and figure out how
old they are? Well, you're going to teach us how to do
that."

"I am? I mean, yes. Yes, I am."

Margaret gives him a quick version of the story of
the painting. At the first mention of the name Pommeroy, Elizabeth, whose walls are littered with paintings
by modern masters such as Matisse, Picasso, and
Warhol, sits up straight.

"Father Julian owns a Pommeroy? I would love to see it. I've been trying to add one to my collection for years. I met him once, with my father, at a downtown gallery—I forget the name. They had a show of his later work. Such a tragic story."

"I'm sure Father Julian would be happy to show it to you," I say. "It's over in the rectory. And you know, speaking of art galleries, Becca and I had a strange experience Saturday morning. Tell them about it, Becca."

"Why don't you tell it?"

"Duh. Because I didn't actually *see* anything."

"Oh, fine."

She finishes telling the story, then adds, "This Gus guy can really *paint*. Soph, remember all those still lifes we saw on the wall? They're all his, and so are the big, dark, swirly ones. Elizabeth, I think one of those would look really good in here."

"Well, thank you, Rebecca. I may just have to go have a look for myself," she says. "I'm always in the market for things that make me feel good."

Margaret opens the shoe box full of photos and sets it on the coffee table in front of Malcolm. "All right. Time to get to work."

Malcolm pulls a pair of reading glasses out of a case and slips them on. "So your theory is that if you can accurately date one of these pictures that shows the painting, you'll have proof that the painting was done prior to 1961, right?"

"Theoretically," Margaret answers. "This is a picture

of Father Julian's great-grandparents in their house in the Bronx, near Yankee Stadium. If you look on the wall behind them, you can see the top right-hand corner of the painting."

Malcolm sets the shoe box on his lap and starts to take a closer look at a few of the pictures. "Well, the good news is that most of these pictures were taken with a good camera—probably an old range finder. Look how clear the image is, all the way to the edges. Wait here a moment while I find a loupe," Malcolm says, heading for the study that once belonged to Elizabeth's father, himself a well-known archaeologist and professor.

"A what?" Leigh Ann asks.

"A loupe. Kind of a fancy magnifying glass—looks like a camera lens," Margaret explains. "I guess archaeologists use them, too."

He returns a few seconds later, polishing the lens with a cotton handkerchief. Then he moves a lamp from a side table to the coffee table. "There. Now let's have a proper look."

He sets the loupe on the corner of the painting in the photograph and squints into it. "Yep, it's a painting all right."

"Yay!" I say, getting into the spirit of things. "Let's call Father Julian and tell him we cracked the case."

"*You're* cracked," Rebecca says, poking me with a pointy elbow.

"What else do you see?" Margaret asks. "Anything on the table? On those bookshelves?"

"Some books, a glass vase, a decanter. A couple of picture frames—hard to see what's in them because of the reflections. Some souvenirs and knickknacks. The usual suspects. Here, Margaret, you take a look. Your young eyes are much better suited to this kind of work than mine."

Margaret takes the loupe from him and zeroes in on the bookcase. "I think I can make out some of the titles. Looks like Father Julian's great-grandfather was a serious reader. There's Plato and Socrates, and *The Decline and Fall of the Roman Empire*. Ah, here's some more modern stuff on the lower shelf. There's a Hemingway, and a couple of Faulkners."

"You know, this really is a fascinating problem," Malcolm says, scratching his chin. "And, I fear, more difficult than I first thought. Not a typical archaeological problem at all."

"That doesn't sound encouraging," Leigh Ann says.

"Let me explain," Malcolm says, peering over his glasses at us. "Archaeologists are always trying to determine the age of things—bones, pieces of pottery, parchment, statues, you name it. But it's usually a matter of *approximately* what year, or even what century, the thing came from. From a more modern perspective, photographs are generally fairly simple to date—to a certain degree. With just a quick glance at these pictures, most people could guess the time frame of the vast majority within fifteen or twenty years. A closer look—like the one we're taking right now—can narrow it down considerably.

For instance, let's consider that copy of Ernest Hemingway's *The Old Man and the Sea*. I happen to know that it was published in 1952, so we now know *this* picture was taken in 1952 *or later*."

"But . . . that's great news, isn't it?" I ask. "As long as it's before 1961, it proves what we need it to prove, right?"

"Not really," Malcolm says. "It's the 'or later' part that complicates things. In pointing out the copy of the Hemingway book, all we did was prove the picture couldn't have been taken *before* 1952. But it could have been taken yesterday for all we know."

It takes a second, but the logic finally sinks into my chlorine-soaked brain. "Ohhhh. Now I see."

"But now for the bad news. This particular picture, I'm sorry to say, was definitely taken after 1963."

"How do you know that?" Margaret asks.

"Do you see this window? Now look closely at the car out in the driveway. I am a hundred percent positive that those are the grille and headlights of a 1964 Ford Thunderbird. The new models would have come out in September or October 1963—a couple of years too late to be useful to you."

"So what can we do?" Leigh Ann asks.

Malcolm rubs his chin a little more, then smooths out his mustache with his fingers. "Well, here's what I would do: go through these pictures and find every single one that shows either the painting or the spot on the wall where it was hung—even the ones that were obviously taken much earlier or much later than 1961. You never know how they might come in handy. Then put those sharp red blazers on and get down to some serious detective work."

"What kinds of things should we be looking for?" Becca asks.

"At this point, anything. Everything. Combinations of things," Malcolm says. "Clothing. Hairstyles. A pen sitting on the desk. A calendar. A pack of matches. A record album. You know what those are, right? It's what we had in the days before CDs and iPods."

"We know what records are," I say, slightly insulted. "Vinyl. They're back in style."

"Ah, forgive me. I momentarily forgot that I am also dealing with famous musicians."

Malcolm and Elizabeth are probably the Blazers' biggest fans; they've been to every one of our shows, and Elizabeth lets us practice in her basement a couple of times a week after school.

Margaret holds up the loupe. "Can we borrow this? I think I'm starting to get some ideas about where we go from here."

"You definitely have your work cut out for you," Malcolm says. "But if the way you handled all the twists and turns in those extravaganzas with the ring and the violin is any indication, the Red Blazer Girls Detective Agency can certainly handle *this* case. I'd stake my reputation on it."

"I would think, dear," Elizabeth chimes in, "that if you were really confident, you'd risk something that actually had some *value*."

"Touché," says Malcolm, holding his heart as if he's been stabbed.

Chapter 9

In which Tillie has an unusual snack

With Becca heading to Chinatown and Leigh Ann off to Queens, Margaret and I walk back to my apartment fully intending to do our homework together. I say "intending" because my new friend Tillie has made other plans.

Mom isn't home from the music school yet, and Tillie meets us at the door. If you're not a dog person, you probably don't understand how unbelievably nice it is to be on the receiving end of that greeting at the end of the day. Dogs are *always* glad to see you; it doesn't matter if it's been three hours or three days. I've only had Tillie for a few days, but it feels like we're old friends and have a routine that we've been following for years.

After her usual tail wagging, rolling over to have her belly rubbed, and excited leaping, she is ready for her afternoon walk. We take her over to Carl Schurz Park, between East End Avenue and the river. There's a small area that's fenced in on three sides, and I bravely (stupidly?) unclip her leash and let her run around while

Margaret and I keep her away from the open side. It's just what she needs—some real exercise—and since she doesn't try to run away, I'm starting to gain the confidence to let her go off-leash in Central Park, which is many, many times larger than Carl Schurz Park.

That is, unless I kill her first.

When we get back to the apartment, Mom is there waiting for us at the door, and the greeting I get from her isn't nearly as nice as the one from Tillie. She is scowling at me.

"Sophie! Have you seen your room?"

"Oh, right. Sorry, Mom. I know, I promised to straighten it up over the weekend. I'll do it tonight, I promise."

"I think you'd better take a look," Mom says. "It's going to be a bigger job than you think. Margaret, if you're smart, you'll disappear before you get roped into helping her."

I glance at Tillie—all innocence and sweetness—and then run back to my room, stopping cold when I get to the doorway.

"Holeeee cow," I gasp. "What happened?"

"Was there an earthquake today that I didn't notice?" Margaret asks. "Some other kind of natural disaster?"

"Hurricane Tillie," I say. *"Tillie!"*

Tillie, wisely, does not come when called.

All my bookshelves are on the floor, with all my books. Hundreds of books.

"How on earth did she . . ." Margaret ponders for a moment, then walks gingerly toward the pile, glancing up at the wall, from which the naked brackets still extend. "Ahhh. The chair," she says, pointing at my sturdy wooden desk chair. "I'll bet she climbed up the back of this chair and then put her feet on the bottom shelf."

"But . . . why?" I ask, sorting through my most precious possessions and one decidedly unlovely brass bowl, now in an ignominious pile on the floor. (In case you're wondering, yes, I've been back to my orthodontist. Another *Reader's Digest,* another "Word Power." Frankly, I don't know what I'll do to expand my vocabulary if I ever get my braces off. It's quite *worrisome.* In fact, I'm rather *disconcerted* by the very *notion.*)

"You must have had something up there that she wanted," Margaret says. "A sandwich?"

"I did *not* have a sandwich on my bookshelves," I insist. "C'mon, I hardly ever bring food in here. Other than the occasional cookie, that is."

Margaret's raised eyebrow tells me that she's not buying whatever I'm selling. "Occasional, my eye."

"Okay, so maybe it's *slightly* more than occasionally. But I would never put a cookie on the bookshelves."

And then I see it. In the corner of the room, over by the window.

Miles and miles of gray yarn. A hint of red stitching. Chewed-up leather.

"Is that—?" Margaret's hand flies to her mouth.

"A baseball," I whisper. It's hard to make much noise

when your heart makes the leap from your chest to your throat.

Margaret picks up Father Julian's tote bag and looks inside. "Were they . . . both . . . in here?"

"Y-yes." I drop to my knees. I'm not praying—well, not yet, anyway. My legs just gave out.

Margaret starts to stuff that mass of yarn and leather formerly known as a baseball into the tote. "This is definitely only one baseball. The other one might still be safe."

I'm still paralyzed, unable to help her.

"Come on, Sophie. Help me find the other ball. I don't see any more yarn. It's probably under all these books."

I force myself to start looking under everything—the bed, my desk, the ginormous pile of books—but it's just not there.

"This can't be happening to me," I sob, looking upward. "First my nose, now this. What did I do wrong?"

And then, the unthinkable: Tillie walks into my room with the other baseball in her mouth.

I scream.

Margaret screams.

Mom comes running.

And a totally terrified Tillie scurries from the room with the two of us right on her tail—a tail that is tucked firmly between her legs. She goes into my parents' room and ducks under the bed.

"C'mon, Tillie," Margaret coaxes. "Good girl. You can come out. We're not going to hurt you."

Actually, *one* of us might. Because, to tell you the truth, I'm not exactly certain of what I'm going to do when I get hold of that scrawny mutt's neck.

Tillie is unconvinced by Margaret's pleasant tone, however, and stays put.

"What does she have?" Mom asks.

"A baseball," Margaret answers. "It belongs to Father Julian. We're—it's kind of a long story."

"It's really valuable," I manage to say. "Maybe."

"I'm going in after her," Margaret says dramatically.

"Be careful," Mom says.

Which is exactly what moms are *supposed* to say in situations like this.

Margaret commando-crawls under the bed, sweet-talking Tillie every inch of the way. "That's a good girl, Tillie. Can I have the ball? I'll trade you that nasty old baseball for a brand-new cookie. Good girl!"

"Did you get it?"

"Got it." Margaret's feet start backing out from under the bed. Tillie pokes her head out, looking up at me with those big ol' sad eyes of hers.

"Don't even talk to me," I say to her.

A dust-covered Margaret finally emerges, holding the ball up triumphantly. She spins it around and around in the light.

With a heavy sigh, she announces: "It's okay. A little

wet, but no damage, and the autographs are all still there."

"Thank God," I say. Then I glare at Tillie, who hides behind her new best friend and protector, Margaret. "You . . . you . . ."

"Maybe Tillie should come with me for a while," Mom says. "While you and Margaret go sort things out in your room."

"Good idea, Kate," Margaret says, pulling me along. "We'll figure something out. We always do."

An hour later, my books are still in a pile on the floor. I'm lying on my bed, staring at the ceiling and trying to figure out how I'm going to tell Father Julian that the baseball his great-uncle caught at Yankee Stadium was eaten by Nate Etan's dog. I wonder if he even knows—or cares—who Nate Etan is. Somehow I doubt he'll think he's *lucky* that his family heirloom was chewed up by some celebrity's mutt.

Margaret attempts to console me by telling me that, no matter what, Father Julian will forgive me.

"He's a *priest,* Sophie. He's in the forgiveness business. And you didn't do anything wrong, or even irresponsible. You had no way of knowing that Tillie has some weird baseball obsession and would tear down a whole wall of shelves to get to one. It was an act of God."

"More like an act of *dog,*" I say through sniffles and sobs.

Margaret's next strategy is hard research. She goes

online, reading article after article on baseball construction throughout the years. Occasionally she spouts some fact or other about how many yards of wool yarn it takes or how the covers changed from horsehide to cowhide because there was a shortage of horses, but I'm too caught up in my own self-pity to really pay attention.

Until now, that is.

"Sophie. Come here. I have some bad news."

"Y-you do?"

"Uh-huh. 'Fraid so."

I drag myself off the bed and slump next to Margaret. The very same Margaret who has saved me so many times. But not, it seems, this time.

She points at the article on the screen, something about World War II–era baseball. "Sorry, but you're not going to be famous."

"Wh-what do you mean?" I feel the tears backing up in my eyes. "Oh no. That *was* the original ball, wasn't it."

Margaret smiles and shakes her head. "What I meant was, you're not going to be famous as the girl whose dog ate a really valuable baseball. Tillie ate the fake one. I'm positive."

"Really?" My knees give out again and I sit on the floor next to her.

"Absolutely." She holds up a rubber ball about an inch in diameter. "This is the center of the ball that Tillie chewed up—they call this 'the pill.' During World War II, the government was rationing rubber, so they had to use inferior, man-made materials for things like baseballs. And *this* is definitely not natural. This baseball may have come from Yankee Stadium, but not in 1928. It wasn't made until 1942 at least."

I jump to my feet and tackle her, pulling her off the chair and onto the floor, where I sit on her. "Margaret Wrobel, I *love* you! You totally saved my life. Again! I am going to dedicate the rest of my life to you. Whatever you want, just ask me and it's yours."

"Easy, Soph. It's not that big a deal. All I did was prove that you got lucky. It was fate; Tillie had a choice of two baseballs to eat, and she ate the 'right' one." She pushes me off her and picks up the other ball, still damp from Tillie's mouth. "And now, thanks to Tillie, we know that *this* is the real baseball."

Upon hearing her name, Tillie trots back into my room, tail wagging like mad. She sniffs the air until she locates what she's looking for: the baseball that we so cruelly and unfairly took from her.

"No way, Tillie," Margaret says, laughing. Then she tucks the ball into her book bag. "Under the circumstances, perhaps it's best if *I* hold on to this."

I glance at the devil-in-a-dog-suit named Tillie. "I think you're right."

"Woof!" says Tillie, who has already shrugged off the loss of the baseball and moved on. Her nose is buried in one of my school blazer pockets, and she sniffs, snuffles, and whines until she finally manages to pull out the folded "Sorry about your nose" note from Livvy—the note that I had purposely not mentioned to anyone. She then stretches out on the floor, holding the paper between her front paws, and starts to lick it.

"What is that?" Margaret asks. "It must smell really good to her."

I take the note from the very disappointed Tillie and hold it out for Margaret to read.

"You see, Sophie? Even Tillie knows the rules: no secrets!"

Chapter 10

A series of inexplicable events

The next couple of days fly past, with only one strange event to report. I'm having a really nice conversation with Leigh Ann on the phone when . . . she bumps me for another call. I don't even have a chance to protest; she just blurts out, "HeyIhavetotakethisI'llcallyouback-later."

But here's the weird part: right after Leigh Ann hangs up on me (which is the way *I* choose to interpret what happened), I call Rebecca, who is on another line with someone—she doesn't say who—and then *she* bumps me off to go back to her first call, promising to call me as soon as she finishes. Which, to her credit, she does, ten seconds after Leigh Ann calls me back. Oy.

Neither one has a reasonable explanation. Leigh Ann mumbles something about having to talk to a classmate about an assignment, and Becca insists she was on with her mom, but I'm not buying either story. My imagination starts to run wild, and it's no time at all until I have convinced myself that they're mad at me because I said something nice about Livvy, and now they want me out of the band.

They're up to something. I'm sure of it.

On Friday, the Blazers have our regular gig at Perkatory, and we're trying to learn a new song, bringing our repertoire up to four, including my own "hit" song—the one inspired by that fateful English project on apostrophes. Our drummer, Mbingu, has been working on the lyrics for a few weeks now, and she is finally satisfied with them, so we can debut the song Friday. This week's show, however, has an added attraction: Nate Etan is coming to Perkatory to see the Blazers.

Wednesday afternoon, we're jamming away in Elizabeth's basement when I get a text message from him:

In NY Fri 4 a few hrs can I c Tillie 7pm.

Rather than try to explain everything in a text message, though, I just tell him yes, and to check his email later for all the details. Movie star or not, we're not going to cancel our Perkatory gig, so if he wants to see Tillie, he's just going to have to come and see us at the coffee shop. Which is a little terrifying, but only slightly more so than an ordinary Friday night.

"Did you tell him about the baseball?" Becca asks.

"Or the howling?" adds Leigh Ann.

Mbingu points at my feet, where my red Chuck Taylors should be. "Or your shoes?"

"No, no, and no," I say. "I don't want him to feel guilty. He's got enough on his mind already. I'll tell him later."

"You don't think he's, you know, taking advantage of you—just a little?" Mbingu asks. "I don't know him, but it seems a little weird that he would ask you to do all this stuff for him when he hardly knows you."

Becca, who had been as excited as anyone to meet him on the set, nods in agreement. "Don't get me wrong, I'm still totally going to marry him, but it *is* a little strange, Soph."

"You guys are crazy," I say. "He asked me for a *favor.* And I'm doing it. That's what friends do."

That's me: friend to the stars. And the fifty dollars a day he's paying me? Absolutely *nothing* to do with it.

Friday night, ten minutes after seven, and no Nate. Seven-fifteen. Seven-twenty. We can't put off our set any longer because Mbingu has an eight-thirty curfew. (Hey, give us a break. We're twelve.) Leigh Ann steps up to her microphone and says, "Hey, everybody. Welcome to Perkatory. We're the Blazers."

And by the way, we're wearing our faux red blazers— T-shirts painted by Becca to look like punked-up versions of our school uniforms. *Très* cool. We open with our old standby, "Twist and Shout," and just as we get started, the door opens and in walks . . . Cam Peterson, Nate's co-star—the one who was so rude to us on the set. He's with a college-age guy who, frankly, doesn't look old enough to be a manager, tough enough to be a bodyguard, or smart enough to be a tutor. After sizing up the place for a few moments, they sit at an empty table next to the one occupied by Margaret and Andrew (the cello player in her string quartet and the recipient of her first-ever kiss), along with Raf and his friend Sean, who has a huge crush on the not-at-all-interested Leigh Ann. Becca and I look at each other, shrug, and keep playing. Cam doesn't exactly seem comfortable, but by the end of the song, he's smiling and cheering along with everyone else. Of course, by then, all of the kids from school have realized that there's a minor celebrity in the audience and are staring in his direction, and to be honest, I'm not sure if they're cheering us or him.

We follow up with the Beatles' "I Want to Hold Your Hand," followed by my song, and then wrap things up with Mbingu's creation, which has kind of a reggae beat that the crowd really gets into.

And still no Nate.

Cam Peterson's head turns toward the door every time it opens, as if he's waiting for someone, too—although my brain is having a hard time grasping just whom he could be waiting for in a tiny coffee shop on the Upper East Side on a Friday night.

With my guitar safely returned to its case, I join

Margaret, Andrew, Raf, and Sean at their table. There are only four chairs, so I guess I'll just have to share one with Raf. Bummer.

"You were great, as usual," Raf says, giving my hand a little squeeze under the table. "So, where's this big movie star you guys are all so in love with?" He uses air quotes around "movie star." "And where's Tillie, anyway? I thought that's why *he* was coming."

Wait a second. Raf's voice has that same tone again, just like the last time the topic was Nate, and it finally occurs to my marble-sized brain that he really is jealous! (Now, can someone please explain why that makes me so happy? Seriously—I don't want to be one of *those* girls.)

"Shhh! Tillie's in the back with the manager's kids. We have to keep her out of sight until the other customers are gone. And I don't know what happened to Nate." I check my phone for messages for the seventeenth time, but there's still no word from him.

Becca and Leigh Ann find chairs at the table next to ours, and a few seconds later Cam Peterson makes his way toward us.

He's smaller than I remembered from that day on the movie set, and as he's standing there between our tables, he's just another nervous, slightly awkward boy— a far cry from the foulmouthed, rude kid we met in that catering tent.

"Um, hi, I don't know if you . . . but you guys rocked. I really enjoyed it."

"Thanks," says Leigh Ann, flashing her million-dollar smile. "Do you want to join us?" She points to the empty chair next to hers.

There's not a boy alive who can say no to that smile of Leigh Ann's.

"Uh, sure. I guess. Thanks."

"Do you want to ask your friend, too?" Leigh Ann asks, pointing to the guy Cam came in with.

"Oh, you mean Will? He's not a friend—just a guy that the producers hired to make sure I don't get lost, or kidnapped, or, you know, in trouble. He's also supposed to be my math tutor, but I don't think he knows what he's talking about. He'll be happy to get rid of me for a while, I'm sure."

"Can I ask you a question?" Becca says. "Did you come here tonight just to see us play? Because that would totally freak me out."

Cam smiles—the first time I've seen him do it—and it's not bad. Not in Raf's league, mind you, but I've seen worse.

"The truth is, no, but I'm glad I got to see you guys play. I am so jealous of people who can play instruments. I tried to learn guitar, but I didn't have time to practice. And by the way, those shirts? Awesome. The real reason I came is that I'm supposed to be meeting Nate Etan here. I got this strange message from him saying he was only going to be in town for a few hours, and he really wanted to talk to me about these scenes we still have to shoot—like a month from now—and that he was meeting his, um, dog here at seven. You haven't seen him, by any chance?"

"No, he told me he'd be here at seven, too," I say. "I've been taking care of Tillie for him while he's off in London or wherever he is."

Cam looks puzzled. "You've had her since he left?"

"Yeah, why?"

"It's just strange. I'm staying at the St. Regis Hotel, and whenever I get a break from shooting, I drag Will out and do some exploring in the park. I'm not supposed to skateboard, in case I break my neck or something. I could swear I saw Tillie with somebody else—at least I don't *think* it was you—Monday or Tuesday of this week. It was by the ball fields up above Ninety-sixth Street. And I'm sure she was calling Tillie's name."

"That probably *was* me. Tillie and I were up there by the Conservatory Garden with my mom. It's her favorite place. Mom's, that is. Although Tillie seemed to enjoy it, too. Funny we didn't see you."

At that moment, Nate Etan bursts through the Perkatory door, stopping just inside so everyone has plenty of opportunity to admire him. Or at least that's the way it looks to us.

"Jeez, what an entrance," Leigh Ann gushes.

"Hey! There they are! My favorite girls. And my favorite co-star! Hey, buddy! *Comment allez-vous?* Sorry I'm late—I had a meeting with my publicist and totally lost track of the time. She's trying to get me on all the talk shows next week—you know how it is. Busy, busy, busy." He looks around the room. "So, where's my girl? Where's my Tillie?"

"I'll go get her," Margaret says, clearly annoyed at him. So much for celebrity worship on her part. Maybe it'd be different if he was a musician; I've seen her blush just running her fingers over her idol's violin.

I sneak a peek at Cam, who seems to share Margaret's (and Raf's, now that I think about it) feelings about Nate Etan.

I make all the introductions around the table, and Nate is very charming, shaking hands with Andrew, Raf, and Sean. I have kind of a weird moment when he and Raf meet, and I cringe when Nate calls him Ralph.

"It's *Raf*," Raf and I say together, but it's already too late. In Nate's mind, I can tell, the good-looking kid with the great hair is going to be Ralph forever.

He seems to have forgotten completely why we were meeting at Perk—the Blazers' gig—until he realizes that Becca, Leigh Ann, and I are all still wearing our faux blazers. "Oh, yeah, your band. The Jackets, right? I *totally* forgot. Did I miss it?"

"The *Blazers*," Becca corrects. "And yeah. We only know a few songs, so, you know—"

But once again, Nate's attention-span-challenged brain has already moved on; he spots Margaret coming back with Tillie.

"There she is! Hey, Tillie girl!" he shouts.

Tillie, however, wants nothing to do with him. She ducks under the table between Raf and me and puts her head on my lap.

"Tillie," I say. "Come on, girl. It's okay." She presses her head harder against me.

"Maybe she's nervous because of all the people," Leigh Ann says.

"This is crazy," Nate says. "Tillie! It's me."

With Ralph's—oops, *Raf's*—help, I coax her out from under the table so Nate can at least get a good look at her and pet her. She sits there stiffly and lets him do it, but she never takes her eyes off me.

"I'm really sorry," I say. "I swear I'm not doing anything special to make her like me more."

"Well, at least I know she's being well cared for," Nate says, forcing a smile. "Which is good news . . . because, I, um, have to go back to London, and I'm going to be there a little longer than I thought. So, what do you think, Sophie? Can you hang in there a few more days? I was paying you forty a day, right? Let's make it fifty, okay?"

"Uh, actually it already was. Um, sure," I say, avoiding eye contact with Margaret. "She's no trouble."

Margaret's eyes grow wide and she practically chokes as she stops herself from screaming at me. (I know I'm going to hear all about it later.)

"Are you okay, Margaret?" Raf asks.

"I'm fine. Just a little . . . surprised."

• • •

102

Raf's mom, sadly, is still not budging on Raf's eight-thirty curfew, so he and Sean need to be out the door by eight in order to catch a crosstown bus. Before he goes, I get exactly two minutes alone with him on the sidewalk outside. I'm still new to this world of dealing with boys as, well, *boys,* but something is definitely different. He's distracted, and doesn't want to make eye contact with me.

"All right—what's going on?" I ask.

He shrugs. "Nothing."

"You really can't stay longer?"

"No. My mom . . . well, you know."

"I'm sorry," I say.

"Yeah, well, I'm sure you'll still have fun without me."

"Raf, you're not seriously jealous, are you? Of Nate? Or Cam?"

"N—nooo."

But he can't look at me.

"Raf! Come on! This is me—Sophie! Those guys are just . . . I don't even know what to call them. In a few days they'll be gone forever. You—and me—that's different. Really."

I throw my arms around his neck and pull him toward me, giving him every opportunity to kiss me.

But he doesn't do it.

The door to Perkatory opens, and as Sean starts up the steps, Raf gently pushes me away.

"I've got to get going," he mumbles.

I watch as he and Sean shuffle off into the darkness.

I wait for him to turn around and wave like he always does, but this time he doesn't. And suddenly I feel sick to my stomach and have to sit down for a few moments.

I try to console myself by telling myself I didn't do anything wrong and that Raf is just overreacting. Yes, Nate is gorgeous. *Really* gorgeous. And rich. And famous. But . . . wait, I do have a point to make here . . . oh, right! Raf and I have history. We're real, and Nate is just make-believe. Beautiful, but make-believe. Have I mentioned how good he looks?

But no matter what I do, I can't seem to get rid of the lump in my throat. A few minutes earlier, I was actually happy that Raf seemed jealous, but now I'm just a mess of conflicting emotions. This whole boy thing really is going to be tough, isn't it? I'm not quite thirteen yet, and I'm already thoroughly confused.

I sit on the stoop outside Perkatory for a few more minutes, collecting myself before going back in. Nate starts to say his good-byes a few minutes later. He glances nervously at his watch, refers vaguely to another "important" meeting downtown, and then buttons his coat.

"Um, Nate," Cam interrupts, "I thought you wanted to meet with me. You made it sound like it was really important, so I canceled dinner with my grandparents tonight. I hardly ever get to see them." He looks like he's going to cry.

"Sorry, dude," Nate says. "I really gotta go. I'll send you an email. Ciao."

Exit Nate Etan, stage left.

Enter reeeaaallly awkward silence, stage right.

Leigh Ann, with her super-cheerful nature, is just the one to break it. "So, you're staying at the St. Regis. We've actually been there—to the King Cole Bar. It's kind of famous."

"And they make a mean piña kidlada," I add. "You know, if you're into pineapple juice."

Cam finally cracks a smile. "I'll have to check it out. Gee, do you think this whole situation could be any *more* embarrassing? Seriously, it's just fantastic. In a few hours, some stupid blogger will be telling the world all about how Nate Etan totally blew me off at some East Side coffee shop."

"Well, nobody's going to hear it from us," Margaret says. "We wouldn't do something like that." Her eyes twinkle mischievously as she adds: "No matter how rude you were to us the first time we met."

Cam's mouth drops open. "That was *you*, that morning in the catering tent—when I was on the phone. Oh my God. The way I acted, I wouldn't blame you if you did send pictures to one of those stalker websites. I am so sorry. You have to believe me when I tell you I was having a really bad day."

I must not be doing a very good job at hiding what I'm thinking, because he smiles and shrugs. "What, you think because I'm a movie star I don't have bad days?"

"Well, except for that part about you being a movie

star, that's *exactly* what I think," I say. Margaret, Becca, and Leigh Ann nod enthusiastically in agreement.

"I see," he says. "Listen, I'm starving. How about we go out for pizza and I'll tell you the whole sad story? And I want to hear about this whole red blazer thing. You guys must know a good place around here. Of course, it won't be as good as the pizza in Chicago, where I grew up, but I'll survive. C'mon, I'm buying."

"Whoa," Becca says, not budging from her chair. "Nobody's going anywhere. Did you just disrespect New York pizza? In front of four New Yorkers?"

Cam, who is already on his feet, freezes when he sees us all still sitting there with arms crossed. "Boy, they aren't kidding about that whole New York attitude thing, are they? Okay, let's try this again. You know, I hear that New York pizza is the *greatest* pizza in the world, and I am just *dying* to try some."

Becca stares him down. "That's better. What do you think, guys? Trantonno's?"

"Perfect," Margaret and I say in unison.

"Chicago-style pizza," Becca says, smirking. "As if."

We're on our way out the door when Aldo, the manager at Perkatory, shouts, "Sophie! Don't leave. I almost forgot—someone left something for you. Didn't see who it was."

The cardboard box he sets on the counter is smaller than the one that held the mysterious and still-unexplained brass bowl. Printed across the top, under my name, are the warnings "This side up! Do not turn over!"

"*Another* strange package?" I say. "When did you find it?"

Aldo scratches his scraggly goatee and hands me a knife to cut the tape. "Right before you went onstage. But, to tell the truth, it could have been sitting there for a while before I noticed it."

I fold back the top of the box and remove an ordinary clay pot—the terra-cotta kind—full of dirt. That's right, dirt. There's nothing growing in it—no orchid, no bamboo plant, not even a weed. Dirt.

I sigh loudly. "What *is* this? Why would someone send me a pot full of dirt?"

"Maybe something is going to grow out of it," Margaret says.

Which is not the most unreasonable thing I've ever heard.

"Is there a card? Instructions?" asks Leigh Ann, peeking into the box.

"Nope. Nada. Just like the bowl. Do you think I should water it?"

"I wouldn't," Becca says. "It might be something poisonous. Or one of those giant Venus flytraps. You fall asleep one night, and when you wake up, that thing is having *you* for breakfast."

"Wow. *Somebody* has a vivid imagination," says

Cam, who moves in to get a closer look. "And *you* have a secret admirer. How romantic."

"Real romantic," Becca scoffs. "A cruddy old bowl and a box of dirt. Woo-hoo. Can we eat now?"

As usual, Becca has a point, but I can't help thinking that there's more to my strange gifts than meets the eye. Is it possible that Raf has something to do with all this? As I trudge along the sidewalk behind everyone (except Cam's bodyguard/tutor, who follows a few steps behind me), I find myself wishing it was Raf's hand I was holding rather than Tillie's leash.

Chapter 11

In which Leigh Ann asks a question for the ages

I don't know if we fully convert him or not, but Cam certainly seems to enjoy the pizza at Trantonno's; he eats half a pie all by himself. And he makes up for his behavior on the movie set by picking up the check. Yesssssss!

The funny thing is, when he first walked in the door at Perkatory, all I could think about was how much I didn't like him. I mean, he showed all the signs of being the worst kind of stereotype: a conceited, sort-of-talented Hollywood brat. But by the time we all say good night and go our separate ways, I feel kind of sorry for him—even though he's heading for a room at one of the nicest hotels in the city! Sure, he has money and a really cool job, but at the end of the day, he seems like a lonely kid. He doesn't really go to school, and he doesn't have any close friends because he's always moving around. When we told him about the adventures of the Red Blazer Girls Detective Agency, he seemed positively jealous of *us*. As I'm walking home with Margaret and Leigh Ann, who's sleeping over at my apartment, I realize that I wouldn't trade my friendships for anything Hollywood could offer.

Leigh Ann and I stay up way too late talking (actually, I do most of the talking, about the situation with Raf and Nate—if what's going on can even be called "a situation") and watching a DVD about a girl who dreams of dancing in a ballet company in New York. We pay dearly for it in the morning when Tillie, who sleeps late for a change, wakes us at six o'clock by pulling the covers off the bed and licking our faces. Very subtle, Tillie.

Leigh Ann's own dance class doesn't start until nine, so I talk her into a nice long walk in the park with the devil dog.

"I'm going to let her off the leash," I say. "I think I can trust her. And she needs to *run*."

And boy, does she ever run.

Suddenly she is no more than a black blur, going in three directions at once. Chasing squirrels. Stalking birds. Playing with the other dogs. It is exactly what she needs, and watching her makes me smile so much that I forget how annoyed I am that she woke me up at six on a Saturday morning—a Saturday morning that I didn't have to get up for swim practice, to be precise.

And then, as Leigh Ann is telling me about the conversation she had with her dad, who just took a new job in Cleveland, Tillie disappears over a hill.

"Uh-oh," I say. "Tillie!"

Nothing. I spin around and around, scanning the park for signs of her.

"Til-lie!" we shout together.

"Tillie!" I hear a voice in the distance say.

"Did you hear that?" Leigh Ann asks.

"Uh-huh. Weird." I pull her in the direction of my last Tillie sighting. "Let's go."

We come over the top of the hill and I breathe a sigh of relief—Tillie is sitting up on a park bench with some-one who is holding her leash.

"Is that . . . Cam?" Leigh Ann asks.

"Uh, yeah. And that Will guy. That's *really* weird."

Cam waves at us as if it's the most natural thing in the world for him to be sitting on a Central Park bench at six-thirty on a Saturday morning, holding the leash of the crazy dog that I'm responsible for.

"Hey, guys," he says.

"What are *you* doing here?" I ask. "I mean—thanks for catching Tillie. Was that you calling her?"

The bewildered look on his face tells me he has no idea what I'm talking about. "Why would I be calling Tillie?"

"Well, someone definitely called her name," Leigh Ann confirms. "Unless we're both going crazy."

"Maybe it was the wind," he says.

I look up at the trees; not a twig is stirring. "What wind? I think you're playing games with us," I say.

"*Moi?* Why would I do something like that?"

I squint at him. "I don't know. Yet. But I'll figure it out."

"Oh, that's right. I forgot—you're detectives."

"You never did answer Sophie's first question," notes Leigh Ann. "What are you doing here?"

"I told you, I like to take walks in the park. And so does Will. Right, Will?"

Will, leaning back with eyes closed, can manage only a grunt in our direction.

"At six in the morning?" Leigh Ann retorts.

"I was up early, because I got a call from my agent, who's in England. He was very excited and couldn't wait to call and tell me that I got a part in a BBC production of *Nicholas Nickleby.*"

"No way!" I shout. "I'm reading that right now. I—we—won copies of it for this skit we did from *Great Expectations,* which Leigh Ann wrote and directed, by the way. Who are you going to be?"

"Smike—do you know who he is?"

"Ohmigosh, that's perfect. I can totally see you as him."

He smiles, nodding. "Thanks. That's nice. Of course, it's just a story by some nobody named Charles Dickens, not a great piece of literature like *No Reflections,*" he says with a telltale roll of his eyes. Then, clearly enjoying teasing us, he adds, "Oops, I forgot, you probably think that *is* a great work of art."

"You know, I was starting to think you're a nice kid," I say, pretending my feelings have been hurt.

"Maybe he just can't help himself," Leigh Ann says. "You know how those Hollywood types are—it's all about *them*."

Cam falls to the cold, damp ground, moaning and acting as if he's been stabbed in the heart.

We look on, unimpressed. "And I was starting to think," Leigh Ann says, "that he could actually *act*."

Will still doesn't open his eyes, but he smiles at that.

On the way home, I almost lose Tillie again. We're just walking along, and then *yank!* My arm almost comes out of its socket as she pulls me down the sidewalk. I finally get my other hand on the leash and bring her to a complete stop.

"What was *that* all about?" I ask. "Did you see a squirrel?"

Leigh Ann points at the sidewalk ahead of us. "Isn't that Livvy?"

She is half a block ahead and has her back to us, pushing a wheelchair, but there's no doubt in my mind that those fashionable jeans and that black TrueNorth jacket belong to Livvy Klack. Even her walk has a certain unmistakable attitude.

"C'mon, let's follow her," I say.

"You think we should?" Leigh Ann asks.

"Woof!" says Tillie. "Woof! Woof!"

"Quiet, Tillie!" I say. "I just want to see who she's with—and what she's doing. We won't let her see us. Aren't you curious?"

"Of course. I'm just, well, you know, a little afraid of her."

"*Everyone's* a little afraid of her," I say. "And with good reason. She's Livvy Klack, for cryin' out loud."

We pick up the pace, with Tillie enthusiastically leading the way, until we cut the distance between us and Livvy in half. When she gets to the next corner, though, she takes an abrupt left turn and we duck behind a car, concerned that she has spotted us. We wait a few seconds before peeking out, and get to the corner just in time to see her push the wheelchair into a diner.

"Whew. That was close," Leigh Ann says. "I thought we were busted for sure."

"Too bad we have Tillie with us, or we'd be going in that diner," I say. "I wonder who that is? And why is Livvy, of all people, being nice to her?"

"I thought you said there was more to Livvy than we thought."

"I did—I do think that. But it's still surprising to actually see it."

It's kind of like seeing a rainbow for the first time. You can see pictures of them and hear people describe them your whole life, but until you see one with your own eyes, you don't really believe it's possible.

While Leigh Ann is showering and getting ready to head over toward Times Square for her dance class, I notice that I have a new voice message—and almost fall off my bed when I hear it.

Hi, Sophie, it's Cam. Hope you don't mind me calling—I got your number from Nate. I'm not a stalker, honest. I'm just calling to make sure you haven't lost any more celebrities' dogs today! And, um, I have a deal for you: I promise not to tell Nate that you lost Tillie if you give me Leigh Ann's number. That's a fair trade, isn't it? Pretty please? I'll even promise not to make any more cracks about New York pizza.

Well now. This is certainly an interesting turn of events, don't you think? Leigh Ann is blow-drying her hair, and it's all I can do not to barge into the bathroom, yank the plug out of the wall, and shriek this incredible news at her. I mean, that's what the old Sophie would have done, but the new, improved, self-controlled Sophie is above such vulgar displays of emotion, right?

Wrong, wrong, wrong.

I barge. I yank. I shriek.

A petrified Leigh Ann finally pries the phone out of my hand and listens to the message for herself. And, bless her heart, she maintains her composure. Totally plays it cool.

"Huh," she deadpans as she hands me back my phone. "Wonder what he wants."

"You're kidding, right?"

A look of utter innocence. "What?" Probably my favorite thing about Leigh Ann is her genuine lack of awareness of her own beauty.

I put my arms on her shoulders and spin her so she's facing the mirror. "*That's* what he wants."

"Don't be ridiculous."

"Leigh Ann. He. Likes. You. I mean, come on. You don't think it's a little strange that he just *happened* to be walking in the park this morning? He heard us talking last night. He was there to see you."

"You're crazy. He's famous. I'm nobody. He can't like me."

"One, you're not a nobody. You're a-flippin'-mazing. You dance. You sing. You're beautiful. You solve crimes. Two, why *can't* he like you? And three, I don't care what you say—I am *so* giving him your number."

"I don't get it. If he wanted my number, why didn't he just ask me?"

"Because he's a boy. Nobody knows why they do *anything* they do. Why did Raf decide to start driving his uncle's scooter all over the city? Or get all weird just because I'm taking care of Nate Etan's dog? Just go with it."

Ah yes. Say hello to daytime television's newest sensation: Dr. Sophie, relationship guru.

Chapter 12

Time for us to put on our detective hats. Let's hope they're fashionable

With everything that's been going on in our lives the past few days, the RBGDA—the Red Blazer Girls Detective Agency, that is—hasn't made much progress with Father Julian's case. The simple fact is, other than figuring out that the baseball that Tillie treated like a double cheeseburger was a fake, we've got nada. Zilch. Bupkis.

"It's disgraceful, really," Margaret tells me Saturday afternoon. "Father Julian is counting on us. We need to get everyone together tonight and get down to some serious detective work. No DVDs, no music, no talking about boys, movies, or movie *stars*. Just the four of us and that old shoe box full of pictures."

Twenty-seven phone calls (at least) and three hours later, Margaret, Becca, and I converge on Leigh Ann's house in Astoria, Queens, where we're all going to spend the night. My mom, who grew up in Queens, rides over on the subway with us and, after dropping us off at Leigh

Ann's, heads out to meet an old friend from school for dinner.

Leigh Ann is the only one of us who actually lives in a house rather than an apartment building. Her brother, Alejandro, who is a senior at St. Thomas Aquinas, where Raf goes, is on his way out the door as we arrive. I wouldn't have thought it possible, but he seems even taller and better-looking than the last time I saw him, which was only a few weeks ago. Shockingly, he doesn't seem at all disappointed that he's going to miss spending time with his little sister and her three best friends. I mean, imagine someone *not* wanting to hang out with us!

So it's just us and Leigh Ann's mom, who cooks Dominican food for us. It's very different from the French stuff I'm used to, but it is delicious, and Ms. Jaimes is in a state of shock after seeing what four twelve-year-old girls can do to a giant casserole dish of chicken, beans, and rice.

While we're eating, Becca tells us the latest twist in the mystery surrounding Gus, the artist who's locked away in the back room of that gallery. On her way home to babysit her younger siblings, Jonathan and Jennifer, on Thursday, she stopped in a diner and ordered two coffees and a tea to be delivered to the gallery. Then she waited across the street to watch as the curtain went up on her little drama.

"At first, the girl tries to send the delivery guy away," Becca says. "I can see her shaking her head. And then he must tell her that it's already paid for, because she peeks into the bag. Which is when she sees what I wrote on the lid of the tea: 'Please serve in a china cup.'"

"You didn't," I say.

"Oh yes I did," she says with a maniacal laugh. "Just to mess with their heads. The girl starts looking around like she's being watched—which she is—and totally freaking out. She follows the delivery guy out the door, asking him who ordered the stuff, but he just shrugs and rides off on his bike. When she goes back inside, she and the guy go to the back room and knock, but Gus doesn't answer. Finally, they dig up a key and unlock the door."

"Did they give him the tea, at least?" Leigh Ann asks.

"Yeah, because after that, I went around to the back window and knocked. He got a kick out of the message, so even though he might be a little paranoid, at least he has a sense of humor. I didn't go in, because I had to go home to watch the twins, but we talked for a minute. Remember I told you he lives upstairs? Well, from some of the things he says, I get the sense that he never leaves the building. He has *everything* delivered, because he's afraid of something—and I don't think it's the guy from the gallery who yelled at us. I think it's something *much* scarier."

At eight o'clock on the button, Margaret dumps the shoe box of pictures onto Leigh Ann's bed.

"Yikes," Becca says, eyeing the pile. "Is that some

kind of magical shoe box or something? There's no way all those came out of that."

"Everybody take a handful," Margaret says.

"Tell me again what we're looking for," says Leigh Ann, staring at the black-and-white picture that Malcolm attached to the lid of the box with a paper clip. "I know there's the painting, and something about a year."

"Nineteen sixty-one. That's the year Pommeroy died," Becca reminds us. "And when his brothers and sister suddenly decided that *they* were great artists, too."

Margaret has Malcolm's loupe pressed to her eye, looking at the picture in Leigh Ann's hand. "Right now, let's just find every picture that has the painting in it, even if it's just a little corner of it. Then we can worry about the *when.*"

I reach in for a fistful of pictures and then sit back on the floor to go through them. Most are your basic family snapshots—you know, the usual birthdays, anniversaries, holidays, vacations, and so on. And while Malcolm may have pointed out that many were obviously taken with a good camera, the photographer—in most cases, anyway—was no expert, believe me.

Out of focus? Check.

Overexposed? Check.

Underexposed? Check.

Grandma and Grandpa "decapitated"? Check. Check.

"Boy, somebody forgot to read the instruction manual for his shiny new camera," I say.

"I have a feeling that cameras in the fifties and sixties were a lot more complicated than the kind we use," Margaret explains.

"Wait a minute," Leigh Ann says. "Look at this one." The picture in her hand is black and white, but it isn't like the others. It's about twice the size, printed on much heavier paper—there's a professional look and feel to it. An elderly couple stands in a very formal pose in front of a fireplace. My eyes, however, go immediately to the wall behind them. Above the mantel, plain as the broken nose on my face, is the Pommeroy painting that Father Julian showed us.

"Hey, that's it!" I shout.

Leigh Ann flips it over. "Huh. 'Rosemont Studios, the Bronx.' But no date. Those must be Father Julian's grandparents."

"*Great*-grandparents," Margaret corrects.

"You know, if this Rosemont Studios is still around, they might have records," says Becca. "I think those places keep the negatives forever."

Margaret pats Becca on the back. "Good thinking. Leigh Ann, can I use your computer to check it out?"

"It's all yours."

That little bit of success really motivates us, and we attack the rest of the pictures while Margaret goes online to see if Rosemont Studios is still in business.

"Rosewood. Rosenberg. Rose and Rose. But no Rosemont."

"That would have been too easy," I say.

"I suppose they could have changed their name," Margaret says.

"Got another one!" Leigh Ann exclaims, waving a snapshot above her head.

"Sheesh," Becca grumbles.

We circle around Leigh Ann to get a good look.

"Yep. There it is again. This one's a lot like that very first picture—the one with the car in the background," Margaret says. "That's the same room—the same furniture, even—and the painting's in the same place on the wall. And look! All kinds of clues!"

"Magazines on the coffee table," notes Becca.

"Bookshelves," I say. "Looks like they're full of little knickknacks—the kind of stuff you pick up on vacations."

"And a dog!" says Leigh Ann. "It looks a lot like Tillie."

I take a closer look at the dog, which *does* look like a slightly beefier Tillie. "Great. That crazy mutt probably ate the evidence. Look, there's something sticking out of the side of her mouth."

"Getting a little tired of Tillie, are we?" Becca teases. "I thought you *loved* her."

"I *do*. She's so sweet. She's just . . . sometimes there's just a lot of her."

Leigh Ann points to a magazine on the coffee table in the picture. "Hey, this one is definitely *Life*—I don't think it's around anymore, but I know I've seen copies of it somewhere."

"The school library," says Margaret. "There's a whole shelf of them behind Mrs. Overmeyer's desk. And *this* one is a *National Geographic*. I'd recognize that anywhere." She sets the picture on the table and begins a closer examination with the loupe.

"Anything?" I ask.

"Well, the titles are clear enough to make out, but everything else is too small to read."

Becca leans over Margaret's shoulder. "Yeah, but what about the *pictures* on the covers? That's just as good, right?"

Margaret leans back, still holding the loupe to her eye. "Of course! Rebecca, you're a genius."

"Finally," Becca says with a quick I-told-you-so glance in my direction. "Somebody noticed. Thank you, Margaret."

"De rien," says Margaret. "All we have to do is look at the covers of *Life* and *National Geographic* and match them to the ones in the picture."

"And if they're from, say, June 1960," I say, "won't that be proof?"

Margaret grins at me. "Nope."

"Pourquoi, ma cherie?"

"Because it's possible they just had a bunch of old magazines lying around. I've seen copies of *Gourmet* from the *nineties* on the coffee table at your house. On the other hand, two magazines from the same month definitely help our case."

"Ah. Circumstantial evidence," I say as it all starts to sink in.

"What's that?" Leigh Ann asks.

"It's like this," I explain. "The police walk into a room, and you're standing there with a gun in your hand and there's a dead guy on the floor. Nobody actually saw you pull the trigger, but it seems obvious what happened, because of the circumstances."

"Ohhh. So you're saying . . . Wait, what are you saying?"

Margaret looks at me. "I think what Sophie's trying to say is that we may not find one magical piece of evidence that solves the case, but there might be a bunch of little things that add up to one obvious conclusion. Well, at least we *hope* it's obvious."

Meanwhile, Rebecca continues to dig through her pile of pictures, determined, she says, to find "the one true ring." I swear, if I hadn't sat through nine hours of *The Lord of the Rings* with her—twice!—I wouldn't know what she's talking about half the time. Her persistence pays off; she leaps to her feet, holding up a picture triumphantly.

"Yessss!" she gloats. "In your face, St. Pierre."

"You're so competitive, Rebecca," Leigh Ann says. "That's really not healthy, you know, when it's about everything."

"It's not everything," I explain. "Just me, and I'm used to it. But it's okay because I *know* she's loony. All right, let's see it." I pull her arm and the picture down to my eye level. "I don't see anything."

"Me neither," admits Leigh Ann.

Becca points at the top right-hand corner and hands the picture to Margaret. "It's right *there*. In the background."

"Oh, I see it," says Margaret. She holds it so Leigh Ann and I can get a clear look. "You can only see a little bit of it." She peers through the loupe once again. "And I think it's a reflection—like we're seeing the painting in a mirror on the wall behind those people."

"Mmmmm. Birthday cake," I say. "Chocolate."

"Wait a second. Now *that's* an interesting clue," Margaret says.

By the tone of her voice, I can tell that her brain is going into its don't-bother-me-now-I'm-onto-something-big mode, and I back away from her. Hey, you never know. One of these days, that gray matter might just blow, and I don't want to be too close.

She hands me the loupe. "Birthday cake. Whose name is on it? And candles. Quick, how many?"

Too much pressure!

"'Happy Birthday . . . Cathy' . . . I think. No, I'm sure. It's Cathy."

"Candles?"

"I'm counting! Ten, twelve, thirteen, fourteen. But these flowers on the table look like they're blocking some."

"She *definitely* looks older than fourteen," Leigh Ann says. "She's got to be seventeen or eighteen at least."

"Aarrgghh," Margaret says. "Stupid flowers. This picture would do it. If we knew when this Cathy was born, we would know what year the picture was taken."

"Lemme see that," Becca says, taking the picture out of my hand. "That guy is really cute. Something about him looks familiar."

"Which guy?" I ask.

"The one in the mirror. He's in the other room, standing by the painting."

"I think he'd look a little different now," I say.

"I know, but I'm tellin' you—I've seen him some-where. Where was it?" She pounds the heels of her hands against her head. "Think, Rebecca! I'm going to remember tonight, and when I do, I'm going to call you, St. Pierre."

"Okay with me, Chen. And then I'll call the loony bin for you."

"For now, let's look for more pictures of the cake," Margaret suggests. "I'll take you both to the loony bin later."

But we turn up no more pictures of the birthday cake, or ones that show the painting, either.

Margaret sits cross-legged on the floor, deep in thought. "All right. We have to expand our search target. From the pictures we have, we know what the living room looks like—the wallpaper, the furniture, everything. So let's go through the pictures one more time, and this time save anything that shows even a *sliver* of that room."

"And then we can do something fun, right?" Becca asks.

"We'll see," Margaret answers.

Leigh Ann nudges me gently. "That's just what my dad always says. I finally figured out that it was his way of saying no without actually having to say that word to me."

Margaret, who still has that silly loupe stuck in her eye, doesn't look up, but I catch a quick glimpse of a sly grin. A few seconds later, she motions for us to look at another photo that she has set on Leigh Ann's bed.

"This is the same room, right? Same rug, same coffee table."

"Looks like it to me," I say. "Just taken from the other side. The fireplace is here." I point to a spot on the quilt that is about an inch past the right edge of the picture. "And the painting would be here."

The loupe reveals that the magazines on the coffee table are a *Life* and a *National Geographic,* just like in the second picture we found, but they're arranged differently. And it's hard to be certain, but it doesn't seem to be the same issue of *Life*.

"Look at the two people sitting on that bench. It's the same couple from the birthday cake picture."

Leigh Ann looks at the young couple. "This was taken on the same day as the birthday cake picture. Same blouse and skirt on her, same shirt and tie on the guy, same hairstyle—although, to be honest, *all* the women in these pictures seem to have their hair done in exactly the same way."

"Yeah, *lots* of hair spray," I note.

"Check out the TV," Becca says. "It looks just like the one Father Julian showed us in the rectory."

Margaret squints through the loupe. "Ohmigosh—look! You can see what's on TV, too—it's a baseball game."

"Let me see," I say, pushing Margaret aside. "Oh yeah. That's a Yankee uniform. A little baggier than they wear now, but I'd know those pinstripes anywhere."

What can I say? Some girls know designer shoes; I know baseball uniforms.

Chapter 13

In which it becomes apparent that I may have spoken too soon

In the morning, Margaret and I head back into Manhattan early—she's anxious to get to work on a new piece on the violin and I have to meet Michelle and the swim team outside Asphalt Green at seven sharp. We're taking a bus up to a pool somewhere north of the city where we have a meet with a school I've never heard of.

I arrive a few minutes before seven and settle into a seat on the bus, which has just enough room for all twelve of us, plus Michelle, who's driving. At seven, we're all buckled in and ready to go, except for Livvy, who is nowhere in sight.

"Has anybody heard from Livvy?" Michelle asks.

Nope.

"Anybody have her cell phone number?"

"I've got it," says Rachel Ungerman, waving her phone. "Hold on. . . . Hey, where are you? Okay, cool. Bye." Rachel looks up at Michelle. "She's on her way— she said she'll be here in five minutes."

Thirteen minutes later (not that I was counting; I just *happened* to look at my watch), a taxi pulls up and out pops a grumpier-and-gloomier-than-usual Livvy Klack.

"Oh man, she looks bad," Carey Petrus says.

"Like she's going to kill somebody," adds Jill Ambrose, who is sitting next to me. And who, for reasons I can't begin to understand, gets up and moves back a row in the van—into the only empty seat.

Which leaves an empty seat next to me. Thanks, Jill. Just see if I remember *you* at Christmas.

I slide over as far as I can against the window. When Livvy gets to the bus door and realizes that I'm her only option, she shoots poison eye darts at the girls in the back and then throws herself into the seat with me. She doesn't look at me, doesn't say a word to me—Sophie St. Pierre *n'existe pas.* She has a truly remarkable ability to do that. They say that everybody is really great at something, and I may have just figured out what Livvy's one true gift is. The girl could share a prison cell with you for twenty years and never acknowledge that you were there.

I decide that maybe this isn't the day to push things with her; let's face it, that nice moment that we almost shared in Mr. Eliot's class is now a distant memory. Instead, I lean my head against the cold window and pretend to sleep all the way to the meet.

The meet is a huge success for us—we win all but two events, and every swimmer on the team wins at least one first-, second-, or third-place medal. I win the 400 individual medley, breaking my old personal record by a second and a half, and win two more first-place medals as a member of relay teams. We win the final event, the 400 medley relay, by almost a full length of the pool, and Livvy, Courtney, and I lift Carey Petrus, who swims the anchor leg, out of the pool for a group scream and hug. On the ride back to the city, the atmosphere on the bus is completely different. We sing along with the radio the whole way. Even Livvy, believe it or not, is smiling—those four first-place medals dangling from her neck have put her in a great mood. It's like we're an actual *team,* and it feels doggone good. Maybe not quite on the same level as the first night the Blazers rocked Perkatory, but it's not bad. Not bad at all.

When we get back to Asphalt Green, a bunch of girls decide to go out for pizza together—Carey, Rachel, Courtney, Amy, Jill, and Livvy. Carey catches me off guard when she asks if I want to go along.

I hesitate at first. "Um, no—but thanks. I've got some homework to—" But then I stop myself. I mean, it's Sunday afternoon. Why not? I have plenty of time to get my homework done, and it could be fun, right? I do everything with Margaret, Rebecca, and Leigh Ann; it wouldn't kill me to hang out a little with my teammates, would it? That whole team-spirit thing wins out against my better judgment, which would have had me going home to finish my science and social studies assignments.

"Okay, why not?" I find myself saying. "Just give me a minute—I need to run inside to use the bathroom."

"Good idea," says Livvy, who follows me inside the building. When I come out of the bathroom, Michelle is standing in the hallway talking to a woman I don't know, and she motions for me to come over. The woman, Cindy Allan, is a former Olympic swimmer who now coaches the swim team at a college in upstate New York. Michelle tells her all about me, bragging about my times from earlier in the day, and Cindy invites me to come and visit the campus whenever I want.

Michelle smiles as she tells me, "You keep improving at the rate you're going, you could be looking at a scholarship."

"It takes a lot of dedication," Cindy says. "But you're definitely on the right track. Keep up the good work, and congratulations on today."

"Thanks. I, um, need to get going, Michelle. I'll see you Tuesday. It was really nice meeting you, Cindy."

I turn and run out the door, only to find that everyone—Livvy included—is gone. I look up and down East End Avenue, but there's no sign of them. It's official: I have been ditched.

Remember all those warm, wonderful feelings I was having about being part of a team just a few minutes ago?

Gone.

I walk home slowly, fighting back tears and the urge to let loose with all the really bad words I feel like screaming—the kind of words Cam Peterson was using on the phone that first time we met him. Oh sure, I could have gone looking for my teammates, but there are, like, forty-seven pizza places they might have gone to. Or they might have decided that they were more in the mood for raw meat, or whatever it is that jackals and hyenas eat. By the time I get to my block, the hurt has morphed into anger—not just at the girls who are allegedly my teammates, but at stupid, stupid me for allowing myself to be vulnerable. Being in seventh grade is a lot like being at war; you don't know where that next ambush is coming from, but you know it's coming. Let your guard down for a second and—poof!—you're toast.

When I get home, I put on my happiest face for Mom and tell her the good parts—the medals, the fun ride home—and leave out the bad. I go back to my room, where Tillie is sacked out on my bed; she rolls over on her back and stretches out her long legs so I can rub her belly.

"Tillie, do you have any idea how good you have it, being a dog?"

She wags her tail and nudges me with her nose. Apparently she *does* know. As she wags and wriggles, she knocks to the floor a small package that I didn't even see.

"Hey, what's this?" I ask. If Tillie knows, she's not talking, so I stick my head out the door and shout, "Mom? Is this from you?"

"Oh, that package? It came in the mail today. I thought maybe you ordered something."

Oy. Here we go again. This time, the box is much

smaller, about four inches square, but sure enough, there's my name and address in that familiar printing. As I open it up, my first thought is that someone has mailed me a dead bird, and my poor brain runs riot trying to remember whom I've offended badly enough to deserve such an ominous message.

It's not a real bird, though, but a lifelike—and life-sized—robin, so I breathe a sigh of relief. Just as I lie down to ponder this latest offering from my mysterious benefactor, my phone rings; it's Margaret, and she wants to hear all about the swim meet.

"Please don't make me talk about it," I plead.

"Um, okay. You're usually dying to tell me about your victories on the field of battle. You didn't hurt your nose, did you?"

"No, nothing like that. I'll tell you later, I promise. I just need a little break from thinking about it. What did you do today?"

"I had a very interesting day. I went to the late Mass at St. V's with my parents, and afterward we ran into Father Julian, so I stuck around to tell him about the pictures we found and ask a few questions. The girl with the birthday cake, the one who's also in that other picture talking to the same boy, is his aunt Cathy. She was born in 1944, which has her turning eighteen in 1962. He's not sure of the exact date, but he says her birthday is definitely in October. If that cake is for her eighteenth birthday, it's no help, but if there's a way to prove it was her seventeenth, we're home free. The good news is that she's still alive and lives a few blocks from the school. And Father Julian says she remembers *everything*. She's kind of the unofficial family historian. So we're going to meet her one day after school, to see what else she can tell us."

"Wow, you were busy."

"Oh, that's not all," she says. "Remember the magazine covers? Well, I did a little research on those, too. The one *Life* magazine is from August 1961, I'm sure of it. The August eighteenth issue has two baseball players on the cover—um, Mickey somebody, I think, and Roger something-or-other. Don't worry, I wrote them down."

"Mantle and Maris," I say. "You really don't know who they are?"

"Should I?"

"Uh, *yeah.* They're only two of the greatest Yankee players ever. I'll bet they were on the cover of a lot of magazines in the summer of '61."

"What was so special about 1961?"

"That's the year Roger Maris broke Babe Ruth's record. He hit sixty-one home runs. And Mantle hit fifty-something."

There's a moment of silence on Margaret's end. Finally, she says, "Wow. I'm impressed. I've known you for five years and I had no idea you were so full of knowledge about baseball."

"Everyone knows about Mantle and Maris," I say. "And it's easy to remember—sixty-one in '61."

"If you say so. Anyway, back to the magazines. The

National Geographic is smaller, so it's a little harder to see, but the picture seems to match the cover from October 1961. It looks like a woman with this crazy hat, or maybe it's a basket of fruit, on her head. I can't be a hundred percent sure."

"Well, two magazine covers from 1961 are a step in the right direction," I say. "We know we're in the, um, ballpark."

Margaret groans. "Say good night, Sophie."

"Good night, Sophie."

Click.

Chapter 14

In which I set loose an army of killer ants on Livvy. Okay, not really, but a girl can fantasize, can't she?

On our Monday morning subway ride to school, I finally get around to telling Margaret about being ditched after the swim meet. Now that I've had a full day to deal with it, I shrug it off as Livvy just being Livvy, but Margaret isn't so quick to forgive and forget.

"I never said I forgive her," I say. "And I don't think I'll *ever* forget it. I'm just saying that it's not worth staying mad about. I learned my lesson. Life goes on."

"What about all that 'there's more to Livvy than you think' stuff you were saying just the other day?"

"Maybe I was wrong," I admit with a shrug.

Margaret smiles. "Thank you. That's all I wanted to hear. You were wrong; I was right."

"And you say *I'm* too competitive. Maybe we shouldn't tell Becca and Leigh Ann about this. They'll want to do something to get even with Livvy, and I want to stop before this turns into one of those *Romeo and Juliet* things where everybody dies in the end. Deal?"

Margaret nods. "Deal."

A few minutes later, we're watching Sister Bernadette steamroll through the school cafeteria, distributing demerits for uniform violations to every girl at one table and confiscating three cell phones from a table of unsuspecting eighth graders. When she approaches our table, we cower and cringe, waiting for the worst. Instead, she holds out a large yellow envelope.

"For you, Miss Wrobel. From Father Julian. Sit up straight, Miss St. Pierre! This isn't your living room."

"Yes, Sister," I say.

That's too much for Rebecca; her face breaks into a huge grin.

Sister Bernadette's eyes narrow as she hovers directly over Rebecca. "Do you find me amusing, Miss Chen?"

"What? No."

"No, *Sister.* And let's do something about that blazer, shall we? It looks like you've been crawling under cars in it. Have you become an auto mechanic?"

Rebecca squirms in her chair, trying to pull the wrinkles out of her sorry-looking blazer. "Yes, Sister. I mean, no, Sister."

"That's better." She storms away, continuing her rampage as she terrorizes table after table.

When she's out of hearing range, Leigh Ann speaks up. "Boy, she's on the warpath this morning."

"What's in the envelope?" I ask.

Margaret opens the clasp and dumps another pile of photos onto the table. Some are black and white, but most are color. The color prints are much, much more recent; based on the clothes and hairstyles, they are from five to ten years ago. Then she removes a large print that is protected by a clear plastic sleeve. It's a notebook-paper-sized version of the one good-quality picture we found—the one of Father Julian's great-grandparents standing in front of the fireplace and the painting.

"Wow, this is a nice picture," Rebecca says. "You can really see the painting. And look at the clock on the mantel. It's so clear you can read the words on the face. Can I borrow this tonight? I want to check something out. I promise to take care of it. Sophie, you weren't planning to bring Tillie over, were you?"

"Ha ha," I say. "I'll have you know that Tillie hasn't chewed anything in days. She's been absolutely *perfect.*"

As we pack up our stuff to head upstairs, Leigh Ann takes me by the arm. "I know this is a sensitive subject," Leigh Ann says softly, "but did you hear from Nate after Friday night? He was really weird."

"No," I admit. "Not a word. How about you? Anything from Cam?"

She can't help grinning a little as she nods. "Last

night. I was going to call you, but I had to finish my homework and then I fell asleep."

Rebecca sticks her head in between us. "What are you two whispering about?"

"I'll tell you at lunch," Leigh Ann promises. "C'mon, we're going to be late for class."

Mr. Eliot's English class is even more entertaining than usual. He assigned a short story, "Leiningen Versus the Ants," over the weekend, and the threat of a quiz ensured that everyone actually did the reading. At the beginning of the story, Leiningen, the owner of a plantation in South America, is warned that a mile-wide horde of man-eating ants is headed right for his land. He stubbornly refuses to leave, convincing himself that he can outsmart a bunch of stupid ants. Seems logical, right?

Not so much, it turns out. These ants are *seriously* intense; they know what they want, and nothing he can do is going to make them change their minds. They cross rivers, walk through fire, and cooperate with one another in a way that's so diabolical it kind of freaks me out.

Somehow Margaret turns this into a discussion about whether "the end justifies the means."

Mr. Eliot just kind of stares at Margaret after she brings it up. "Well, I wasn't really expecting anyone to be familiar with means-end analysis, but I seem to have underestimated you once again."

"Not all of us," someone in the back of the room says.

"Amen," I say, turning around to see that I'm

agreeing, probably for the first time in my life, with Jessica Glenn. "Margaret, what are you talking about?"

Margaret explains, "It's really not that complicated. People are always asking whether the end—in other words, your goal—justifies *any* means of achieving it. So, is it okay to do whatever you have to in order to make something good happen?"

"Can you give us an example?" Leigh Ann asks. "Like, from real life?"

Margaret scrunches up her nose and thinks for a second. Then her eyes open wide. "Let's say the police arrest Sophie because they heard that she's going to blow up the world. When they question her, she admits that she is planning to do just what they say, and that she already started the timer on the bomb. She's not about to tell them where the bomb is hidden, though, so the police have to ask themselves: Does the end—saving the world—justify *any* means of getting it, like torture?"

"Yes!" cries Jessica. "Rip her fingernails out!"

"Hey!" I protest, making fists to protect my nails. They may not look like much (I'm a biter), but I still don't want anyone yanking them out.

Mr. Eliot nods in admiration at Margaret. "Good example. But it doesn't always have to be a life-and-death situation. Sophie, you make the calculation all the time; you just don't realize you're doing it. Remember when you made the decision to disobey Father Danahey's order to stop snooping around the church for the Ring of

Rocamadour? Finding the ring was an end that, for you, justified almost any means, including breaking the rules."

"So you're saying it's okay to do whatever it takes to get what you want," Leigh Ann concludes.

"No, no, no," Mr. Eliot says. "And *please* don't tell your parents that's what I said. There is no easy answer. Philosophers have been arguing about it for centuries. The point is that you have to really weigh the two sides in your mind every time. You have to use your own conscience as a guide."

The Blazers meet in Elizabeth Harriman's basement after school, and we decide to stick with the songs we know for our regular Friday evening gig at Perkatory. We know that we need to add a few more to our repertoire, but it's hard with the limited time we have for rehearsal.

"Maybe we should just drop out of school now," Becca suggests. "Think of all the time we'd have to rehearse then. And you know, lots of famous musicians didn't go to college."

"But I think most of them at least went to high school," I say. "I don't think that's a very practical solution."

"Yeah, Becca, something tells me your mom wouldn't be too thrilled," says Leigh Ann.

"Or my dad," says Mbingu, shivering. "I think you would hear him screaming at me all the way from Africa."

"I was *kidding*," Becca says. "It's just frustrating sometimes. Especially when I see some of these people on TV—I mean, we are so much cooler than some of them. And we're starting to sound better, too."

"We just have to keep working at it, doing what we're doing," Leigh Ann says. "Cam says we sound great—especially when you know we've only been playing together a couple of months."

Mbingu, Becca, and I stare at her. "*Cam* says?" we all say together.

With a flash of perfect white teeth, Leigh Ann brightens the dim basement with her smile, and I remember her (broken) promise to tell us about him at lunchtime.

"Oh yeah. I guess I forgot to tell you. We were so busy arguing about all that means-and-end stuff that it just—"

"Slipped your mind?" I say, finishing her thought. "A movie star calls you and you forget to tell us."

"Oh, come on—you guys met him, too."

"Yeah, but he didn't ask for *our* number," I point out.

Becca looks like she's going to explode. "He asked for your number? When did this happen?"

I explain about the Saturday morning encounter in the park and the voice message that followed, which leaves Becca and Mbingu shaking their heads.

"Man, life is so unfair," Becca notes.

"Tell me about it," says Mbingu.

"Guys, it was just one phone call. We talked. That's it. He's nice, and funny, and he's not even conceited—not like Nate at all. I mean, Nate is really good-looking and everything, but he *so* knows it. Cam totally admits that he just got lucky."

Becca wags her eyebrows at me, which makes me and Mbingu laugh. A couple of seconds later, Leigh Ann realizes what she has said. "I mean, with his acting career! It all started with one commercial when he was a little kid in Chicago. But guess what—he's coming to Perkatory again on Friday. We have to keep it secret, though. If everybody finds out ahead of time, there will be, like, a million girls there, and then he'll never get in. Heck, *we* probably wouldn't get in. So, promise?"

We all make a solemn vow to keep the secret, *if* Leigh Ann agrees to dish on everything they talked about.

"So, does he *like* you?" Becca asks.

Leigh Ann shrugs, her perfect skin blushing slightly. "I don't know. I mean, I guess he does a little."

"Do you like *him*?" asks Mbingu, diving right into the heart of the matter.

"He is cute," Leigh Ann admits. "But it's all so . . . temporary. I mean, I'm trying to be realistic. They'll be done shooting the movie in a couple of weeks, and then he'll be gone. It's not like you and Raf, where he just lives on the other side of town. I'll probably never see him again."

"*Or,*" I say, "he falls madly in love with you and never forgets you, even when he's starring in a really romantic movie with some beautiful actress, and then he comes back for you and you two live happily ever after."

Becca scoffs at my vision of Leigh Ann's future. "And let me guess, in this little fairy-tale fantasy of yours, they live right next door to you and Raf—and Tillie, of course—and your kids play together every day."

Wait a minute. Has Rebecca been reading my diary?

Leigh Ann uses the mention of Raf's name to steer the conversation away from her and in my direction. "What's the latest with you two, anyway? Is he still acting weird?"

Despite my best efforts to hide it, my friends know I've been obsessing about Raf's Friday night good-night non-kiss.

"It's been a pretty quiet week so far," I say. "He won't admit that anything's wrong, but he still isn't really talking to me. I tried calling him last night, but he said he had to do his homework."

"Ouch," says Becca. "That doesn't sound good."

"Gee, thanks, Bec," I say. "Now I feel *much* better."

"Hey, that's what I'm here for," she adds, grinning.

Leigh Ann throws her arm around my shoulders. "Don't listen to her, Sophie. Just give him a little time. He'll call. I promise."

Chapter 15

Maybe she has a sister named Raisinella

Later, while Tillie is helping me study for a Spanish quiz by eating my vocabulary flash cards, my phone rings. I cross my fingers as I flip it over to see the screen; it's *still* not Raf. I try not to sound too disappointed when I answer.

"Hey, Bec."

"We have a problem," says a more-serious-than-I'm-used-to Rebecca.

"Who's we?" The first thought that races through my brain is that this is where she tells me that she's really sorry, but Raf is dropping me to go out with her. The second is that the rest of the Blazers have decided to kick me out of the band. I brace for the worst, wondering how I'll respond to either piece of news.

I'm dead wrong, of course; it's something completely different. "You, me. Margaret. Leigh Ann. The Agency."

"Ooh, I like the sound of that: the *Agency.* Sounds very clandestine."

"Clan—what?"

"Secret. So, big problem or little problem?"

"Huge. It's about the painting."

"What? Did you find something?"

"Uh-huh."

"Bummer. So it *was* painted after 1961."

"I dunno. Probably."

"Becca, what are you talking about? Was it or wasn't it?"

"This is a different problem. Remember that nice big picture that Father Julian gave us? Where the painting is really clear? Well, I was looking at it, and then comparing it to the picture that I took of the actual painting that Father Julian showed us in the rectory. And guess what—they're not the same. It's just a slight difference, but they are two different paintings—I'm positive."

"How can that be?"

"Somebody made a copy—an *almost*-perfect copy. They made one little mistake in the bottom right-hand corner, six or eight inches up. There's a place where two squares are on top of each other. In Father Julian's painting, the darker square overlaps the lighter one, but in the old photo with his great-grandparents, it's the other way around. There are dozens of overlapping squares, so this one doesn't stand out. The only way anyone can possibly tell is by doing what I did—comparing the original to the copy."

"We need to tell Margaret and Leigh Ann," I say. "And Father Julian. This changes everything. If the painting is a fake, then it really doesn't matter when it was painted. Can you print out a nice big copy of your picture for tomorrow?"

"Way ahead of you, St. Pierre. Oh, and, Soph?"

"Yeah?"

"About Raf."

Uh-oh. Here it comes.

"Uh-huh. What about him?"

"I'm sorry about earlier—you know, when I said that about it not sounding good. L.A.'s right. He's gonna call. And if he doesn't, I'm gonna go over to the West Side and kick his skinny little butt."

"Thanks. That's really sweet."

After school on Tuesday, Becca presents her two-paintings theory to a bewildered Father Julian. It is hard to argue with her analysis of the two pictures. Even though the portrait of his great-grandparents is black and white, the contrast of the light and dark squares is unmistakable, especially when viewed through the loupe. When Father Julian breaks out the painting, we go over every square inch, comparing it to the painting shown in the portrait. Everything else about it is perfect, down to the little curlicue in the bottom of the y in Pommeroy.

"This is remarkable, Rebecca," Father Julian marvels. "I might have looked at those two pictures side by side for ten years and not seen what you saw in a few moments."

"I guess that's what they mean by an 'artistic eye,'" I say.

"So now what?" Margaret asks. "Even if we know this painting isn't the same as the one in the old picture, it still doesn't tell us about *that* picture. Do you have any idea how—or when—the two paintings could have been switched? Or where the other one might be?"

"No, but I know who would know, if anyone does," says Father Julian, standing. "Girls, it's time for a visit with Aunt Cathy."

"Right now?" Leigh Ann asks.

"No time like the present," he replies. "And besides, I know she's home today. You'll get to meet my cousin Debbie, too. You know, this makes me wonder about *everything* those folks in that gallery said. I'm more convinced than ever that they weren't being completely honest with me."

Margaret gives me a nudge with her elbow and whispers in my ear, "Maybe this is a good time to tell him about the baseball."

"What? Oh. Yeah. Why don't you start, and I'll jump in if you leave anything out."

She shakes her head slowly. "Chicken. Um, Father Julian, before we go, Sophie and I have something to tell you. Sort of in the interest of complete honesty."

"Oh? Something else about the painting?"

"No, it's the baseballs this time. It's one of those good-news, bad-news stories. The good news is that we figured out which baseball is the real thing."

"Really?" he says. "That's *terrific*. What's the bad news?"

"Tell him, Soph," Margaret orders.

"Well, we had a little accident with the other ball. Tillie ate it."

"Who's Tillie?"

"Tillie is a dog. She's not mine. She belongs to Nate Etan—you know, the actor? We met him, and, well, it's a long story, but now I'm taking care of her for a while."

"And she ate a baseball?"

"Yes, but it was the fake," I add quickly.

"Lucky for you," Becca snorts. "I'd love to hear how this would have turned out if she'd eaten the real one."

"Is she okay?" Father Julian asks. He seems genuinely concerned about the stupid dog that almost ate a valuable family heirloom.

"Oh, she's fine," I say. "She didn't actually eat much of it. Mostly she just tore it into a million pieces. But even if she did, I think she's pretty much indestructible."

"Unlike the baseball," says Becca. "Sorry, I couldn't resist."

"And the other ball—how can you be sure it's the original?"

Margaret explains about the fake rubber center that proves the ball that Tillie ate was made well after the 1928 World Series.

"Not exactly the way the experts would have done it," Father Julian says with a broad smile, "but the result is the same—so no harm done. Now let's go see Aunt Cathy."

He grabs his coat from a hall closet and leads us out the door. His aunt lives in a doorman building just off Third Avenue at Fifty-sixth Street, and we take the elevator up to her apartment on the ninth floor, where she's waiting for us with the door open. She's dressed in that classy-but-comfy cashmere-and-pearls style, like a grandmother from a sixties sitcom. And even though it's almost fifty years later, I would still recognize her from that picture of her standing in front of her birthday cake. I don't think her hairstyle has changed a bit; there's a big ol' aerosol can of hair spray lurking somewhere in her apartment.

"Aunt Cathy, you look great!" Father Julian exclaims, kissing her on both cheeks.

"My goodness, look at you," she says with a disapproving look at his jeans and sweater. "Traveling incognito, I see. No one would even know you're a priest."

"I'm undercover today," he answers with a wink.

"Oh, leave him alone, Mom," says a young woman's voice from another room.

"Hi, Deb!" shouts Father Julian. "Come here, there are some people I want you to meet." He gathers his four crimson-blazer-attired friends around him as Debbie, a pretty, round-faced woman of twenty-seven or twenty-eight, barrels into the room and attempts to squeeze the life out of him.

"Uhhhnnn. Good to see you, Deb," he says, catching his breath.

Debbie takes a step back to get all four of us into her

frame of vision. "Hey, I remember reading about you girls. You solved a big case a couple of months back and found a valuable necklace, is that right?"

"A ring," Margaret corrects. "It was hidden in the church for twenty years."

"And they've been very busy since then," Father Julian says. "They recently solved a case involving a violin that was stolen—twice!"

Once we're all settled in, with glasses of milk for us, coffees for Aunt Cathy and Father Julian, and a glass of wine for Debbie, he explains the situation with the painting, including the newest detail.

"So, one reason we're here is to see if you would have any idea of how or when or why this happened. For instance, do you remember anyone talking about making a copy and then hiding the original for safekeeping? Dad certainly never mentioned anything like that."

Cathy looks at the photograph of her grandparents, standing proudly in front of the fireplace, the painting hanging above the mantel. "Now that you mention it, my sisters and I raised a bit of a fuss with your great-uncle Phillip. When Mom died, she left the painting to your father in her will, no doubt about that. Oliver didn't want the painting, but Phillip was not pleased by that. He swore that Mom had promised him the painting. After her funeral, your father was away on business for a few days, and Phillip used that opportunity to take the picture from her house. We begged him to return it, but he finally stopped answering his phone. But then, just before your father came back, Phillip suddenly returned the painting, saying that his conscience was bothering him."

"You're kidding," says Father Julian.

"Oh no. It's all true. We never said anything because we didn't want to cause any hard feelings between your father and Phillip. And then, remember, Phillip dropped dead six months later."

Margaret absorbs all the information and then says, "Maybe Phillip made a copy—or had one made. Rebecca, how long would it take you to make a really good copy of this painting?"

"A couple of days, maybe three or four, to do a nice job," Becca answers. "The paint wouldn't really be dry all the way through, but you probably wouldn't notice anything like that unless you were looking for it. And I'm sure there are ways to help that along, too."

"It sounds like a possibility," Father Julian acknowledges. "Which just raises a whole slew of other questions, the most important of which is, if Uncle Phillip kept the original, what did he do with it?"

"You'll need to ask Miss Pennsylvania about that one," answers Aunt Cathy.

Leigh Ann makes a quizzical face. "Miss Pennsylvania?"

"Miss Prunella Scroggins. We called her Miss Pennsylvania—not to her face, of course—because she always had her hair done up on the top of her head like a beauty queen. She was Phillip's, ahem, *girlfriend*. For more than forty years."

"Goodness. I haven't thought about her in years," Father Julian says. "Good old Prunella."

"Something tells me there's a great story connected with her," Margaret says.

Aunt Cathy chuckles quietly. "Oh boy. About a million stories. One thing I can say about Prunella: life was never dull when she was around. She was from some tiny town up in the Pennsylvania mountains, I believe. Eagle's Lake, or Eagle Mountain, I think. Eagle something. Phillip used to go fishing a couple of times a year, and he met her on one of his trips. Something of a local *character* up there, if you know what I mean. The woman could hold her liquor like no one I've ever seen, before or since. Phillip found her in a tavern and, for reasons no sane person can imagine, he was absolutely smitten. And her language—oh my."

"I do seem to remember it being on the spicy side," Father Julian recalls.

"That's putting it lightly," Aunt Cathy says. "It could peel paint off the walls. It was the sixties, and civil rights marches were in the news all the time. Let's just say that Prunella did *not* approve of Martin Luther King. I don't think I've ever met anyone quite so bigoted—certainly no one so *outspoken* in her bigotry, at least. Phillip dragged her out of that bar in the early sixties, and she stuck with him to the bitter end. Because they weren't married and he didn't leave a will, all of his possessions should have gone to your father, your aunts, and me, as we were his closest living relatives. Nobody really cared about the money; after all, life with Phillip was no bed of roses. He was a pain in the neck, and frankly, Prunella was welcome to whatever he had. But some family heirlooms—items with sentimental value only—disappeared. Family photos, jewelry, my grandfather's pocket watch—things she had no right to. I guess she had adapted to life in the city, because she didn't go back to Pennsylvania when Phillip died. She moved right into his rent-controlled apartment uptown."

"Whatever happened to her?" Margaret asks.

"Thankfully, she stopped coming to family functions," Aunt Cathy says with a relieved expression. "The first couple of years after Phillip's funeral, I ran into her a handful of times. I know it sounds quite juvenile of me, but if I saw her first, I turned and *ran* in the other direction, as fast as my legs would carry me."

"Is she still alive?" I ask.

"Last I heard, yes. Still in that same apartment."

"Father Julian, you *have* to go visit her," Margaret declares. "She can't be hard to find—how many Prunellas can there possibly be?"

"Oh, let's hope she's the last. One is more than enough," Aunt Cathy says.

"If Phillip made a copy of the painting and kept the original," I say, "she might still have it. And even if she doesn't, she can probably tell you what happened to it."

"Have you shown your aunt the pictures from her birthday?" Leigh Ann asks.

"No, but I have them right here," Father Julian says, handing an envelope to Aunt Cathy. "Although I'm not sure it matters anymore. If the original painting is gone, the year the pictures were taken just isn't that important."

Aunt Cathy smiles when she sees her birthday pictures. "Oh my. This handsome young man is Denny McCormack. He lived next door, and my parents were always hopeful that we would fall in love, but neither of us was much interested in the other, except as good friends. He went away to Indiana or Illinois for college, and the summer after his senior year, he came back married."

"Can you tell which birthday you're celebrating?" Margaret asks.

"Seventeen? Could be eighteen or even nineteen. Honestly, I can't be sure. Denny was always around at family affairs. I'll bet our families took a dozen pictures of the two of us in front of birthday cakes over the years."

She flips through a few more pictures, stopping to laugh at two grumpy-looking old people on the couch in one of the more recent color snapshots. "Ask and ye shall receive. You wanted to see Prunella and Phillip, and here they are. And don't they seem just *thrilled* to be with one another?"

She hands the picture to Debbie, whose mouth drops

open when she sees it. Her eyes get a little watery right away.

"Oh my," Debbie says. "Cale Winokum."

"Who's that?" Father Julian asks.

"He's the young man in the picture standing in front of the fireplace," Debbie says. "He taught art at some school in the city—Bramwell, on the West Side—but he really just wanted to be an artist. I met him through Phillip, but I don't remember how they knew each other. They didn't exactly have much in common, to put it mildly. Cale was this gentle, quiet, shy person. He was . . . well, wonderful, and *so* talented."

"Was?" I ask tentatively.

But before she can answer, Margaret points to the older man standing in the background of the picture. "Who's this?" she asks.

Aunt Cathy squints at the picture and shakes her head. "I have no idea. If I had to guess, I'd say he's a friend of Phillip's—they're about the same age. I don't ever remember seeing him again. To tell the truth, I don't really remember him from this party, but I guess photographs don't lie."

"I want to hear more about this Cale Winokum guy," Becca says to Debbie. "Whatever happened to him? Did you two ever, uh, get together?"

"Becca, that's kind of personal," I say, even though I'm dying to hear her answer.

"No, it's all right," Debbie assures me. "We went out

on a few dates, but then, seven years ago, he just disappeared from the face of the earth, right in the middle of the school year. The school where he taught went crazy looking for him. Someone told me he joined the army, but I never believed it. He wasn't the type, not at all. Others said he went to Europe to study painting and never came back. That one always seemed more likely to me, so that's what I've chosen to believe all these years."

Leigh Ann sighs. "That is so sad. And you never even heard from him? A letter, a postcard, even?"

"Not a one. I thought about looking up his family, but I never did. He made his choice, and I had to get on with my life."

"You, however, should go see Prunella—but *please* don't tell her I sent you," Aunt Cathy says to Father Julian. "I don't want her looking me up. Do tell me about your visit, though. I can't wait to hear."

That makes two of us, at least.

Chapter 16

In which Tillie provides invaluable assistance

Finding Miss Prunella Scroggins requires some serious detective work; the four and a half brains (Margaret has the extra half) of the Red Blazer Girls are pushed to their absolute limits. And it doesn't happen without some sacrifice; we lose a lot of good people on the way.

Okay, so I'm exaggerating. The truth is, Rebecca opens a Manhattan phone book and—bam!—we have a phone number and address for a P. Scroggins.

Father Julian tells us about the phone call and visit after school the next day. Despite some initial reluctance on her part to see a member of Phillip's family, she changes her mind when she learns that he is now a priest.

"I suppose to her that means I'm not a threat," Father Julian says. "She was—is—definitely suspicious of my motives."

"What did you tell her?" Rebecca asks, grinning mischievously. "You didn't *lie,* did you?"

"Let's say I shaded the truth a little," he admits. "I

told her that I'm doing some research about the family, and I wanted to learn more about Uncle Phillip. All of which is true, by the way."

"What's she like?" Leigh Ann asks. "Is she as nutty as your aunt says?"

"Wait, wait, wait!" Margaret insists. "First—what about the painting? Does she still have it?"

Father Julian smiles slyly. "You girls will be proud of me. I was a regular Father Dowling in there." He takes out his cell phone. (Yes, *Father* Julian has a cell phone. Weird, isn't it? He even knows how to text, which I suppose gives him something to do during really boring confessions. His ring tone? Church bells, naturally.) "I have a picture," he says, and hands the phone to Rebecca.

"Did you ask her about it?" I ask.

"I didn't want to make her too suspicious, but when I casually remarked that I liked it, she said, 'You too?' which definitely struck me as odd. When I asked what she meant, she told me that a few days ago, an art gallery contacted her out of the blue about it. They told her they knew from their records that she had owned a Pommeroy—which is complete nonsense, because that painting never spent a second in their gallery—and wondered if she still did. They told her that the market for his work is down a little, but even if they couldn't produce a buyer, they would be willing to buy it themselves and take their chances."

"It does seem like too much of a coincidence to be a coincidence," Margaret says. "Did she say who it was?"

"No, but I'll bet you it's the people I talked to—the Svindahl Gallery. Phillip must have done business with them; how else would they know about her owning the painting?"

"Wait a minute!" Becca shouts. "The Svindahl Gallery? *That's* where you went? Sophie, that's the gallery where Gus works! I knew it. They're running some kind of scam down there."

I have to admit, it does seem a bit odd, their contacting Prunella about a Pommeroy just days after telling Father Julian that his painting—by the same artist—isn't worth anything unless he can prove its age. Maybe it's not a scam, but something strange is going on.

"So what's Prunella going to do?" Margaret asks. "Do you think she'll sell it?"

Father Julian shrugs. "It seems likely. She's no art lover, believe me, and any sentimental attachment she may have had is long gone. But back to your question, Leigh Ann. Yes, Prunella is everything Aunt Cathy said, and more. She certainly is . . . colorful."

Becca tips an imaginary bottle to her lips and staggers around.

Father Julian's eyes widen and he laughs out loud. "Like you wouldn't believe! Ten in the morning and already going strong. I took a small glass of sherry to be polite; meanwhile, she's drinking Manhattans—heavy on the bourbon—like they're going out of style."

"So, what do we do now?" Margaret, ever the detective, asks.

"I don't think there's anything we *can* do," says Father Julian, scratching his head.

Margaret digs in her heels at the injustice of it all. "This Prunella woman doesn't have any right to the painting. And now she's going to sell it! Even if she was married to Phillip, *he* never had the right to the painting. Let's face it, he was a crook; he *stole* it from his own family. And then he either painted the fake or had someone else do it. Father Julian, you *have* to get it back."

"She's right," Leigh Ann says, with Becca and me chiming in with our agreement.

"What do you want me to do? Take her to court? That could take years—and cost thousands and thousands of dollars."

But my sweet, brilliant—and sometimes devious—best friend has something else entirely in mind. "We switch the paintings," she says.

"Margaret, you really are a genius," I say. "That's perfect."

"And exactly how do you think you're going to pull that off?" a doubtful Becca says. "You can't just walk into her apartment carrying a big ol' painting and switch it with the one on her wall. I think she'd notice."

Margaret's index fingers press against her temples. "I don't know . . . yet. But we'll figure it out. We always manage to find a way. We snagged the ring right out of Mr. Winterbottom's hands, and had to solve a locked-room mystery in order to recover the violin. We can do this. I'm sure."

Father Julian holds up his hand. "Girls, hold on a second. Before you start planning something, uh, illegal, or even questionable, keep in mind that at this point we don't even know if *either* painting is real. None of this matters if the original painting is post-1961. Unless—"

"Unless what?"

"It's possible she has some other way of proving the date—like a letter from Pommeroy."

"All right, so we prove, once and for all, in our own way, when that thing was painted," Margaret says. "*Then* we go after it."

"Yeah," Becca agrees. "I mean, let's face it. Even though we haven't proved it yet, *you* know that Pommeroy gave a painting to your great-grandfather, right? Which means that he at least *started out* with a real Pommeroy. It's like a jigsaw puzzle where you know what the final result looks like, but you're missing one stupid little piece."

"One really *important* piece," I correct.

A piece that I am determined to find.

That shoe box full of photographs has taken on new significance for me. Yes, part of me sincerely wants to help out Father Julian and his family, but a more selfish part of me is motivated by something else entirely: I am craving a little adventure. It's hard to describe the rush of adrenaline I got at that moment when I totally pulled the rug out from under Mr. Winterbottom, or when Raf drove me across town on his uncle's scooter, my arms wrapped around his waist, the wind blowing in my face. And while I don't know how we're going to switch paintings with Miss Prunella Scroggins, I'm starting to imagine the four of us on the roof of her apartment in the middle of the night, dressed head to toe in black, and crawling between the red laser beams of her super-sophisticated security system.

Then again, maybe I've seen too many movies.

Whatever the case, I push Tillie, who is sprawled across the middle of my bed, off to one side and arrange the pictures that we've already targeted as helpful:

"Come on, Tillie, help me out here. What do you see?"

She tilts her head at me in a way that makes her look like she understands every word I'm saying. Instead of telling me the solution to the problem, however, she rolls over on her back and grunts at me—her way of saying, "Rub my belly, you simpleminded human."

She kicks out her back legs, knocking the shoe box to the floor, and hundreds of pictures spill out in all directions.

"Tillie!" I roll myself off the bed and am just about to start scooping when something catches my eye. It's a picture I haven't seen before, but one that might easily have been overlooked by any of us. Five kids are posed in the yard outside a house—not at all what we had been looking for. It's the picture window *behind* them, though, that's interesting. You see, it's clearly the *same* picture window that you can see behind the people on the couch in that other photo.

Now take a good look at the two people facing each other. Do you see it? It's the same two people sitting on that bench next to the TV—Aunt Cathy and Denny McCormack. She has a drink in her hand, and he's holding a plate with a big piece of cake. That picture must have been taken a few seconds before the one that shows the TV.

Behind the kids on the other side of the picture are the sliding glass doors that lead into the kitchen—the doors that are barely visible behind Aunt Cathy and Denny in the birthday cake picture. There's a floor vase filled with fresh flowers and a dog with its nose pressed against the glass. But no sign of the painting, and nothing else that screams out a date at me. I know I'm onto something, but I just can't quite fit the pieces together. Yet.

"There just has to be a way to put a date on *one* of these pictures, Tillie."

She woofs at me, and jumps off the bed in search of something to chew on, no doubt. A few moments later, she's standing at the threshold to my bedroom, a piece of the cover of the baseball she destroyed hanging proudly from her mouth.

"Woof," she says.

"If I were you, I wouldn't be bragging about that. You're lucky to be alive. If you weren't Nate Etan's dog, you'd be *dead.*"

When I say the word "dead," Tillie drops to the floor as if she's been shot, lying on her side with her eyes closed, legs sticking out stiffly, and pink tongue lolling out of the side of her mouth.

My heart skips two full beats. I just killed Nate Etan's dog! I can hear those fangirls beating down my door already, pitchforks and torches at the ready.

"Tillie!" I shout, frantically trying to remember how to do CPR on a dog.

She opens her eyes and leaps to her feet, licking my face. It was a trick!

"What the . . . Tillie, you almost gave me a heart attack!"

She nudges me with her cold, wet nose and then sets the soggy remains of the baseball on my lap.

"Gee, thanks," I say.

And then, like a bucket of ice water over the head, it hits me: crazy as it sounds, I think Tillie is trying to tell me that the baseball is a clue!

"Good girl!" I dig through the shoe box to find Malcolm's loupe, so I can take a closer look at the photograph with the Yankees game on the TV. Two players are visible in the image, which appears to be from a camera behind home plate. The batter is definitely a Yankee player, and although the number is partially obscured, I'm sure it's none other than number seven, Mickey Mantle himself. The pitcher is clearly number thirty, but it takes me a few minutes to be certain that the block letters across his chest read "Cincinnati."

Which is strange. After all, the Cincinnati Reds are a National League team. Why would Mickey Mantle be batting against a National League pitcher in October? There's only one possible answer.

"It's the World Series!" I yell at Tillie as I hug her. She gives me a look that says, "Duh!" and lies back down.

"Okay, Till, if you're so smart," I say, "what year did the Reds and the Yankees play in the World Series?"

Tillie just tilts her head to the side and stares at me this time.

"That's what I thought. You're not so smart. It was 1961. The Yankees won in five games. In thirty seconds I'll tell you who the pitcher is, and the exact date of this picture."

She puts her head down, unimpressed.

Okay, so it takes me *slightly* longer than thirty seconds to establish that the pitcher is Joey Jay (who won the game for the Reds) and the date of the game was October 5, 1961—Aunt Cathy's seventeenth birthday. But I still did it faster than Tillie could have.

And the painting now has a date!

Except it doesn't. The painting! It's not visible in the picture with the TV—or in the new one I found.

I pound my forehead with the heel of my hand. "Oh man. There has to be a way to connect all these dots."

My phone rings, and when Nate Etan's name lights up, I take a panicky look in the mirror to make sure my hair looks okay and that there are no big chunks of food stuck in my braces.

"Hey, *bonjour, Mademoiselle Sophie! Comment vas-tu?*"

For someone who supposedly spent so much time in France, his accent is truly atrocious.

"Um, *très bien,* I guess. How are you? *Where* are you?"

"Uh, yeah, that's the *raison* for the call. I'm still in London, and now it looks like I'm going to have to fly to Japan for a few days to make a commercial. How are you and Tillie getting along? Food holding out? Any problems?"

Tillie looks up at me, still chewing on the cover of "her" baseball.

"No, not at all. We bought some more food. She's great. In fact, she showed me a new trick today. You didn't tell me she could play dead."

"*What?* I never taught her that. I don't know much about dog training."

"Well, somebody taught her. She scared me half to death. I said the word 'dead' and she dropped like a shot."

"You're kidding. My Tillie?"

"Honest. And she's really good at it. It looks like she has rigor mortis—her legs stick straight out and her tongue hangs to one side. Once I realized she wasn't actually dead, I cracked up."

"Son of a gun. I had no idea. Somebody else taught her, because the only real trick I've ever been able to teach her is 'jump.' When you say that word, she jumps straight up in the air, like she's on springs. And that wasn't hard to teach; she did it every time I got ready to put her leash on. All I had to do was keep saying 'jump.' Go on, try it."

"Hey, Tillie! Jump!"

Tillie tilts her head questioningly at me and wags her tail, but all four feet remain glued to the floor.

"Jump!"

More tail wagging, but still no defying of gravity.

"Well?"

"Nope. Nothing. She's staring at me like I'm crazy."

"Huh. Maybe she only does it for me. Well, look, Sophie, I just called to tell you how much I appreciate all this—I know you didn't expect to have her for this long. I *promise* I will make it up to you."

"Don't worry about it," I say. "She just helped me solve a little problem, and even my mom is starting to love her."

"Cool. Give me a shout if you need anything. Ciao!"

And just like that—poof!—he's gone.

Chapter 17

Oh, great-now my dreams are getting complicated

I'm on the back of a scooter, arms wrapped around Raf's waist, flying down the Champs-Elysées in Paris. All around us, taxis are honking and people are waving and shouting at me like I'm some kind of celebrity. I smile and wave back, my hair streaming behind me like the tail on a kite. There's a sharp right-hand turn just ahead, so I squeeze Raf tighter as he revs the engine even faster.

"Hold on," he says, leaning into the corner. "Just a little bit farther."

A few seconds later, he parks the scooter in front of a café. "This is the place," he says, turning around to face me.

At the exact moment I realize that my arms have been wrapped around Nate Etan and not Raf, Mom wakes me up.

"Sophie! Time to take Tillie out."

Completely disoriented, I instinctively reach out to

stop myself from falling off the scooter. I sit up on my bed—still fully dressed, with Father Julian's pictures still strewn all around me, and Tillie curled up with her head on my pillow.

"Wha—what time is it?"

"A little after nine."

I panic, leaping to my feet so fast that I see stars. "Nine! Why did you let me sleep so long? I'm late for school."

Mom laughs. "Nine at night, you goose. Come on, I'll go with you. I could use the fresh air." She glances at the pictures on my quilt. "What were you doing in here, anyway? I thought you were studying."

"I was, kind of. We're doing a special project for Father Julian—you remember him, right? And having a really, um, *strange* dream."

"Oh yeah? Anything you'd like to share with your dear old mom?"

"Uh, no. Definitely not."

When we come back from our walk, I get ready for bed, but after my two-hour nap, I'm wide awake. I scroll through all my missed text messages; in addition to the fifteen from Margaret, Becca, and Leigh Ann, sent while I was unconscious, there are three from Raf. Boy, do I feel guilty. Here he is, thinking about me, asking what I want to do next weekend, and what am I doing? Dreaming about another guy. Oy. Just what was Nate Etan doing in my dream version of Paris, anyway? That little fantasy world is supposed to be exclusively for me and Raf.

As I'm holding the phone, it rings—it's Raf.

"Hey, you," I say. "I was just about to call."

I mean, I *was*, wasn't I?

"I was starting to wonder—when you didn't answer my texts, I figured you were probably out with that movie star boyfriend of yours again."

Another moment of panic as I check myself out in the mirror to see if guilt is, like, literally written all over my face. I compose myself enough to laugh—a little nervously—at the idea of Nate Etan being my boyfriend.

"Ha ha. No, nothing that, um, interesting. You know that case we're working on for Father Julian? One minute it's seven o'clock and I'm staring at all these old pictures, and the next thing I know, my mom is yelling at me to take Tillie out. I slept for two hours! *That's* why I didn't answer. And now I'll be up for hours. So talk to me. Seems like we haven't talked—actual conversation, not just texting—in days. And the last time I saw you— well, you weren't exactly talkative." And then a teensy white lie: "I was just thinking about your uncle's scooter, and how much fun we had."

"Yeah, until I got grounded for life."

"How much longer, seriously, until your mom lets you stay out past eight-thirty?"

"Oh, she's starting to crack. I got a hundred on my last French test—see, I told you that one quiz was a fluke—and that made her really happy. Do you want to go to a movie this weekend? If she knows it's you, she'll probably let me go. She likes you."

"That's because you didn't tell her I was on the scooter with you," I say. "If she knew, she'd probably think I talked her perfect little angel into it. Whose turn is it to pick the movie?"

"Mine. If you're okay coming over to this side of town, they're showing the original *Frankenstein* on Saturday. It's a true classic. You *have* to see it; Boris Karloff is amazing."

"Is he the guy with the square head?"

"That's makeup, Sophie."

"I knew that."

As Raf reminds me of the superiority of classic black-and-white movies, I pick up the picture that I discovered (with Tillie's help)—the one with the kids posing out in the yard.

Then I'm digging madly through the pile for the loupe, all but ignoring poor Raf.

Ten more seconds and several pictures go sailing as I search frantically for the birthday cake picture and the TV picture, which got mixed in with the others when I fell asleep. When I locate them, I place them all in a neat row so I can give each a close look.

Finally, I lift my eyes and stare at Tillie, my mouth falling open in astonishment.

"That's it!"

There's an awkward moment of silence from Raf's

side of the conversation, followed by, "Uh, that's *what*? Were you even listening to me?"

"Of course. I mean, well, mostly. Listen, Raf, can I call you back in a few minutes? I need to call Margaret right now. It's super-important. I'll explain later."

Chapter 18

I know it's not fair, leaving you (and Raf–oh no!) hanging like that, but . . .

So, do you see the answer yet? I'll give you a little time to solve it for yourself, because I know that, deep down, you really want to do it on your own. Meanwhile, now that we have proof that the original painting was done before October 1961 (and we do, trust me), the Red Blazer Girls have a job to do, a job that's going to take the three C's—creativity, cunning, and good old-fashioned chutzpah.

The adventure begins on a C-squared Friday; it's cold and clammy. After a quick run-through of our songs in Elizabeth's basement, the Blazers, along with our manager, Margaret, head uptown to stake out Miss Prunella's apartment. After we told him the good news about the date of the picture, Father Julian provided us with one tidbit of information to get us started, even though he continues to insist that he wants nothing to do with our efforts to get the painting back. Prunella, he learned, goes out for the early-bird special at a local diner at four-thirty every Friday afternoon. What we do with that little nugget, he says, is completely up to us.

On the way there, Margaret explains to Mbingu that we are on an intelligence-gathering mission, pure and simple. "Before we can formulate a plan, we need to find out everything we can about her. Everyone has a weakness; we have to find hers, and then figure out a way to exploit it."

Mbingu looks at me. "Does she always talk like that?"

"Pretty much," I say. "Especially when she's working on a case."

According to the information we got from the phone book, Miss Prunella lives on Ninety-fourth Street—the same street, I note, where we saw Livvy and that old woman.

"How weird would it be if Miss Prunella and that lady we saw with Livvy are the same person," Leigh Ann says.

"*Too* weird," I say.

"*That* would be a coincidence worthy of Dickens," says Margaret. She stops and points across the street at a building with an iron fence surrounding it. "That's the place."

"Okay, you're not going to believe this," I say, "but that's the same building I saw Livvy go in."

Margaret considers the circumstances for a few seconds. "Well, I think Father Julian would have mentioned that Prunella was on crutches or in a wheelchair, so it's probably just a *minor* coincidence. Well, I guess we'll see; it's five after four, so she should be leaving soon. Let's just wait here for her to come out."

One of those creepy iron fences—the kind that looks like hundreds of long, spiky spears sticking straight up and just waiting for people to impale themselves on— stands between Prunella's apartment building, a place that clearly has seen better days, and the sidewalk. It may not be the high-tech security system I had imagined, but it looks like it does the job of keeping the occasional cat burglar out. I wince when I think about trying to climb over those spears . . . and slipping. Yee- ouch.

At four-ten on the nose, the door to the apartment building opens, and a few seconds later a short, wiry woman with hair the color of a shiny new penny pushes open the iron gate and steps through.

"Is that her?" Mbingu asks.

"Mmm—bingo!" says Margaret. "Her hair is just like Father Julian described. Sorry, Sophie—no crutches."

"*C'est la vie,*" I say.

"You're kidding," Becca says when she sees the person we're talking about. "*That's* who we're up against? She's a little old lady. She looks kinda like my kinder- garten teacher."

"As a detective, however, you have to remember that she's a little old lady who has something that belongs to someone else," Margaret reminds her. "And don't underestimate her because of her size. Remember what Father Julian said? She drinks and swears like a sailor."

"Ah . . . the end justifies the means, *n'est-ce pas?*" I say. "So, even if we have to tie up and rob an old woman to do it, it's okay, because we're doing it for a good reason, right?"

"First of all, we are *not* going to tie her up or rob her," Margaret insists. "All right, I guess if you really wanted to get *technical,* maybe we are going to rob her, but we're not leaving her empty-handed. And we're righting a wrong that was done a long time ago, so that, um, balances things out. Come on, let's go."

We trail Prunella to a diner on Second Avenue, and a minute after she goes inside, we follow, sliding into the booth right behind her gaudy orange head. And that's when we get the bonus. A man and a woman, both in their early twenties, approach her table.

"Miss Scroggins?" the man asks. "I'm Arthur Svindahl. Junior, that is. From the Svindahl Gallery. We spoke on the phone. This is my sister, Amelia. It's a pleasure to meet you."

Becca's eyes widen and she leans her head in to whisper, "That's them! From the gallery. He's the one who yelled at us."

We exchange silent glances at our table while Margaret scribbles this message on a napkin: "Keep talking so I can listen to them."

Even though we hadn't planned on eating, I am suddenly ravenous when our waiter shoves a menu in my face, coming perilously close to my still-tender nose. And besides, it looks kind of suspicious if we just sit there without anything to eat or drink. I don't want to be the one to blow our cover, so I turn to Margaret. "You want to split a turkey club with me?"

She has her head turned, eavesdropping on Prunella and the Svindahls, but she nods at me. *"Oui. Avec frites, s'il te plaît."*

After we place our order, we pretend to have a conversation while straining our ears to hear everything we can.

And boy, do we get an earful. It's going to take a week's worth of showers before I feel clean again, just from *listening* to Prunella, who has, as Leigh Ann puts it, a mouth "like a sewer." And frankly, I think that's doing an injustice to sewers; the stuff coming out of her mouth is filthier than anything I've ever seen in a New York sewer.

Instead of a blow-by-blow description of every offensive thing that Prunella said, let me start with a list of emotions registered at our table in the time it takes to eat half a sandwich and some soggy, undercooked fries that no Frenchman would admit to having invented:

Disbelief
Indignation
Irritation
Exasperation
Annoyance
Anger
Wrath

Outrage

Fury

Borderline homicidal rage

So much for feeling sorry for the little old lady. By the time I snag the last fry from Margaret's plate, the five of us are ready to climb over the booth and steal her purse!

Occasionally, Arthur Svindahl steers the subject back to the painting and whether she's made a decision about selling it, but somehow she always seems to get back to her original topic.

Amelia, clearly frustrated with Prunella's behavior and her brother's inability to deal with it, finally takes charge. "Miss Scroggins, if we can just focus for a few moments on the painting that we looked at in your apartment. We are prepared to write you a check for this amount for the painting *today.*" She slides a piece of the gallery's stationery across the table to Prunella. "Now, you're perfectly welcome to talk to other galleries, but I doubt you'll find any who are willing to pay this amount—especially since you don't have a certificate of authenticity or other real proof of provenance."

"Oh, it's real enough, all right," Prunella says loudly enough for every ear at our table to perk up. "Phillip took it from his sister's house. I told him to do it and he did it."

She seems almost proud of that fact, the crazy old bat.

"I want to think about it," Prunella says. "I know I ought to take your money and run, because I have a hard time believing that *anybody* would want that monstrosity, but I need a little time to get used to the idea."

"Then let's say the offer is good for a week," says Arthur. "We will get in touch with you next Thursday or Friday. We'll have a cashier's check ready for you."

"Fair enough," Prunella says.

The diner door swings open and I instinctively duck down in my seat when I realize that it is Livvy Klack. She is pushing a woman in a wheelchair, and the brisk November wind is making it hard for her to hold the door open and maneuver the wheelchair inside.

Our waiter hustles over to the door. "One second, Olivia. Let me help you," he says.

Olivia? How often does she come here?

When everyone is safely inside, he greets the woman in the wheelchair. "Good afternoon, Miss Demarest. The special today is roast chicken with mashed potatoes and green beans. Get you started with some coffee?"

I lean over the table and whisper, "Code red, everybody. Livvy Klack is in the building. Repeat, Livvy Klack is in the building."

"Where?" Becca says, spinning around to see for herself.

"Don't look!" I hiss, but it's too late. We've been spotted.

There is an awkward moment of recognition when Livvy's eyes and mine meet. I sort of half smile, half wave at her, but she doesn't return either; she seems to look right through me. I don't know what it is, but at that moment, even with all the rotten things she's done to me, I feel kind of sorry for her. She's so used to being in control that she must absolutely hate situations like this, where people might see a side of her she doesn't want to be seen.

"We should go," I say.

Leigh Ann nods. "Yeah, I don't think I can take any more of you-know-who."

"You don't want to snoop a little?" Becca asks. "You're tellin' me you're not a little curious about Livvy?"

And that's when good ol' Miss Prunella puts the icing on the cake. As the Svindahls get up to leave, she points at Livvy and Miss Demarest and says, loudly enough to be heard by nearly everyone in the place, "Well. Now I've seen everything. A pretty white girl pushing a crippled old *colored* woman around in a wheelchair. I'll bet you there's nothing wrong with her; she just likes having a white girl do all her work for her."

I close my eyes, cringing. My face feels like I have a sunburn as the blood rushes to it, but I don't know what to do. A quick peek at my friends' faces, mouths hanging open in sheer horror, tells me that they're all struggling with the same dilemma. Do we butt in and stand up for Livvy, Miss Demarest, and, well, common *decency,* for crying out loud, or do we just pretend we didn't hear a thing and walk away?

Livvy spares us that decision. Whatever discomfort she felt at seeing us in the diner is gone, and she stands up and unloads on Miss Prunella.

"How dare you, you ignorant old bigot!"

Arthur Svindahl starts to come to Prunella's defense. "Now hold on. There's no need to . . ."

But Livvy aims her death-ray vision at him for a microsecond, and when he wisely backs off, she turns her attention back to Prunella.

"You aren't worthy to even be in the same room, to breathe the same *air,* as this woman. She's done more in her life than you—"

This time, she is interrupted by Miss Demarest, who has calmly placed her hand on Livvy's arm. "Olivia, dear, sit. Don't let her spoil our nice dinner. Please."

Livvy, whose face has turned the color of a nice piece of tuna sashimi, takes a deep breath, glares one last time at Prunella, and sits down.

When the Svindahls finally leave, I stand up and pull on my coat. "Okay, now it's definitely time to leave."

But believe it or not, Prunella's *still* not done. This time, however, she has the sense to mutter under her breath—quietly enough that Livvy doesn't hear, thank God.

"With a temper like that, she must be *Irish.* It's a shame—she's a pretty young thing, too."

As we walk out the door and into the darkness of a November evening, we are uncharacteristically quiet— but, I'm convinced, more determined than ever.

Chapter 19

The stuff nightmares are made of

An hour later, the Blazers are still filled with enough adrenaline to rock Perkatory from the sticky floor tiles to the stained and peeling ceiling. Before launching into our final number, however, I take the microphone in hand for a mysterious announcement.

"We'd like to dedicate this next song to a . . . well, she's not really a friend, but she's somebody I have new-found admiration for—somebody who did something really brave today. Um, that's all I can say about it right now, but trust me, she did a good thing. This one's called 'You Rock,' and it's by our very own Leigh Ann Jaimes and Becca Chen!"

"Amen!" shouts Mbingu, who hits her cymbals like she's imagining they're Prunella's face, I think. We all play with a kind of reckless abandon; it's not our best performance, but it certainly is our most passionate.

As promised, Cam Peterson shows up right on time and sits at a table with Margaret and Andrew. Except for their Saturday morning quartet practice at my apartment—with my mom three feet away—it's the only time those two get to see each other. And unfortunately for them, that situation isn't likely to change for a while. Margaret's dad is super-protective and old-fashioned in a way that would be charming if it wasn't affecting my best friend's love life, and has forbidden dating of any kind until she is sixteen. It's only because of her status as our official manager that she's getting away with these little Friday evening rendezvous. The final notes from "You Rock" are still hanging in the air when Alex, Leigh Ann's gorgeous older brother, walks in.

Leigh Ann runs off the stage to hug him, and the disappointment shows immediately on Cam's face.

"Don't worry—that's her brother," I whisper in his ear. "He's a senior."

Cam's face brightens. "Ohhh. Phew."

Alex, who is a full head taller than Cam, turns to introduce himself and then kids Cam in a good-natured, protective-big-brother way. Leigh Ann blushes and pushes him away from the table.

"Alex! Leave him alone—he's a really nice guy. And at least *he* got here in time to hear us play."

"Uh, yeah. Sorry about that. Slow train. I'll make it one of these weeks."

"Speaking of *slow,*" Becca says with a devious smile, "where's Raf? Grounded again? Hee hee hee."

"He's *not* slow, Becca," I say. "*One* time he got grounded for flunking *one* test. And for your information, he's staying in tonight so we can go to a movie tomorrow night—the original *Frankenstein*. It's one of his favorites. His mom is finally starting to crack. She's giving him a whole extra hour. So there." I stick my tongue out at her to punctuate my defense of Raf's honor. "But I do have to go home early tonight, too. I promised Mom, 'cause I've been leaving her alone with Tillie a lot."

Margaret and Andrew offer to walk with me, but I don't want to spoil their once-a-week chance to talk in person. Besides, I have a lot on my mind, and I'm looking forward to the chance to just walk and think. That little scene with Prunella and Livvy really has me wondering. If Livvy hadn't stood up and confronted that raving lunatic, would I have done it? Or would I have just sat there, fuming? I desperately want to be the kind of person who will do the right thing—who will stand up to injustice when I see it—but I'm not sure I have the courage. I did stand up to Livvy that one time outside the movie theater, when she was insulting Margaret, but that was different; I know Livvy, and Margaret's my best friend in the world. Could I do the same thing for a complete stranger?

Another really good reason to make it an early night is that I have to be back at St. Veronica's at five-fifteen on Saturday morning for a swim meet. At our practice Friday morning, Michelle told us about an important development. All the girls on the team come from either St. Veronica's or Faircastle Academy. When the

Faircastle kids announced that they'll be leaving because their school is forming its own team, Michelle called Sister Bernadette to find out if we could work out a similar deal. Sister Bernadette loved the idea, so effective immediately, we are officially the St. Veronica's School Swim Team. It's not going to be much of a change; we'll still be practicing at Asphalt Green, and we'll still have red swimsuits, although maybe Sister B will pay to have the school name embroidered on them. We immediately start dreaming of matching warm-up suits and sneakers, but Michelle warns us not to get carried away. I guess the private luxury bus I requested is out of the question, too.

It promises to be a long day; our team, half the size it was a week ago, is taking a van to Haworth Prep, a school near Princeton, New Jersey, for an invitational meet. When Michelle shows me where we're going on the map, I start to worry about being back in time to meet Raf at Lincoln Center for the movie. With all the stuff about Nate, the weird conversation outside Perkatory, and my practically hanging up on him the last time we talked, I can't help thinking that Raf is a little annoyed with me—maybe even with good reason. Showing up late for the movie probably won't help things.

The one good thing, if there is anything positive about getting up at four-thirty on a Saturday morning, is that no one expects you to talk. Even Carey Petrus, who, as Mr. Eliot would say, "could talk the ear off a brass monkey," is basically comatose as we wait for Michelle to unlock the van. Livvy already has her hand on the door handle for the front passenger seat—the only one that reclines—and no one has the gumption to challenge her for it, especially at this time of day. Without a word to any of us, she closes her eyes and drifts off to Livvyland, which, if the smile on her face means anything, is a much happier place.

The meet itself is not such a great beginning for the St. Veronica's School Swim Team. Haworth Prep looks like a college campus, and basically, we get our little red-swimsuit-wearing butts kicked by a bunch of snooty New Jersey kids. We win only three events: Livvy dominates in both the 200 and 400 backstroke, and our 400 medley relay team pulls out a victory—but only because the anchor swimmer for the other team took off too soon. To be fair to us, though, if the Haworth swimmer had waited and made a legal start, the finish would have been *really* close.

Despite our "crushing defeat" (as Carey, a wannabe sportscaster, has dubbed it in her running commentary), we're all in good spirits for the van ride back to the city. In fact, it is an absolute blast; to someone passing our van on the New Jersey Turnpike, we must look like the crushers, not the crushees.

A funny moment occurs when Carey and Rachel are teasing Livvy—a dangerous activity most days—about how she's so much better than the rest of us that she'll probably ditch us to join a better team.

"And just think," says Jill Ambrose, "of all those fresh new noses, just waiting for you to break them."

There's an awkward silence as everyone, including me, turns to see what Livvy's going to say. After my return to the team following the Nose Affair, nobody ever mentioned it again (in front of me, at least), and they *certainly* haven't ever talked about it in front of Livvy and me.

The corners of Livvy's mouth turn up ever so slightly and I swear I detect a good-natured twinkle in her eye as she looks up at all the faces staring expectantly at her.

"That's very funny, Jill," she says. "But I'm just getting started on *this* team." Her face lights up further as an idea strikes her. "Hey, Michelle, can you put me in the lane next to Jill at practice next week? I want to, um, *help* her work on her kick."

Michelle, who has heard everything, looks up in the rearview mirror. "Sure, Liv."

"Nooo!" cries Jill.

"What are you worried about?" Rachel asks. "I thought you *wanted* a nose job. This way, you'll be damaged goods. Your parents will have to give in. Someday you'll be thanking Livvy."

"What do you think, Sophie?" Carey asks. "Will she be thanking Livvy?"

And suddenly the spotlight's on me.

• • •

While we're stuck in traffic at the entrance to the Lincoln Tunnel, I get a text from Nate telling me that he's *definitely* returning to New York on Friday to take Tillie off my hands. They have to shoot a few more scenes in the city before the whole production moves up to an old inn in northern New Hampshire, where there's already snow on the ground.

Instead of being relieved, however, I'm saddened by the thought of losing Tillie. I've gotten used to her sleeping on my feet, to having her face be the first thing I see in the morning, to our walks, to . . . well, everything about her. I've even forgiven her for making an afternoon snack of my favorite sneakers. And I know I'm not the only one who feels this way; I caught my dad sharing a croque-monsieur with her, and when Mom stretches out on the couch to read in the evenings, she invites Tillie to lie next to her. The silly mutt is part of the family.

Half an hour later, Michelle pulls the van into a parking space across the street from St. Veronica's. We all scramble out with soggy duffel bags slung over our shoulders, desperate to use the school bathroom after drinking way too much soda at a rest stop on the turnpike.

"Okay, girls, you have five minutes," she warns. "I have to get the van back to the garage."

What happens in the next few minutes is kind of a blur. After I leave the bathroom, I remember that I meant to take my math textbook home for the weekend, so I hop on the elevator for a ride up to my locker on the fifth floor. It's after five o'clock, and the red glow of the exit signs, the only light on the floor, is not enough for me to read the numbers on my lock. While I struggle with it, straining my eyes, the elevator opens and Livvy gets out. She takes two steps into the shadowy void before she realizes she's not alone.

"Oh! God, you scared me," she says.

"Yeah, it's kind of dark up here. I'm having trouble seeing my lock. You don't have a flashlight, do you?"

"Um, yeah, I guess. A little one." She sounds annoyed—the old Livvy. "It's on my key chain." She digs around in her coat pockets, uses it to open her own locker, and then shines it in my direction. "Here."

"Thanks. I forgot my—"

But there's no point in continuing; she's engrossed in a message on her phone. Once again, I have ceased to exist.

I toss my math book into the duffel with my wet towel and swimsuit and head for the elevator at the end of the hall. Normally, I would just take the stairs, but a peek through the doors tells me that the stairs are even darker than the fifth floor, and climbing down several flights in the dim, nearly empty school sounds really scary to me. When the elevator arrives, Livvy runs down the hall toward me, shouting a good-bye to whomever she's talking to on the phone.

I push the button for the first floor as the elevator

door closes with its characteristic *cha-clunk*. We start our slow descent in silence—fourth floor, third floor . . . All of a sudden, the elevator jerks to a stop with an earsplitting *sssccccrrreeeeeeeeeeeccchhh.*

And then the lights go out.

"What did you do?" Livvy asks accusingly.

"I didn't do anything. I just pushed the button." I can't see Livvy at all—the darkness is absolute. "Do you have that flashlight? There must be an alarm button on this thing."

Once again, Livvy finds her key chain light and shines it on the control panel. The alarm button rings a surprisingly loud bell, and I breathe a sigh of relief.

"Michelle *has* to be able to hear that," I say. "She'll figure out how to get us out of here." I ring the bell a few more times for good measure, then press my ear against the crack in the door.

"What are you *doing*?" Livvy asks.

"Listening." I push the alarm button some more, and then try another tactic: when in doubt, scream. "*Hello! Michelle!* Can you hear me?"

Livvy and I stay perfectly still, not even breathing, listening for a sign that someone's trying to get us out. But there's nothing.

"Hmmm," I say. Then I remember the last time I was trapped in a small space: Rebecca and I were locked in a closet that we'd crawled into when we were convinced there was a secret passage between Mr. Chernofsky's violin shop and the apartment upstairs.

And to get out we . . . my phone! Of course! Jeez, how did I not think of that sooner?

Although I'm sure she arrived at it in a very different way, Livvy has reached the same obvious solution at exactly the same time. The glow of her cell phone lights up the elevator.

"No service," she says. "Super." Which *really* sounds like the Livvy of old.

I look at mine. "Hey, I have one bar—oops, nope. Spoke too soon. Nothing. No service." I don't tell her that my battery is down to its last gasp, and that even if I had service, my stupid phone would probably die before I got through to anyone.

"Ring that bell thing again," Livvy demands. "Michelle has to be there. She wouldn't just leave us."

She wouldn't, right?

An hour goes by.

We're sitting on the cold linoleum floor.

In the dark.

And neither of us has said anything for a long, long time. Occasionally, Livvy lets loose with a big, dramatic sigh and mutters something under her breath. She doesn't want me to respond; she's just making sure I know how miserable she is, and that she blames me for our predicament.

"I have some food in my bag," I say. "My dad always packs me extra, just in case."

"In case you get stuck in an elevator?"

"I guess," I answer, choosing to ignore the sarcasm. "It's just some veggies. You want some?"

"No."

A few more seconds of silence, then, "Um, okay. A few." She shines the light just long enough to see where I'm holding the plastic bag full of lukewarm carrots, celery, and red peppers.

We munch quietly—well, as quietly as you can munch raw vegetables—in the darkness and . . .

Another hour passes. It's now almost ten after seven; I'm supposed to meet Raf at Lincoln Center in twenty minutes and I can't even call to tell him I'll be late. He's going to *hate* me.

"This stinks," I say.

"Uh, *yeah.*"

"I can't believe they just left us here. We could be stuck in here till Monday."

"Somehow I think *your* parents will start to wonder what happened to you long before then."

"Well, I'm sure yours will be worried, too," I say.

It feels like the right thing to say in this situation, even though I have no idea if it's true.

Livvy scoffs, and in the dark I swear I can *hear* her eyes roll. "Ha. That's a good one. *My* parents giving a crap about me."

"Oh. Sorry. Didn't mean to—"

"Don't worry about it," she says curtly.

After thirty seconds of silence, I suddenly blurt out, "I know it was an accident."

"What was?"

"When you broke my nose."

"Oh. That."

Maybe it's the lack of oxygen, or the ridiculousness of the situation—stuck in a school elevator on a Saturday night—but Livvy starts to giggle. Probably because I've never actually heard her make a happy sound before, my first thought is that she's sobbing because she thinks her parents don't care about her, and I freak out a little, because I have absolutely no idea how to deal with *that*. Should I ignore it? Offer a shoulder to cry on? Luckily, the second wave is undoubtedly laughter. Of course, her laughter makes me nervous, too; this is Livvy Klack, after all. In my experience, if she's laughing, it must be *at* someone—and right now, I'm the only someone in the vicinity.

"What's so funny?" I ask tentatively.

"I'm sorry, I have a little confession to make. It *was* an accident, I swear. I never meant to hit you. But after it happened . . . I didn't feel guilty. At all. I felt *good*." She giggles again, and this time, it's contagious.

"Livvy! That is so mean."

"I *know*. I'm terrible." Giggle, giggle.

Wait a minute. What is happening here? Is it possible that Livvy Klack and I are . . . having a moment?

Chapter 20

In which many questions are answered

Mr. Eliot is always yammering on about how "life imitates art," and I'm afraid this whole wacky situation with Livvy and me and the elevator is a perfect example. Maybe I'd better explain.

Remember that short story that Livvy and I worked on together in Mr. Eliot's class? The one where we made the really clever graph that he liked so much? The story is called "The Interlopers" by Saki, and it's the story of two men who have hated one another their whole lives because of an old legal dispute over which of them owned a certain piece of land. One day—a cold, snowy day, in fact—they run into one another out in the woods, and just as they're about to fight it out like men, a tree falls, pinning them both to the ground.

Sound familiar? Except for that part about the tree, that is. Weird, huh?

At first, they continue their bickering, each one threatening the other, bragging about all the bad things he's going to do when *his* men show up. But they're both lying. Nobody knows they're out there, and nobody's coming to rescue either one of them. And it's getting darker and colder by the minute.

Finally, one of the men comes to his senses. He remembers that he has a little wine in his coat, and after a bitter struggle between his conscience and the half of him that still hates the man he's trapped with (that would be, ahem, the internal conflict of which we spoke so eloquently in class), he offers to share it. At first, the other guy refuses, but I guess the cold finally gets to him, because the next thing you know, they're chattin' it up like a couple of, well, twelve-year-old girls stuck in an elevator.

I explain my life-and-literature-connection theory to Livvy as she listens in silence. Sitting there in complete darkness is maddening; now that we have had this little breakthrough, I'm dying to see her face. I confess that a small(ish) part of me is convinced that she's making faces and obscene gestures at me in the dark.

"It *is* kind of ironic, I guess," she admits. "Especially since we worked on that story together. But I think you're forgetting something really important. The *ending*."

"What, about the . . . Oh, *yeah*."

Livvy is right. The ending of "The Interlopers" isn't exactly like a hug from a warm puppy; it's more like a bucket of ice water in the face.

And suddenly that elevator is a very dark and very cold place.

• • •

A few minutes after eight. By now, Raf has called and texted me several times (or at least I hope he has) and, as a last resort, probably called the landline in my apartment. I'm hoping—praying, even—that Mom is home, not freaking out too badly, and starting to put two and two together. A call to Michelle, and then another to Margaret, who will call the other girls on the team to find out where I went after we got back to the school. My best friend is an honest-to-God genius, and if *anyone* can figure out where I am, it's Margaret.

"How're you doing over there, Liv?" I ask. It's a strange feeling, me asking—sincerely—how she is.

"My butt hurts."

"Yeah, mine too. I'd sit on my coat but then the rest of me would freeze. I had no idea it got so cold in here on the weekends."

"Uh, Sophie?"

"Yeah?"

"Can I ask you a question? About yesterday, at the diner."

Uh-oh. "Um, yeah. What?"

"I was just wondering—was that really just a coincidence that you guys were there at the same time as me? The reason I'm asking is because we—er, I—go there almost every Friday and I've never seen you there. But one other time, two girls with a dog were following me, and I swear it was you and that Leigh Ann girl. Maybe I'm just being paranoid."

"Oh," I say, feeling myself blush. "You're not paranoid.

That was us. I thought for sure we ducked behind that car in time. Jeez, this is embarrassing. We weren't being intentionally nosy; we were just on our way back from the park and we saw you. I'm sorry. We were just curious—honest."

"I didn't know you had a dog."

"I don't, really. I'm watching her for, um, a friend for a few weeks."

I could tell her that it's Nate Etan's dog, but one, I doubt that she would believe me, and two, I hate people who name-drop like that. It's *so* pretentious.

But now that we're on the subject of the diner, I wonder if this is a good time to ask her about the woman in the wheelchair. I don't want her to think I'm prying into her personal life, even if that is exactly what I'm doing.

It's like Livvy reads my mind. "Look, I know you're wondering who I was with."

I play it cool. "Now that you mention it, yeah, I am a *little* curious."

"She's my old nanny; her name is Julia Demarest, and she basically raised me while my parents were both working a million hours a week and traveling all the time. Then, about four or five years ago, she found out she has MS—multiple sclerosis—and it finally got so bad that she had to stop working."

"Ohmigosh. That's terrible. It's nice, though, that you help her out like that."

I hear Livvy's coat rustle as she shrugs. "It's the least

I can do. I owe her so much. Everything. She's amazing. All the good parts of me are because of her." She lets that sink in for a moment. "I know what you're thinking: Livvy has *good* parts? But I do, really."

"I believe you," I say. "Especially now."

"And I don't know why—maybe it's because she's more like family than my real family—but I love spending time with her. Here she has this horrible, incredibly painful disease, and she never complains. I know I'm not always a good person . . . okay, I'm never a good person, but she makes me want to *try* at least. I don't know how she does it, but she's always positive. Even when that *awful* woman in the diner said that stuff about me and her, she just laughed it off. She's like, 'Life is too short to worry about what people like that say.' God, I can't believe I'm telling you all this. I've never talked about her to *anyone.*"

"Well, we all thought you were going to strangle that lady, and we were ready to jump in and help you. We'd been sitting there for a while; she was loony tunes. I mean, I knew there were people like that, but I've never actually met one before. Have you ever seen her? I mean, since she lives in the same building as your friend and everything."

"She *what*?"

"I'm afraid so. We've sort of been snooping on her, and she came out of the same building where we saw you that day—over on Ninety-fourth, right?"

"Why were you snooping on *her*?"

"It's kind of a long story; we're doing a favor for Father Julian."

"A priest hired you to spy on a crazy old lady with fluorescent orange hair?"

When you put it like that, it does sound a bit peculiar, I guess. "They're kinda sorta related, and there's a . . . 'family dispute,'" I say, adding air quotes even though Livvy can't see them in the dark.

"Ohhh."

"Livvy?"

"Yeah?"

"Can I ask you one more question?"

She doesn't answer immediately. Finally, she says, "About that time we ditched you after the meet, right?"

"How'd you know?"

"Because I know how it must have made you feel. It was stupid, and I am so sorry."

"But . . . why? I mean, we worked on that project in English, and then we were having so much fun on the bus ride back from that meet, and then . . ."

Livvy sniffs. "I don't know why I do it," she says. "I had this big fight with my parents that morning when they told me that they'll be leaving me home with my aunt—who I hate—for *two months* while they go off to Europe for *business*. Or so they say. They just got back from a month in China. And before that, three weeks in Singapore. So they're doing all that—without me—but then they say they can't afford to send me to Quincy, where I really want to go; it's where all my real friends go. Or at least I thought they were my friends, because that was also the day I found out that one of them had this huge birthday party—and I didn't get invited. It was just for kids from Quincy, they all said. You have to believe me, Sophie, that when I ditched you, it wasn't about *you*. After that day in class, I was actually starting to like you. It was just, well, I was having a really crappy day, and I needed to get even with the world."

"And I happened to have a bull's-eye painted on my back."

"Something like that. I know it's too late now, but I really am sorry. It was a crummy thing to do."

"Oh, it wasn't that bad," I lie. "And you know, Livvy, the girls at St. Veronica's—even Margaret—we're not so bad, either. Maybe if you gave us a chance. We might surprise you."

"I don't doubt it," she says.

Nine twenty-three. I jerk awake, completely disoriented and shivering from the icy floor. Was I dreaming, or did I hear voices outside the elevator? I pull my coat zipper as high as it will go and wrap my arms around myself, listening for sounds other than Livvy's soft breathing.

Wait! Voices!

"Livvy! I think someone's here. Ring the bell!"

She fumbles around with her keys for a few seconds, looking for her flashlight, but then gives up and starts pounding away on the panel until she hits the button for the bell. She holds it down for a couple of good long rings, and then we listen.

"Sophie! Livvy!"

It's Michelle, and even through the elevator walls, I can hear the guilt in her voice.

"Hello!" we shout.

I hear a few people say "Thank God" on the other side of the elevator door. Mom is there, too, along with Margaret and Sister Bernadette.

"Are you two okay?" Mom asks.

"We're cold. And a little hungry. But yeah, we're good."

Okay. Stop and think about *that* for a second (I'm sure Margaret did): Livvy and me, together in an elevator for four hours . . . and we're *good*. To some eyes, the fact that we're both alive could be viewed as a minor miracle.

"We're going to get you out of there, but it's going to take a few minutes," Sister Bernadette announces. "The last time he was here, the elevator serviceman showed me how to reset the system—sometimes that's all it needs. Say a little prayer, and sit tight."

Livvy snorts. "I don't think we're going anywhere."

"You poor kids," Mom says.

"Ohmigosh, you guys, I am *so* sorry," says Michelle. "I feel just terrible."

A minute later, the light inside the elevator comes on. Livvy and I shield our eyes and then drop our hands, squinting at each other. I hold out my hand to shake hers. She takes it, a little sheepishly.

"Thanks, Sophie."

"For what?"

"For listening. For just being, I don't know, a friend. In case you hadn't noticed, most of my other friends are jerks. I don't want to go all *Breakfast Club* on you, but you're, um, okay."

"Yeah, you too. But I forget—on Monday morning, didn't all those kids go back to who they were before?"

She hesitates just a moment too long before insisting that isn't going to happen. "We're more like those two guys in 'The Interlopers' than those dumb kids in the movie," she says. "Remember, after they become friends, they talk about how surprised everyone will be when they walk into town together. That'll be us."

I nod at her, touching her on the arm.

We'll see. I haven't forgotten how *that* story ends.

In the last few lines, the two men are still trapped, their feud now a thing of the past, with the temperature, darkness, and snow falling all around them. Suddenly one of the men spots several figures running toward them, and the only question remaining seems to be whether they're Georg's or Ulrich's men.

When Mr. Eliot gave us the copies of the story, he deliberately left off the last line, which answers the question. We had a great discussion about how the story *should* end. In wrapping things up, the writer had a choice: the "happy" ending, in which the two former enemies are rescued and we can imagine them going forward with their lives as friends; the "realistic" ending, in which they are rescued but immediately resume their quarrel; or the cruelly ironic ending, where fate takes a hand.

The class was about evenly divided among the three endings. For me, though, there was no choice; the writer absolutely *had* to go with the ironic one. What would be the point, I argued, of a story like that with a happy ending? The two men walking off into the sunset together and unharmed isn't an ending—it's a cop-out.

Saki, apparently, agreed with me.

The story's last sentence: "Wolves."

Now *that's* an ending.

A few minutes later, the elevator lurches, and four hours after we began our journey from the fifth floor, Livvy and I reach our destination. The door opens and I am immediately smothered by my mom, who is crying uncontrollably. Michelle is hugging Livvy, apologizing over and over, and explaining how it all happened.

"I went into the office to make a quick call, and when I came out, the other girls said that everyone was out of the bathrooms. They said you two were nowhere in sight—that you must have been in a hurry and taken off."

"We went to our lockers," I say. "And then . . ."

"Margaret figured it out," Mom says. "She knew exactly where you'd be."

I give Margaret a big hug. "I knew she would. That's why I love her."

Meanwhile, I realize that poor Raf is just standing

there looking extremely cute, and more than a little lost at the back of this pack of very emotional women.

"I'm sorry," I tell him. Even though I'm dying to throw my arms around him and give him a big kiss, I'm not ready to do that in front of Mom—or, for that matter, Sister Bernadette. So I take his hands and ask, "How long did you wait for me?"

"At first, I just figured you forgot to charge your phone *again*. But after about half an hour, I called your apartment."

"And scared me to death!" says Mom. "I thought you were late getting back from New Jersey, and then when no one could get hold of you . . ."

More sobbing.

"Well, thank the Lord we have a happy ending," says Sister Bernadette. "Miss Klack, do you need to call anyone?"

"Nobody will be home, anyway," Livvy says matter-of-factly. "My parents have plans, I'm sure."

"Then you're coming with us," Mom announces. "You girls must be *starving*. And *freezing*. Come on, what is everybody hungry for? My treat."

I consider my favorite sushi place because it is nearby, but my body is crying out for something besides cold, raw fish. I need a hot, juicy burger. With lots of gooey cheese. And onion rings. And maybe an order of fried calamari to start. (All right, so maybe it's not going to be the healthiest dinner ever, but I just lived through a traumatic experience.)

We try our best, but there's no talking Livvy into joining us.

I can kind of see why. Being stuck in the elevator with me is one thing; it was neutral territory. Dinner with my mom, my best friend, and my friend-who's-a-boy-but-not-my-boyfriend, on the other hand, is a whole different kettle of crustaceans.

"Thanks, but I'm going home and going right to bed," Livvy says, and I think I believe her.

"See you Monday," I say as we prepare to go our separate ways.

With a quick wave, but not another word, she turns and walks off into the cold New York night.

And there's not a single wolf in sight.

Chapter 21

Margaret Wrobel: blackmailer, rabble-rouser

"What did you two do for four hours?" Margaret asks, handing me another napkin to wipe the cheeseburger juice from my chin.

"Froze, mostly. It was dark. And really cold."

"But, you know, what did you do? What did you talk about?"

I give her a very uncharacteristic shrug. Maybe I'm just hungry and trying to get my body temperature up above ninety-five degrees, but I really don't feel like talking about Livvy and everything that happened in the elevator. Livvy and I have had some ups and downs in the past, but I saw a different, private side of her and don't feel like I need to blab about it to everyone—or even to Margaret.

"Oh, nothing. I'll tell you all about it later."

Margaret's eyes narrow and she leans her head across the table, motioning to Raf and me to come closer.

Uh-oh. I can tell she means it, so I lean in and take what I have coming.

"Now you listen to me, Sophie Jeanette," she says. "I understand you've had a long day. *However,* unless you two would like me to share with your mom a certain story about a ride around the city with a certain boy on a certain *motorized* vehicle, I would advise you to start talking. Fast. So, one more time: what happened on that elevator for four hours?"

"Tell her," says Raf. "Unless you want your dad to use those crazy knives of his on me."

"All right, all right," I say.

I don't tell her *everything,* but I do hit most of the important stuff. Margaret is not happy when I get to the part where Livvy was laughing about how good it felt to clunk me on the head.

"No, really, it's okay," I assure her. "We're cool."

"Humph." Clearly, she is not at all convinced that Livvy is worthy of my trust.

"So, how did you figure out where I was, anyway?" I ask, hoping to change the subject.

"Simple logic, really," Margaret says. "It only took me a few phone calls to the other girls on the team for Michelle and me to figure out that no one actually *saw* either you or Livvy leave the building. Since nobody could get in touch with either of you, it made sense that you were together. I also remembered that you mentioned to me that you forgot your math book yesterday. That *is* why you went upstairs in the first place, isn't it?"

"Right again, Sherlock," I admit.

"After that, the hard part was convincing Sister Bernadette to meet us at the school. She thought it was some kind of practical joke. I had to put your mom on the phone to convince her."

Mom raises her glass of soda for a toast. "Thank you—all of you—for finding my Sophie. She is very lucky to have such wonderful friends."

As the waitress clears away my plate—so clean it looks like Tillie licked it—Margaret puts her arm around my shoulders. "I know you didn't tell me everything that went on in there," she says. "But I'm willing to wait for the rest."

As she's talking, I reach under the table to give Raf's hand a squeeze. He locks his fingers into mine, and in two seconds, he warms me up more than the half-pound burger I've just devoured.

Mom is right about one thing, at least: I do have wonderful friends. And unless I'm really mistaken about what happened in that elevator, I have one more than I did when the day started.

Even with all the extra attention I get from my parents on Sunday (Dad cooks me all of my favorites and Mom surprises me with a gift certificate to a bookstore on the Upper West Side that specializes in mysteries), Monday comes quickly.

"So, guess what?" Margaret says as we all take our usual seats in the cafeteria before the first-period bell.

"I saw Father Julian after Mass yesterday; he's really nervous that we're planning something illegal."

"Are we?" I'm thinking it might be good to know.

Margaret gives me her don't-worry grin and a wave of her hand. "It's kind of a gray area. He's dying to know what we're doing, but he doesn't want to just come out and ask, because he's afraid to know the truth. I told him about our plan to pay Prunella a visit. He almost had a heart attack when I told him I was thinking about taking Elizabeth with us."

Three voices in perfect harmony shout: "You said *what*?"

"What are you afraid of?"

"Don't get me wrong," I say. "I love Elizabeth. She's just . . . unpredictable. If Pruneface says something crazy—which, let's face it, is almost guaranteed—Elizabeth might explode or something."

"Well, I've been thinking about it, too," Margaret admits. "Here's the situation: Father Julian doesn't want to confront her about the painting, because he's afraid that she'll think that the family is accusing her and Phillip of something—"

"Something that she basically admitted to," I say.

Margaret nods. "True. But he's afraid of pushing her into selling it to the Svindahls. If that happens, we'll never see it again. So we have to do something—and fast. We're going to *borrow* Prunella's painting for a while."

Now it's Leigh Ann's turn to raise an eyebrow. "Borrow?"

"Exactly," confirms Margaret. "We get it checked out, and if it's a fake, we return it unharmed. But if the painting is the real thing, which is likely when you consider that the Svindahls have already made her an offer, it's totally up to Father Julian to decide what to do. He has the will, which proves who the rightful owner is, and on top of that, there are witnesses who were there back when Phillip swiped and then later returned the painting—although it seems pretty clear he wasn't returning the original at all. He had replaced it with one he obviously *knew* was forged. Legally, I think Father Julian is on pretty solid ground."

"Sounds good to me," says Becca, who does not seem at all concerned with the legality of what we're planning. "When do we make our move?"

Margaret looks around the table at each of us. "Today. To borrow one of Becca's favorite expressions, Prunella Scroggins is going *down.*"

"Like a rotten tree in a hurricane," Becca adds. "I like it."

"And if it means taking the Svindahls with her, then so be it," adds Margaret.

"So, do you have a plan worked out for the switch?" I ask.

"Ninety-nine percent."

"What about the other one percent?"

"We improvise. Even Sherlock Holmes has to deal with unforeseen problems. Part of being a good detective is being able to think on your feet. Problem number one: we have to get ourselves and the fake painting into Prunella's apartment. *Legally,* I should add. No break-ins."

"Why does everyone look at me when she says that?" Rebecca says, suddenly full of mock indignation. She's plenty proud of her reputation.

"I *wonder,*" I say.

"And then part two: we have to switch the paintings on the wall and get the real one out of her apartment, all without her seeing," Margaret adds.

"Eh, that doesn't sound so bad," Leigh Ann says.

"Unless she has an alarm system," I warn. "Or a mean dog. These things always have a way of being more complicated than they look. And it seems like I'm the one who always ends up hiding under an altar or locked in a closet."

Margaret smiles at the memory of our shared experience under the altar in St. Veronica's when we were looking for the Ring of Rocamadour.

"So, just how do we get in?" Becca asks.

"Through the front door," says Margaret. "But you're not going to have to pick the lock, Rebecca. Prunella's going to open it for us."

"Like when we pretended to be reporters for the school paper so we could check out those Russian ladies in the apartment over the violin shop?" Leigh Ann asks.

"Romanian ladies," Margaret corrects. "But yes, something like that. Something more . . . original, though. Something truly inspired. Something that will have Miss Prunella eating out of our hands. Our grimy little Polish/French/Chinese/Dominican American immigrant hands. Hee hee."

"Uh-oh," I say, almost feeling a twinge of pity for Prunella. You don't want to be on the bad side of somebody as smart as Margaret. It is *not* pretty. "What are you thinking, Margaret?"

She starts to unfold a sheet of bright orange paper and motions for us to huddle closely around her. "I *really* don't want anyone else to see this. It might be hard to explain."

REAL NEW YORKERS UNITE!
JOIN THE LEAGUE OF ORDINARY AND ORIGINAL NEW YORKERS FOR BOLD IDEAS NOW

ARE YOU TIRED OF WATCHING THE BEST JOBS GO TO IMMIGRANTS INSTEAD OF REAL NEW YORKERS?

ARE YOU TIRED OF HEARING LANGUAGES OTHER THAN ENGLISH SPOKEN IN NEW YORK?

DO YOU FEEL THAT NO ONE IN GOVERNMENT LISTENS TO REAL NEW YORKERS ANYMORE?

ARE OUR OFFICIALS OUT OF TOUCH WITH REAL NEW YORKERS?

IF YOU ANSWERED YES TO ANY OF THE QUESTIONS, JOIN US! IT IS TIME FOR BOLD IDEAS NOW!!!

BOLD IDEA #1: SPECIAL RIGHTS AND PRIVILEGES FOR REAL AMERICANS.

BOLD IDEA #2: ABOLISH ALL OF THE SO-CALLED PRIDE PARADES IN THE CITY. IF YOU'RE NOT PROUD OF BEING AMERICAN, WHY ARE YOU HERE?

BOLD IDEA #3: WHY ARE WE GIVING AWAY CITIZENSHIP WHEN PEOPLE ARE WILLING TO PAY FOR IT?

COME TO OUR NEXT MEETING TO LEARN MORE AND SHARE YOUR

BOLD IDEAS!
WE NEED YOU!

"Why, Margaret Wrobel," I say. "I had no idea you were so . . ."

"Crazy?" suggests Becca. "What are you going to do with this?"

"This," Margaret says, waving the flyer in Becca's face, "is like peanut butter in a mousetrap. And Prunella's the mouse."

"More like a rat," Leigh Ann says.

"We knock on her door and shove this in her face, and I guarantee you she'll invite us in. People like her are dying for somebody to listen to their wacky ranting and raving. I'll bet she has ideas that will put my made-up ones to shame."

I have to laugh, because the whole thing is so preposterous. It's hard to imagine four less likely candidates for an organization like the one Margaret created. Let's examine the evidence, shall we? Exhibit A: Margaret Wrobel. Born in Poland. Spoke Polish before she spoke

English. Her parents still speak more Polish than English at home. Exhibit B: Rebecca Chen. Second-generation Chinese American. Exhibit C: Leigh Ann Jaimes, who is from the Dominican Republic. And Exhibit D: me. Mother American-born of Welsh/Irish/German ancestry; father born in France (gasp!). Out of eight parents, my mom is the only one with more than two generations under her American belt. Face it, we're a mini–United Nations. And to somebody like Prunella Scroggins, we *are* the enemy.

"You guys are missing the best part," says Margaret. "Look at the name of the organization again."

" 'The League of Ordinary and Original New Yorkers for Bold Ideas Now,' " reads Leigh Ann. "Is this for real, or did you make it up?"

"LOONYBIN!" I shout, which earns me a puzzled look from Mr. Eliot, who is walking past.

"Patience, Miss St. Pierre," he says, not missing a beat. "You'll get there one day."

"I'm sure I'll see you there, too!" I say, but darn it, he's already inside his classroom.

Meanwhile, Becca and Leigh Ann have spotted the acronym.

Becca snickers. "Loony bin. Pretty good, Margaret. Anybody who thinks these are good ideas *belongs* in one, that's for sure."

Leigh Ann shakes her head in wonder. "You're a funny kid, Margaret. How did you think of this?"

Margaret shrugs modestly. "I don't know; it just

comes to me. I figured the easiest way into her apartment is if she *trusts* us. We already have an in—Father Julian. That should get us up to her door. He's going to call her today and tell her that we're friends of his, and when he learned of our interest in, um, politics, he suggested we meet her. When that door opens and we start yakking about how bad immigrants are for the country, she'll be all over us. She'll probably get out her checkbook."

"Back up a second. We're gonna talk about *what?*" Leigh Ann asks.

I put my arm around her shoulders. "Easy, Leigh Ann. It's all part of the plan. The end justifies the means, right?"

"I don't know," she says. "If she starts talking bad about Dominicans or Jamaicans, I might have to justify her one right on the nose. Oops, sorry, Sophie. Didn't mean to . . ."

Almost involuntarily, I touch my nose, pressing on the spot where Livvy broke it until I wince from the pain. "It's okay—it's almost healed."

The first-period bell rings, and Livvy and her Klackpack (of wolves?) stroll past. I smile to myself at the memory of the giggling fit that we had about my nose, and wonder if she'll acknowledge me in class. Despite everything we said in that cold, dark elevator, two days is a *lifetime* in the universe of seventh graders.

Anything can happen.

Chapter 22

If you listen closely, you can hear that *Twilight Zone* music in the background—things get that strange

In Mr. Eliot's class, we're discussing another short story by Saki, whose real name, I learned, is Hector Hugh Munro. (I don't know about you, but I *like* the sound of Hector Hugh Munro; I can't imagine why he felt compelled to use a pen name. That, and I'm generally suspicious of people who go by only one name. It's entirely too presumptuous.) "The Open Window" is about a young girl who entertains herself by telling one outrageous lie after another to a visitor who is a real nervous Nellie type, and scares the poor guy half to death.

When Mr. Eliot calls on me, I say, "It's an okay story, but it just doesn't have that, you know, totally butt-kicking ending of 'The Interlopers.' "

Margaret's eyebrows rise at my answer. She would throw herself under the wheels of the 6 train before she'd use an adjective like "butt-kicking."

Mr. Eliot looks in Livvy's direction. "How about you,

Miss Klack? Do you agree with Miss St. Pierre's assessment of the story?"

Curious—him calling on Livvy right after me. I wonder if he has already heard about the elevator ordeal, and that's why he's picking on us. That would be so like him. I resist the temptation to turn around and look at Livvy, but I hear the familiar annoyed sigh of someone who would rather be left alone.

"Yeah, I mean, no. It was better than 'The Interlopers'—that one just wasn't very realistic. True enemies don't just become friends like *that.*" She snaps her fingers—inches behind my head—for emphasis.

Was that a not-so-subtle message for me?

"Interesting point," Mr. Eliot says. "Sophie, care to rebut?"

"Well, I think it *is* possible. Especially if they, you know, *share* some kind of, um, traumatic experience." I know Livvy is looking right at the back of my head, and I can feel my ears turning red.

Leave it to Margaret, who seems to be sensing my discomfort, to change the subject by pointing out something in the story that I (and everyone else in the class) had completely missed.

"I agree with Sophie that maybe 'The Open Window' doesn't have that same kind of 'wow' ending, but the story itself is still *full* of irony. The girl's name is Vera—and well, to me, that just says it all."

There's a moment of silence as everyone waits for the punch line.

Finally, a befuddled Leigh Ann asks, "Says *what,* exactly?"

"Vera. From the Latin *veritas,* meaning 'truth.' Get it? Her name is Vera, but she's practically incapable of telling the truth. She's pathological. It's *incredibly* ironic."

The rest of us mere mortals stare openmouthed, first at her and then at Mr. Eliot, who's looking at Margaret like a proud parent.

"Well played, Miss Wrobel." He writes the word *veritas* on the board.

Behind me, I hear Livvy mutter, "Good Lord. Latin? Is there anything she *doesn't* know?"

I'll let you know when I find something, Liv.

After school, I find a strange package sitting on my shelf in the locker that I share with Margaret. It's not at all like Margaret to put something of hers on my shelf; we have strict rules about whose stuff goes where.

When Margaret squeezes in next to me to pack up her book bag for the night, she notices it, too.

"That yours?" she asks.

"Nope. I thought it was yours."

"You're saying you didn't put it there?"

"Nope."

"Nope, you didn't put it there, or nope, that's not what you're saying?"

"You're making my brain hurt," I say as I lift the package out. It's the size and weight of a book, wrapped in plain brown kraft paper. My name has been printed diagonally across the paper. "That's the same printing as on all the other boxes."

We both look around at the noisy crush of girls that surrounds us.

"Open it," Margaret commands.

I peel off the paper to find a hardcover copy of *The Secret Garden,* which happens to be one of my all-time favorite books. Right away I notice that this isn't just any old copy; it is *my* copy, the very same one that disappeared when I was in the fifth grade. My mom bought it for me in London, and it has a little sticker that reads "£5.99"—which I left on because I thought that having a foreign price tag was just the coolest thing *ever.* I touch the sticker affectionately and open to the inside cover, where my own handwriting confirms: "This book is the property of Sophie Jeanette St. Pierre."

"Is that—" Margaret starts.

"The one I lost," I say, hugging it to my chest. "I remember I had it with me in school for a book report. I left it on my desk when we went down for lunch, and when we came back, it was gone."

"So how did it get into our locker two years later? Have you told anyone our combination?"

"I don't think so. Except Becca and Leigh Ann, of course. But they wouldn't . . . I mean, there's no way one of them took it. We didn't even know Leigh Ann then."

Before she can respond, I have a moment of panic. I lunge into the locker and dig into my jacket pockets. My fingers wrap around my iPod and phone, and I breathe a sigh of relief. "Whew! My stuff's still there."

"Yeah, everything else looks normal," Margaret says. "Save the paper it was wrapped in. There might be clues."

"Clues? Where? For what?" Becca asks.

Leigh Ann pokes her head into the huddle. "What did I miss?"

I show them *The Secret Garden.* "Somebody swiped this from my desk in fifth grade, and now it suddenly appears in my locker. You guys—you're not messing with me, are you, sending me all this stuff?"

Becca shakes her head. "Scout's honor."

"Never seen it before," adds Leigh Ann.

"Okay, this is officially creepy," I announce. "We need a new lock, Marg."

"I'll check with Sister Eugenia tomorrow," Margaret says. "She'll let us trade this one in. In the meantime, don't leave anything valuable inside." She pauses, rubbing her hands together in anticipation. "So, is everybody ready to pay Miss Prunella a visit?"

First stop: the red door of Elizabeth's townhouse. Father Julian left his father's copy of the painting with her, and Elizabeth, with the help of a friend at the Metropolitan Museum of Art, has confirmed our suspicions. It is definitely a fake; there is no underpainting. They didn't have time to do a full analysis of the paint, but it doesn't appear to be the same kind Pommeroy usually used.

"It's a beautiful forgery, though," Elizabeth says. "Skillfully done. Whoever did it had some talent. He— or she—simply wasn't aware of Pommeroy's unusual method of working. Or didn't expect anyone to look quite so carefully at it."

Before we leave for Prunella's apartment, Margaret goes through the painting's backstory one more time for Elizabeth's sake, emphasizing the word "borrow."

"We just want to make sure you're okay with it," she adds.

Elizabeth nods enthusiastically. "Oh, I'm always up for a little adventure. And this is a mystery that needs solving."

Just as we're leaving Elizabeth's, Mom calls to tell me that she's going to be late getting home, and that I need to go home and walk Tillie right away.

"It's okay," I tell Margaret. "I'll run ahead of you guys, pick up Tillie, and meet you outside of Prunella's. Becca and Leigh Ann can watch her while I go inside."

"For a price," Becca shouts at me as I skedaddle up Lexington.

Tillie greets me at the door like she hasn't seen another human in months. She almost knocks me over, and then lies down flat on her back so I can rub her belly. Reality hits me: I am going to miss her craziness when Nate finally returns. In a few days, she'll be gone forever and I'll be back to begging and pleading with my parents to let me adopt a poor, defenseless mutt from a shelter.

We bound out of the building and Tillie pulls me all the way to Prunella's. She seems to know exactly where we're going, and the sight of everyone waiting outside the scary iron fence sends her into a full-blown tizzy.

"What's she so excited about?" Leigh Ann asks.

"Who knows? It's like she's going to visit her best friend."

Tillie looks up at the apartment building and barks.

"Okay, Becca. She's all yours." I transfer a handful of small dog biscuits from my coat pocket to Becca's. "If she gets too excited, give her one of these."

Margaret hands me a coiled length of vivid yellow twine with a sturdy safety pin tied to one end. "Hold on to this. And *please* don't leave it behind when we leave."

Sheesh. Make *one* little mistake and you pay for it the rest of your life.

"Oh, stop pouting," Margaret says. "If you stick that lip out any farther, a little bird is going to land on it."

"I'm not pouting," I lie.

"Good, because it's time to get to work." The gate swings open and all five of us (plus Tillie) go through, but Becca and Leigh Ann, our "ground crew," take a hard left turn once inside the fence, ducking down behind the hedges with Father Julian's painting.

Prunella is expecting us, thanks to Father Julian's phone call. He assured her that we weren't looking for donations; we were simply recruiting new, like-minded members for an organization that she would almost certainly want to join.

Margaret presses the button for apartment 5B, and after we identify ourselves, Prunella buzzes us into the building.

When she opens her front door, Prunella seems normal—almost charming, even.

"It's nice to see young people taking an interest in their country," she says after Margaret has explained the purpose of our visit—recruiting new LOONYBIN members. (Of course, we're not referring to the organization by its acronym in front of her.)

"And such nice, fair-skinned girls, too," she continues. "There aren't too many of us left—what with all these immigrants taking over everything. Come inside."

My skin starts to crawl as she leads us into the room she calls the sitting room, which is not at all what I expect. Instead of floral wallpaper and maybe a doll collection, or even a big-screen TV, the walls are covered with dead animals. There are several deer heads, including one that looks suspiciously like Bambi's mother; a moose head that is, I admit, *much* bigger than I expected a moose head to be; a bearskin with the head still attached; the head of some animal that looks like a really ticked-off pig; a fox; a bobcat; four fish; and strangest of all, in the corner of the room, a complete stuffed coyote, its nose raised as if on high alert.

Elizabeth turns in a performance equal to one of my

finest. She gushes over all the dead animals in a way that makes me believe that every interior decorator in New York will be hanging deer heads and bearskins in apartments all over town.

Frankly, I think the whole place is positively creepy—especially that poor coyote, who, to me, looks a bit too much like a lighter-colored Tillie. And, unlike his cartoon character cousin, not wily at all. I stop for a moment, perching on a stool (supported by real deer legs—yuck!), and try not to focus on all the eyes that seem to follow my every move.

"We're just trying to make America a better place," Margaret says convincingly as our hostess continues the tour of her very peculiar theme park: Prunella's Tacky Treasures of Taxidermy. "We need to start taking care of the *real* Americans—like us. The ones who have been here the longest."

Oy. Margaret's family has been in America for all of five years. My phone is resting in the pleats of my uniform skirt, and Becca and Leigh Ann, listening in from outside the building, are laughing so loud that I have to cough to cover it up.

But Margaret is on a roll. "As you can see here on our flyer, one of our boldest ideas is to sell American citizenship. Every year, millions of immigrants come to America, and we don't charge them a cent, when we could be charging them *thousands* of dollars. If they really want to come here, they'll be willing to pay—don't you think?"

There's no doubt that we have Prunella's undivided

attention, so Elizabeth suggests that she and Prunella go into the kitchen and make a pot of tea before we all continue this important discussion in the living room. She *insists* on helping out in the kitchen, leaving Margaret and me alone with the Pommeroy, which, in the midst of all those dead animals, sticks out like a Michelangelo in a room full of macaroni sculptures. Elizabeth's job is to keep her new best friend in the kitchen for an absolute minimum of two minutes, even if it means blocking the door with her own body—something I would pay *plenty* to see.

As soon as the kitchen door closes behind Elizabeth, Margaret swings into action. We can't risk using the front window, where everybody in the neighborhood can watch, so she yanks open a window on the side of the apartment and signals to Becca and Leigh Ann to get into position.

"Okay, Soph, unwind that piece of twine and hand me the safety pin."

While I'm doing that, she takes the painting off the wall and heads for the window.

The kitchen door squeaks, and we freeze. "Do you girls want tea?" Elizabeth sticks her head out the door and gives us the okay sign.

Margaret snaps the safety pin onto the wire across the back of the frame after giving it a good tug to make sure it is solidly attached to both sides. She then starts lowering the painting out the window while I try to keep it away from the building, tree branches, and the nasty, sharp points of the iron fence on the way down. Becca reaches up and snags the painting just as a gust of wind hits it, almost pulling the twine out of Margaret's hands.

"Got it!" Becca yells up at us.

Leigh Ann makes the switch, attaching the twine to the wire stretched across the back of Father Julian's almost-but-not-quite-perfect copy of the Pommeroy.

"Okay!" she shouts. "Take it away!"

Margaret starts quickly reeling in the twine hand over hand. Five feet. Ten. And then . . . disaster! A strong gust of wind gets under the painting and blows it sideways, and the twine wraps itself around a section of the scary iron fence.

"Uh-oh," I say.

For a few precious seconds, no one has anything to add to my rather astute analysis; "uh-oh" seems to have said it all.

But wait. We don't *do* quitting. It's simply not in the RBGDA playbook.

"I have an idea," I tell Margaret. "It might just work, but I have to leave you here for a minute. I'm going downstairs; if you don't see me in thirty seconds, tell Becca to bring the other one back to the lobby. We'll put it back if we have to." I make a beeline for the door.

"Where are you going?" Margaret asks. She glances worriedly at the kitchen door. "Never mind. Just go!"

It's an old building, the kind in which the stairs are not enclosed, and as I'm racing for the third floor, I hear the unmistakable sound of a dog skittering across the tile floor in the lobby and then bounding up the steps. Tillie practically knocks me off my feet when she sees me. But we're in the middle of a crisis situation and I simply don't have time to ask how or why. I grab her by the collar and knock firmly on the door to apartment 3B—the one belonging to Livvy's former nanny, Julia Demarest, and two floors directly below Prunella's. (How do I know which apartment is hers? Easy—her name was right there on the door buzzer panel. A simple matter of observation, as Sherlock would say.)

The door opens, and suddenly I am in the twilight zone, facing the strangest sight I have ever seen. For a moment, I'm not sure if I'm looking into a mirror, or if that is a *different* girl and dog in front of me. When I finally focus, I realize that the blond girl I'm staring at is, of course, Livvy, and the dog she's trying to hold back could be Tillie's identical twin.

"Sophie? What are you—" But Livvy is cut off by Tillie, who leaps out of my hands and almost tackles her, wagging her tail and whining and licking Livvy's face. Livvy's dog watches this for a few seconds, and then starts barking.

"Tillie, *sit*!" The words leave Livvy's and my lips at precisely the same moment, and for the next ten seconds I completely forget that I've left Margaret (and a certain painting!) hanging two floors above me.

"You have a dog named Tillie?" I say. "This is Tillie, too, but she's not really mine. She's Nate Etan's— she . . . we . . . I . . . it's kind of a long story."

Livvy is still petting my Tillie, who continues to tell her the story of her life.

"Ohmigosh, I almost forgot . . . I, um, need a huge favor. Do your side windows open?"

"The . . . windows? Uh, yeah, I guess so." "Bewildered" doesn't *begin* to describe the look on her face.

"Look, I promise to explain everything later. It's kind of an emergency."

The two Tillies sniff and circle each other as Livvy steps aside and waves me in. "Which window do you need?"

"Far wall. *That* one."

I can see the yellow twine curving into the tree branches that are only a few feet from the window, and as I stick my head out, Margaret looks down at me. "I think I can reach it," I say. "Livvy, can you hold on to my feet so I can reach out a little farther?"

Poor Livvy is in some kind of shock—she just nods and wraps her arms around my ankles. (Livvy Klack! Helping me! A few weeks ago I would have been worried that she'd toss me out the window.)

I stretch my arms and fingers to their limit, and with the help of a swirling gust of wind, I first touch and then get a firm grip on the edge of the painting's frame.

And then . . . I freeze.

Pointing directly at my head is a black iron spear; its razor-sharp tip seems only inches away.

"Ohhh. Whoa." The ability to think clearly disappears as my imagination goes haywire. Please, please,

please don't let go, Livvy. I swear I will never say another bad word about you.

Margaret calls down to me. "Sophie? What's wrong?" A pause, and then, "Oh. My. Gosh. Okay, I see it, too, but you can do this, Soph. Focus on the painting. Deep breaths."

Those are the magic words for me. Margaret knows that when I get overly excited or stressed out, I sometimes forget to breathe, which makes thinking—or just about anything else—extremely difficult.

Inhale. Exhale. Repeat.

I pull the painting toward me, untangling the string from the fence. Success!

"Go!" I shout up to Margaret, who pulls it up and into the fifth-floor window.

I close the window and turn to face Livvy, who *smiles* at me.

"I've gotta go right now, but—"

"Go," she says. "You can tell me later. I can't wait to hear what this is all about."

"Thanks—for, you know, not dropping me. I owe you, big-time. Come on, Tillie," I say. Both dogs make a move for me, and I hesitate before choosing the one with the collar. "Let's go, girl." She wags her tail at me but looks back at Livvy with a sad whine as I pull her out the door and up to the fifth floor.

I knock softly and Margaret opens the door; she gets a wild look in her eyes when she realizes that Tillie is with me.

"Where did *she* come from?"

"Becca must have let go of her leash when she was trying to climb the fence," I say, stepping into the foyer with Tillie. "How did everything go up here? Is the painting on the wall? She didn't see or hear anything?"

"It's perfect. Everything looks exactly like it did before she went into the kitchen," Margaret answers. "Come on, they're going to be back in the living room any second now."

"I can't stay in here with *her*," I say, pointing at Tillie. "And I can't just leave her in the hall."

"Ah, there you are!" Elizabeth says. "Tea's ready, girls."

Without warning, our hostess suddenly appears behind Elizabeth and peers around her at Margaret, Tillie, and me.

Batten down the hatches: Tropical Storm Prunella has made landfall. Her face clouds over when she spots Tillie. She sputters for a moment before spitting out the words, "What is *that* filthy beast doing in here?"

Now, before I go any further, let me remind you that this outburst is coming from a woman with a hundred dead animals hanging on her walls.

"She's *not* filthy," I say, seriously insulted on Tillie's behalf. I brush her coat every day, and even wash and dry her feet when we get back from the park. She's cleaner than lots of people I know.

"Out! Out, out, out! All of you! I invite you into my

home and you bring a *dog*. I should have you all arrested."

"For what?" I ask. I'm not trying to be a smart aleck; I really want to know what crime she thinks we're committing.

"But what about the League?" Elizabeth says. "We haven't had a chance to talk about a role for you."

"As if I would join an organization that includes dog owners! I know when I'm being cheated! Now, out with you!" She reaches into the hall closet for a broom and literally starts to sweep us out of her apartment. "Out, out, out."

The door slams shut and we practically fall on the hallway floor laughing.

"*Now* do you believe us?" I say to Elizabeth. "We tried to tell you she belongs in the loony bin."

"Now, girls," she says. "Be nice. You probably thought the same thing about me the first time we met."

Margaret shakes her head emphatically as we start down the stairs. "No, we thought you were interesting. Maybe a little eccentric. But never crazy."

"At the moment, I am a bit confused," Elizabeth admits. "Where did Tillie come from? Was she part of the plan all along?"

"That's a *very* good question, isn't it, Sophie?" Margaret says. "But then, I have a *lot* of questions for Miss St. Pierre. Starting with how you got into that apartment on the third floor."

"Magic," I say. "Tell you what—I have to go thank somebody, and, uh, sort some things out. I'll come over later. Tell Becca and Leigh Ann I'll call them."

I give Elizabeth a kiss and a big hug and knock once more at the door to apartment 3B.

Chapter 23

In which Malcolm delivers some disturbing news

Livvy opens the door to apartment 3B, and once again I have the uncanny feeling that I'm staring into a mirror.

"Man, this is weird," she says.

I hold up my hand. "Before you say anything else, I have a question for you. Does your Tillie know any tricks? You know, like play dead or roll over?"

"Um, she *used* to. She had a whole act; we'd go through them all the time. Then all of a sudden, she stopped. Now I can't get her to do anything."

"Hmmm. Do me a favor: try it again, right now."

Livvy looks at her Tillie and shrugs. "Okay, but I know she won't do it. Hey, Tillie! Play dead!"

Livvy is right; her Tillie stands there unmoving, staring blankly up at her. My Tillie—er, Nate's Tillie—on the other hand, spins in a tight circle three times, stands stiff as an ironing board momentarily, and then flops to the floor, as if some unseen force has pushed her over.

"Oh. My." Livvy's jaw drops. "T-Tillie? Is that . . .

you?" She looks at the other Tillie. "But . . . then who are you?" She drops to the floor, dazed by the revelation that she's been living with somebody else's dog.

"I think I know," I say. "Would you say that her behavior changed about two weeks ago? Maybe after a walk in the park?"

Livvy nods. "Yeah, that sounds about right."

I then have to explain how I know Nate Etan, and how I ended up with his dog. Which is actually Livvy's dog.

"So, the bottom line is, you've been taking care of *his* dog, and I've been taking care of yours. Who started barking the second she saw this building, and who ate a pair of my shoes and a baseball. My personal favorite, though, is when she howls at the moon."

"Oh my God!" Livvy cries. "She *does* do that! Isn't it spooky? But . . . how?"

"When they were shooting those scenes in the park, Nate used to take Tillie—his Tillie, that is—for walks around the park and let her off-leash in the mornings—"

"And I did that, too! I usually stay here with Julia on Friday nights, and Saturday mornings I take Tillie over to the park. There are always a million dogs off-leash, and I let her have a good run. A couple of weeks ago, she disappeared for a while, but then I found her. It's funny, but now that I think about it, I remember that something seemed wrong at the time. She had the same collar, but something about the way it was put on was different, and the way she looked at me when I called her. Like she didn't really know me. And then she was really picky about the food that she's always eaten. How did I *not* know it was the wrong dog?"

"That's easy. Look at them. They're impossible to tell apart by looks. And remember, you weren't the only one fooled. Nate didn't know, either. It's a good thing I knocked on your door today. Nate's coming back for Tillie on Friday. They're going up to New Hampshire and then back to California. But then again, who knows? If we hadn't figured this out, Tillie might have become a movie star."

"Are you going to tell him?"

"Yeah, I think so. And he should probably see the two Tillies together so he doesn't think we're scamming him or something. You want to meet him?"

Her eyes light up. "Yes!"

"I think we can arrange that."

Livvy, thrilled to be reunited with her Tillie, is greatly amused by the Tales of Prune-hell-a.

"Now that I know she hates dogs, I'll have to make sure that Tillie and I run into her more often," she says with a smidgen of that old Livvy sass. (Which doesn't seem so bad when it's not being directed at me.) "I still owe her from that day in the diner."

"You'd need ten dogs, a couple of horses, and maybe a *goat* to get even with her for that. But let me know when you're ready. I'd *love* to help."

Before I leave—*not* with the same dog I brought—I invite Livvy to stop by my apartment on Friday night, at the time Nate is allegedly picking up Tillie. "I have to warn you, he probably won't come. He's . . . well, he's not exactly the most reliable person."

"Does he look as good in person as he does on TV?"

"Better."

"Then I don't care if he's unreliable. I'll be there."

Confession time: I fell asleep while reading *Nicholas Nickleby*. But before you Dickens-haters out there start in with your chants of "I told you he's boring," let me explain. I've been getting up at five in the morning, swimming for two hours, and then running around like a maniac every day, and it has finally caught up with me. End of story. So just lose those smug smiles right now; Charles Dickens still *rules*.

In my dream, I'm sitting at my favorite Parisian café with Leigh Ann and Cam . . . and Nate, doggone it. The waiter arrives on a mint-green Vespa and fills everyone's water glass except mine. Then he scoots away, his white apron flapping in the breeze.

"Excusez-moi," I say, trying to get his attention. "You forgot me!"

He stops and turns around to see what I want. For the first time, I see his face—it's *Raf's* wonderfully familiar face!—and he's aiming that licensed-to-kill smile of his directly at me. He opens his mouth to say something, and—

"Sophie! Wake up!" Mom says. "You'll be late for swim practice."

Groan. "I'm moving," I fib while trying to come up with a legitimate reason to stay in bed.

But Tillie's cold, wet nose takes care of that little fantasy, and I trudge off in the dark to the pool.

After practice, I meet Margaret outside her building. She is standing there, arms crossed and tapping her foot.

"What happened to you last night?" she asks. "I thought you were coming over to study Spanish."

"I know—I'm sorry about that. I just ended up talking to, um, Livvy for a while." I intentionally mumble the key word in that sentence, but Margaret has the hearing of a hoot owl.

"Did you say *Livvy*? Where did you—oh, right, that woman she knows lives in Prunella's building. How did you know which apartment she was in?"

"I *observed,*" I say proudly. "Just like you're always telling me I need to. Her name was right there outside the lobby, with all the buzzers."

"Good work, Sophie! I'm impressed. And Livvy was there? I can't believe you didn't tell me."

And then the moment of truth.

"Ohmigosh, Sophie. Are you and Livvy . . . friends?"

Jeez. For once, couldn't she just ask me something simple, like . . . what is the meaning of life?

Malcolm and Elizabeth take the Pommeroy to their friend at the Metropolitan Museum of Art in the morning, and Malcolm sends Margaret an email asking to meet us after school at Perkatory for some very surprising news.

He sets the painting on the table in front of us. "It's a fake," he blurts out, not even waiting for our drinks to arrive at the table.

"What?" our voices cry out in perfect four-part harmony.

"How is that even possible?" I ask. "I mean, we're sure the one we just hung on Prunella's wall is a fake, right?"

"Absolutely," Margaret says. "So, after all that running around, all we did was trade a fake for a fake?"

"Which means—" Malcolm starts.

"That somebody must have conned Phillip!" exclaims Margaret. "Phillip hired someone to make a copy that he could pass off to his sister so he could keep the original. But it sounds to me like the forger made *two* copies and then kept the original for himself. Or herself."

"Is this fake exactly like the other one?" I ask.

"Yes and no," Malcolm says. "According to the expert at the Met, the visible parts of the two paintings are very, very similar—probably done by the same hand. But while the other had no underpainting whatsoever, this one was painted over another artist's work, completely unrelated to Pommeroy in style. My guess is that the forger simply recycled a canvas that was the size he needed—most likely something that he had done himself. Lots of gallery owners and employees are amateur artists."

Something about it just doesn't add up.

"But . . . we're assuming that somebody from the Svindahl Gallery created that other forgery because they knew just where to look after Father Julian brought in that first fake, right? And that there just had to be some connection between Phillip and the Svindahls. Well, if one of the Svindahls was the forger, they would know that *this* is a fake, too. Right? So why are they willing to pay *anything* to get it back? It just doesn't add up."

A moment of stunned silence, followed by several heavy sighs.

"A truly excellent question," says Malcolm.

"It *doesn't* make sense," Margaret admits. "It's not very likely, but I suppose it's possible that they're trying to right a wrong. Maybe they're afraid it will be discovered and ruin the gallery's reputation."

"Then why didn't they want the fake that Father Julian showed them?" I ask.

Margaret pats me on the back. "Excellent logic, Soph. You really have been reading your Sherlock, haven't you?"

"Sophie, my dear, I'm afraid I don't have a good answer for you, either," Malcolm says. "But see what you girls can make of this; it was taped to the hidden side of the stretcher bar in the back." He takes a folded envelope from a pocket inside his tweed blazer and sets it on the table.

Margaret opens the envelope and removes an address book that's no more than two inches square.

"My, my," she says, flipping through the gold-edged pages. "Phillip's 'little black book.' So he kept some secrets from his beloved Prunella. Tsk, tsk. And look, some of the women's names have stars by them. Malcolm, maybe you'd like to explain what those mean."

"Not in a million years!" Malcolm says with a hearty laugh. "But you never know what else you might find in there. Good luck—I'll send you a message if I learn anything new." He wraps up the painting and heads out the door.

Chapter 24

Maybe they just have trouble with algebra

Margaret, convinced that the Svindahls hold the secret to whatever is going on and desperately searching for proof of the connection between them and Phillip, discovers an interesting detail in the picture where Phillip and Prunella are sitting on the couch, looking so pleased with each other. She sets it on a table in the school library and takes Malcolm's loupe from her bag.

"This photograph is important because it shows the painting clearly. And thanks to Becca noticing that little difference in those two squares, we know that *this* painting is definitely *not* the one that Father Julian had, *nor* the one that was hanging on Prunella's wall. Based on what Father Julian's cousin Debbie said, this picture must have been taken seven years ago—that's when she met Cale Winokum. And we know that within a few weeks of this picture being taken, Phillip walked off with the painting until his 'conscience' made him bring it back. Now, take a close look at the three men in this picture. There's Phillip, Cale Winokum, and this mystery man," she says. "What do they have in common?"

"Um . . . nothing," I say. "Phillip is old and kind of sleazy-looking. Cale is cute, in a scruffy, artsy-geeky kind of way. And it's hard to tell about the mystery guy. He looks pretty normal, I guess."

Fashion expert Leigh Ann zooms in on the clothes. "They're all wearing dark blazers and light-colored pants."

"And . . . anything else?" Margaret prods.

"Their ties!" Leigh Ann says. "The ties are all the same."

"Bingo!" Margaret says. "Now, what are the odds that three men would be wearing the exact same tie, unless—"

"They're school ties!" I say. "Stripes and crests. Definitely private school stuff."

"Precisely," Margaret says. "The Bramwell School, to be exact."

Leigh Ann looks skeptical. "Um, aren't they a little old to be wearing school uniforms?"

"True," says Margaret, "but Bramwell alumni are lifetime members of a very exclusive club. Haven't you noticed that Malcolm wears that one maroon and gold bow tie a lot? Those are the colors from *his* old prep school."

"And that's how these three know each other?" Becca asks.

"Well, I know Phillip went there, and I had Father Julian ask Debbie about Cale. He graduated from there—before going to . . . *art* school."

"Ohmigosh! He could be the forger!" I say.

"And I'll bet you anything," Becca says, "that this 'mystery man' is from the Svindahl Gallery. Look at him. He could be the father of the guy who yelled at us—the one who was at the diner with Prunehead."

"He's Arthur Svindahl Sr.," Leigh Ann says, looking up from the computer where she has pulled up the Svindahl Gallery website.

She turns the screen so we can all see. Sure enough,

there he is: a little grayer, a little heavier, but there's no doubt it's the same guy.

"So . . . these three got together and hatched this little scheme," I say.

"But somebody got greedy," Becca adds. "Instead of making one forgery for Phillip, I'll bet you that Svindahl had Cale make *two,* and then he kept the original for himself."

"Not a bad plan," Margaret says.

"But it still doesn't explain why they want it back," I point out.

Margaret nods her agreement. "There's a logical explanation. We just have to find it."

Chapter 25

In which I dig up a "key" piece of evidence

I've been assigned the job of returning the address book to Prunella, and I decide that I can kill two birds with one stone. Livvy's parents are out of town—again—so she and Tillie are staying at Julia Demarest's apartment for a few days. Now that we have switched dogs and I have the "right" Tillie, I miss the old one. I was really getting used to all of her strange habits—even her howling. Nate's Tillie is a bit of a couch potato, I'm afraid. When I come home, I get a wag of the tail, but not that look of utter joy that makes me feel that all is right with the world. And she won't even get up on the bed with me; she sleeps on the floor next to the bed—like a *dog*. On top of all that, I have to wake *her* up in the morning! It's just not the same.

My plan is to run up to the fifth floor, slide Phillip's little black book under Prunella's door, and then swing by Julia's to say a quick hello to Tillie—and Livvy. As I'm approaching the fifth floor, however, I hear Prunella's door close and two people arguing in the hallway as they wait for the elevator. I duck behind a column and prepare to snoop, ready to make a run for it if necessary.

It's Amelia Svindahl and her brother, Arthur.

"This is just unbelievable," she says in a high, whiny voice. "I don't understand. It's impossible. Inconceivable."

"You're absolutely sure that's a different painting from the one you and Dad saw last week?" Arthur asks.

"Positive. Gus's notes are very clear. You know how *meticulous* he is. He's totally insane about details like that—leaving his little identification marks that only he understands on everything he paints, whether he's doing his own thing or copying somebody else's. I saw his marks on the Pommeroy copy that that nosy little hobbit of a priest brought in a few weeks ago, and I saw different ones on the copy that *was* on the wall here a week ago. Somehow—don't ask me how or why—those two paintings have been switched."

"Well, we simply *have* to get that painting back, even if it means giving up the original Pommeroy," Arthur says. "Of course, Dad will have an absolute fit about that. He just loves that godawful thing."

"Serves him right. He's the one who got Gus involved in the first place. Painting over a Werkman. How could anyone be so stupid?"

The elevator finally arrives, but before the door closes, they drop one more little gem for me to take home.

"It wasn't entirely Gus's fault," Amelia says. "Seven years ago, Werkman was a complete nobody. Who knew his stuff would end up worth more than the Pommeroy?"

Did I say "little gem"?

More like the crown jewel.

When the Svindahls disappear behind the elevator door, I spend the next five minutes with my ear pressed to Prunella's, listening to her sing along with a 1940s big-band record. She's not bad, either—although it practically kills me to admit that. There's a good half-inch gap at the bottom of her door, and when I give the address book a healthy kick, it slides well into her apartment. When she suddenly stops singing, I make a run for the stairs, stopping on the third floor for a nice visit with Livvy and a very exuberant Tillie.

I stop by Margaret's apartment on my way home and reenact the Svindahls' conversation for her. Everything about her, from her toes, which are tapping like mad, to her oversize brain, vibrates with the energy of a genius on the verge of a major discovery.

"Do you know what this means?" she asks. "This changes *everything*. We have the upper hand. I can't wait to tell Father Julian."

"What are we going to do? Call the police?"

Margaret shakes her head. "That won't do any good. We can't prove anything—and the Svindahls have had the Pommeroy for years. The cops would laugh at us.

No, this is up to us. We need a really good plan . . . a 'butt-kicking' plan, I think you'd call it."

"RBGDA sleepover tomorrow at my place," I say. "The Blazers have the week off because Aldo is trying out a poetry slam at Perk, whatever that is. I'll get Dad to make us something good. I think better after a good meal."

"That sounds perfect. Can you call Becca and Leigh Ann to make sure they can do it?"

"Got it. We will have a couple of other visitors—for a while, anyway."

"Visitors, plural?"

"Nate's coming to pick up Tillie."

"And? That's one."

"Oh, right. Um . . . Livvy . . . is going to stop by," I mumble without making eye contact with Margaret. "I promised she could meet Nate, you know, especially since she was the one actually taking care of his dog. I'm sure she won't stay long."

"Okay. That's, um, good."

"You're not mad?"

"Of course not. Sophie, you're my best friend. I trust you. I'm even—I don't know—*proud* of you for working things out with Livvy. I'm not sure I'm ready to take that step, but I promise not to go after her or anything like that. Of course, I can't speak for Becca and Leigh Ann."

"Especially Leigh Ann," I say. "I think she still fantasizes about slugging her. Let's hope Livvy doesn't say anything bad about Queens, eh?"

. . .

As I barge through the front door of our apartment building, Tony, the afternoon doorman, shouts at me to stop.

"Gotsomethingforyou," he says, digging through the
pile of envelopes and papers that litter the lobby desk.
"Ah! Hereyougo."

He hands me a white envelope, plain except for my
name printed across the front. No stamps, no return address, not even an apartment number.

"Who dropped this off?"

Tony shrugs. "Dunno. Iwasawayfromthedeskfora-
minute. Camebackandthereitwas."

I rip open the envelope on the way to the elevator
and find this inside, cut from a piece of poster board:

*The pleasure of your company is requested on
Saturday at two o'clock in the afternoon.
Please bring all your gifts.*

"What the . . . Who is *doing* this?" I demand.

The nervous-looking old man who is waiting for the
elevator sidesteps away from me.

I smile at him. "Sorry."

When the elevator comes, he doesn't get in with me, which makes me smile. Call me evil if you want, but sometimes I get a little thrill from the sort-of superpower that we kids have to make grown-ups uncomfortable. It's amazing how many adults suddenly become incapable of coherent speech when they're trapped in an elevator with a kid.

I line up on the floor of my bedroom the strange gifts I have received: a brass bowl, a flowerpot full of dirt, the almost-real robin, my long-lost copy of *The Secret Garden,* and finally, the cryptic handmade invitation that seems to be missing some key information. For starters, exactly *where* am I invited?

And then I stare at them, waiting for an epiphany— some sudden understanding of what has been right in front of my eyes all along. When nothing comes after a few minutes of that, I stretch out on my bed with *The Secret Garden,* hoping that a few chapters of Mary and Dickon and Colin will help. As I flip through the pages, stopping to read some of my favorite parts, a receipt flutters out of the book and onto the bed. I can't read the name of the store, but it's for a flute that cost $4.99. I am quite certain that I have never bought a flute in my life, which means I was probably *meant* to find this receipt.

"Okay, Tillie," I say. "This has gone on long enough. And I call myself a detective."

Thinking aloud, I continue: "The robin and the flute are part of the story of *The Secret Garden.* Dickon plays the flute, and in chapter eight, it's a robin that shows

Mary the way to the secret garden. But first, he . . . digs up the key!"

The dirt! I never even thought to dump it out; I've been watering it, waiting for something to start growing. I push aside a little at the top of the pot and immediately notice a bright green gummy worm. My fingers wrap around it and gently pull it free of the soil. A piece of thread is tied to the end, so I start pulling. Two feet, three, four, and . . . YES! The biggest skeleton key I've ever seen plops out, bringing a handful of dirt with it. After I rub it clean and examine it with my trusty magnifying glass, I find the letter *V*—or is it the Roman numeral for five?—freshly engraved into the flat surface of the key. At the moment, the only place I can recall that might need a key like this one is the gate outside Prunella's building. Somehow, I doubt that she's the one sending me gifts, but now that I think about it, she's not the only person I know in that building. Livvy spends a fair bit of time there, too. And *she* was in my class in the fifth grade, back when my copy of *The Secret Garden* disappeared. Could she have something to do with this?

I pick up the invitation once again, running my finger around the curves of the handmade card. Something about that shape seems vaguely familiar, and suddenly the slide show in my brain is running at full speed as images flash into and out of my mind. A heavy iron gate. Lots of flowers. A boy with a flute. A bird. A girl with a bowl. My imagination, I'm afraid, is getting the best of me. I've read *The Secret Garden* so many times it's starting to feel real to me. I honestly can't separate what I've imagined from the places and things I've actually seen.

I close my eyes for a second, and when I open them, the invitation in my hand is no longer merely a piece of poster board.

It's a *map*.

"No. Way." It can't be this simple. I run to my computer and immediately search for the official Central Park site. I pull up the map of the park and there it is: the shape of the invitation matches the shape of the Conservatory Garden exactly.

But as I keep reading, I realize there's more. Much more.

I know where I'm going on Saturday. The who and the why? Not so much—yet.

Chapter 26

Hey, I think I'd look good in red tights and that snazzy cape

Father Julian meets us at Elizabeth's on Friday afternoon and shares the details of a conversation that's *almost* as interesting as the one I overheard between those sleazy Svindahl siblings.

"Oddly enough," he says with a coy smile, "the Svindahl Gallery has had a change of heart. Arthur Svindahl's exact words were, 'We've reconsidered our position on the Pommeroy you brought in, and we'd like to take another look.'"

"I'll bet they would," I say. "They must be going crazy, trying to figure out how your copy ended up in Prunella's living room."

"What did you tell them?" Margaret asks.

Father Julian sets the painting beside his chair and exhales loudly. "I said I'd think about it. It is quite a dilemma. Unless we're misinterpreting the conversation that Sophie overheard, they have the original Pommeroy in their possession. I'd love to hear their explanation for how they happen to have it, but ultimately, I just want that painting back in the family so Dad can decide what to do with it."

"You're not thinking about making a trade, are you?" Leigh Ann asks. "Don't do it. They're crooks. They'll cheat you."

The front door swings open and Malcolm glides in as if on skates, doffing his tweed cap to us before flinging it perfectly onto a hook on the foyer wall ten feet away. He turns back to us with his steeliest gaze. "The name's Chance. Malcolm Chance."

"I don't care if you're Henry the Eighth," Elizabeth scolds. "Wipe your feet. And take off that coat. You're dripping all over the foyer."

"Lovely to see you, too, dear," he says. He then catches us all by surprise when he scoops Elizabeth into his arms and kisses her.

She pretends to push him away for our benefit, but she's enjoying it. "Why are you in such a good mood?"

"Because I just got back from the Met, where I got some absolutely astounding news. News that is worthy of a celebration." He holds up the Pommeroy from Prunella's apartment. "Remember when I told you that this is a fake? Well, I was only half right."

"Nothing unusual about *that*," Elizabeth chides. I give her a high five.

Malcolm chooses to ignore us. "As I was saying, beneath this lovely forgery is—"

"A painting by Paul Werkman," I say.

Malcolm's chin bounces off the plush Oriental rug. "Wh—what? How can you possibly know that?"

"X-ray vision," I say. "After thirteen years on your planet, my superpowers are finally beginning to develop. I'll be flying soon."

I don't think he's buying the Supergirl story.

"All right, the truth is that, for once, I happened to be in the right place at the right time, and I overheard the Svindahls talking about it. But thanks for confirming the story. And, for the record, I *didn't* get caught. Or leave anything behind."

"Astonishing," he says. "The CIA doesn't know what it's missing, not hiring you girls right now."

"Well, if it's worth what they say, it certainly explains why the Svindahls were willing to pay to get a 'worthless' forgery back," Margaret says.

"Oh, it explains it and then some," Elizabeth remarks. "A Werkman is worth at least four or five Pommeroys in today's market."

Father Julian buries his head in his hands. "It just gets better and better. What am I going to do?"

"The preservationist I've been working with at the Met tells me that it is possible to remove the top layer of paint without damaging the Werkman," Malcolm says. "It will take some time, and it won't be cheap, but it can be done. All you have to do is give the word, and I'll take care of the rest."

"I don't understand why someone would have

painted over the Werkman in the first place," Elizabeth says. "If it was in a gallery, certainly they would have known its value."

"From what I heard," I say, "the Svindahls totally blame Rebecca's buddy Gus—the guy who works in the back."

"I know you guys are going to think this is terrible," Leigh Ann says, "but I can *totally* see how it happened. After Sophie told me what she overheard, I went online and looked up this Paul Werkman. Do you know what his paintings look like? One that I saw was all white, with a circle of not-quite-as-white white painted in the middle. You can barely even see the circle. And even if you could see it—I mean, so what? I'm sorry, but I just don't get modern art."

"Don't feel bad, Leigh Ann," says Malcolm, leaning in her direction. "Most of it is a mystery to me, too. Give me a nice Rembrandt or a Vermeer any day."

Before Rebecca and Elizabeth have a chance to defend modern art, however, Margaret holds up her hand to call a truce.

"Father Julian, you trust us, right?" she says. "Give me twenty-four hours to come up with a plan."

"To do what, exactly?" he asks.

"I'm not sure yet, but I may have a way to get your family's painting back without handing the Werkman over to that family of felons. And then you can do whatever you want with it. Heck, you can even hand it over to Prunella if you want."

"Ewww. Don't do that!" Leigh Ann says. "Donate it to charity or something. I mean, as far as she knows, she still has the same painting. It's like my dad says: what she doesn't know won't hurt her."

"I do trust you girls," says Father Julian. "I promise not to make a decision until I hear your plan."

"Oh, how exciting," Elizabeth says. "I do love a good caper."

Don't we all?

Dad's coat is on and he is on his way out the apartment door as the four of us barge in, chattering away about the Svindahls and how much we're going to enjoy sticking it to them.

"Ah—*bonjour, Monsieur St. Pierre,*" says Margaret. "*Comment allez-vous?*"

"*Ça va, merci,*" Dad replies.

Leigh Ann's eyes open wide when she sees him. "Ohmigosh. Did you cook for us? Please, please, tell me you made that killer macaroni and cheese."

I've begun to suspect that Leigh Ann is friends with me for one reason: my dad's cooking.

Dad pulls the corners of his mouth down, forming an exaggerated frown. "So sorry, mademoiselle. No *fromage* today. Monsieur Etan is coming and he asked for his favorite: *poulet au vinaigre.*"

Leigh Ann's nose crinkles up—just a teensy bit. "What's *that*?"

"Chicken with vinegar," I say. "Don't worry. You're going to love it. *Au revoir, Papa!*"

"Be good," he says.

As if we need to be told.

After considering Nate's past record of tardiness, we decide not to wait for him, and dig into the first of the two enormous dishes of Dad's *poulet*. Moments after Leigh Ann threatens to lick her plate clean, there's a knock at the door. It's Nate, and he has brought a special surprise guest: Cam Peterson. Leigh Ann, who had been so nonchalant about Cam asking for her number, suddenly sits up straight in her chair and checks her teeth for bits of fresh parsley in the reflection of her knife while Becca teases her mercilessly.

"Hey, So-So Sophie! Good to see you," Nate says, catching me by surprise with a bear hug. He then takes my head between his hands and examines my nose. "I can hardly see where that chick clocked you."

"Yeah, it's almost like new."

Suddenly Tillie bursts out of the bedroom where she's been napping with Mom. She takes two steps and then leaps at Nate from a good ten feet away.

"Now *that's* the Tillie I know," he says. "What happened, girl? The last time I saw you, you wanted nothing to do with me. It's like you're a different dog."

"Uh, yeah, about that," I say. "Funny story."

Another knock, and as I open the door, the two Tillies stand face to face once again, with a speechless

263

Livvy Klack staring in at the gorgeous Nate Etan and the rest of us mere mortals.

I introduce Livvy to everybody ("This is the chick who clocked me," I inform Nate), and while Nate and Cam compete to see who can eat more of the chicken, Livvy and I join forces to tell the Tale of Two Tillies.

"If I hadn't met you in that coffee shop and seen for myself how she acted, I wouldn't believe you," Nate says. "I *knew* she was acting strange—tackling Cam on the set that day, and doing tricks for you, but I never thought for a second that she literally was a different dog."

"And poor Livvy here thought something was really wrong with her Tillie," I say.

"I was ready to take her to the vet," Livvy says, "because she didn't want to sleep in the bed with me, wouldn't do any of her tricks, and refused to eat her usual food. I was convinced she had cancer or something horrible."

"That's it!" Margaret cries. When we all turn and stare at her, she shoots back, "Sorry, I didn't mean to interrupt. A great idea—no, make that an *incredible* idea—just popped into my head. Nate, how long are you going to be in town? And Tillie—we're going to need her."

"Till Thursday or Friday, probably."

"Cam, how about you?"

"Sometime next weekend. Depends on . . . Well, I hope, anyway," he says with a glance in Leigh Ann's direction.

Margaret next turns to Livvy and takes a deep

2 6 4

breath. Those two haven't spoken since that fateful English project, which now seems eons ago.

"Livvy, how'd you like to be part of a little drama I'm putting together?"

"Me? Really? I, um, uh, what do you mean, drama? Like a play?"

"Yeah, kind of," Margaret answers.

I poke the Brainy One in her side. "What are you up to?"

"Okay, this may take a while to explain. First, we have to . . ."

Chapter 27

We discover the only person alive who apparently never heard that old "sticks and stones" line

When Margaret's grand scheme is finally clear to everyone, the boys and Livvy make their exits—with, sadly, *both* Tillies. There is a bright spot, however; I get paid for dog-sitting Tillie!

Nate is almost out the door when he remembers. "Ohmigosh! Sophie, your money!" He digs into his wallet and pulls out a thick wad of bills. "Are hundreds okay? I don't have any small bills. So, let's see, fifty a day times three weeks, so that's fifty times twenty-one days— somebody help me out, I'm not that good at math."

"One thousand and fifty," Margaret says without hesitation.

"Thanks. Plus an extra hundred for your sneakers and the food you had to buy . . . Tell you what, let's make it an even twelve hundred. That okay with you? Sophie? You in there?"

"T-t-twelve hundred dollars?" I stammer. I guess I've

been too busy to actually do the calculations myself before now. I was thinking it would be a few hundred dollars, and I was all set to be thrilled with that.

"Is that wrong?" Nate asks. "Did I mess up the math?"

"No, no—it's just . . . that's a *lot* of money."

"Well, you did me a huge favor," he says. "You earned it. Just don't go and blow it all on *books* or something." He's grinning; somebody must have told him about my "little problem."

"Holy crap, St. Pierre," Becca says. "You're loaded. If I were you, I wouldn't tell my parents. They'll make you put it in the bank or in some stupid college fund."

"Well, if she doesn't tell, I will," Margaret says.

Becca sticks her tongue out at Margaret. "Buzzkill."

With Mom in hiding in her room with a book and (I suspect) a pair of much-used earplugs, the four Red Blazer Girls get comfortable in my bedroom. I just love it when everybody sleeps over, and with Tillie gone for good, I feel like I really need my best friends around to make me forget how much I miss that mutt. Of course, those twelve hundred smackers won't hurt, either.

Leigh Ann sits at my desk, checking her email until she's too distracted by the assortment of strange gifts I've received over the past couple weeks to continue.

"What is going on with all this stuff?" she asks. "Have you figured out who's sending it yet?"

"What? Oh, *that* stuff," I say with all the nonchalance I can gather. "Um, no. Still working on it."

"Well, tell us what you have so far," Leigh Ann says. "We've got time."

"Nah, we have to work on the plan for Wednesday. There's still lots to do." I take a notebook and a pen from my desk and pretend to jot down some notes to myself.

My friends? They're not buying a word of it. When I look up, they're all staring at me with arms crossed.

"All right. What's going on?" Leigh Ann insists.

"What?"

"You're not fooling anyone, Sophie," right-as-usual Margaret says. "Spill it."

I really am out of options. If I don't tell them something, they'll tickle me or threaten to do something to my beloved books.

"It's Raf," I admit.

They are silent for a second as they exchange glances. Finally, Margaret says, "Are you *sure*? This doesn't really sound like Raf to me. It's not that he's not smart enough to do it, I just don't know how he could pull it off. Like, where did he get the book? And how did he get it into our locker—in the middle of the school day?"

Good point.

"He must have had an accomplice," I say, locking eyes on Rebecca.

"Hey, why are you pickin' on me? Margaret is a much more likely suspect. She shares the locker with you, for cryin' out loud. Plus, she lives right by you, which would explain those packages that showed up at your apartment."

"Hmmm," I say. "I hadn't thought of that."

"Me?" Margaret says. "Becca, you're crazy. You're always sneaking into our locker. And everyone knows how good you are with locks."

"That's true," says Leigh Ann. "And you and Raf *are* always joking around together."

"*Me* and Raf! What about *you*? You two—"

"Stop!" I shout. "Before somebody says something . . . This is just stupid. It doesn't matter. I know where I'm going on Saturday, but I'm not telling *any* of you. You're just going to have to wait to hear about it."

When everyone finally accepts that I'm really not going to tell them any more about Saturday's rendezvous, we finally get back to work on our primary objective, which is to recover the original Pommeroy from the Svindahls. As the RBGDA's art expert, Rebecca is responsible for learning as much as possible about the Svindahls and their gallery. She goes online and starts snooping around the New York art world for information about the three family members and the artists they represent. According to their website, Gus Olienna has been associated with the gallery for about eight years and is a "modern master of the still life." Although an extensive biography exists for every other artist whose work is sold by the gallery, with a picture of the artist and a long list of schools, studios, and ateliers where they learned their craft, the bio page for Gus Olienna consists of one sentence: "Gus Olienna studied painting at the prestigious Eve I. Lebekam Academy of Fine Arts in Paris."

Becca does a search of his name, but the only place it shows up in the entire Internet universe is on the Svindahl Gallery's site.

"And when I search for Eve I. Lebekam," she says, "I get absolutely nothing. No matches. Zero. That's pretty hard to do in this day and age."

"Go back to the bio page," Margaret says. "I want to see something."

Margaret stares at the page for a few seconds, then smiles. "Oh my, Mr. Olienna. Nicely done. Eve I. Lebekam. Look at it backward."

"Makebel I. Eve," Becca says. "So?"

"Make believe," Leigh Ann says.

"Your friend Gus is very clever," Margaret says.

Becca, always on the lookout for a conspiracy, adds, "Or maybe he's trying to hide something. If they gave a make-believe name for the school, why not him, too? He never really seemed like a Gus to me."

"You may be onto something, Rebecca," Margaret says. "I wonder . . . Hey, what was that Cale guy's last name? The guy in the picture with Phillip and Svindahl where they're all wearing their Bramwell ties. It was Winokum, right? The guy who used to go out with Father Julian's cousin Debbie."

She taps out "Cale Winokum" and "Gus Olienna" on my computer, and we all gather around the screen.

"What are you thinking, Marg?" I ask.

"If you say the names backward, they're Mukoniw Elac and Anne Ilosug," Becca says. "The second one at least sounds like it *could be* a name."

"Becca, take a good look at that picture," Margaret says. "Especially Cale. Does he look familiar at all?"

Becca stares at the picture for a few seconds before the corners of her mouth start to turn north.

"So? What do you think?" Margaret asks.

"About what?" I ask, completely in the dark.

"Cale and Gus are the same person," Becca says. "Take away the beard, give him a good haircut—yep, I'm sure. How did you know, Margaret? You've never even seen Gus."

"Look at the two names again," Margaret says. "That made me suspicious—and everything else just fell into place."

CALE WINOKUM
GUS OLIENNA

Becca, Leigh Ann, and I stare at the two names until Leigh Ann finally sees it. "The vowels! Both names have all five vowels: *a*, *e*, *i*, *o*, and *u*. And they're in order."

"Yeah, they're just reversed," I say. "Why would Cale change his name?"

"A million possible reasons," Margaret says. "Maybe the Svindahls have some kind of hold on him."

"This must have something to do with that 'nasty little man' that Gus was talking about," Becca says. "After class tomorrow, I'm going back to see him—with some tea. In a china cup. Gus is going to tell me the whole story before I leave."

"Can I come with you?" I ask. "I have swim practice in the morning, but I'll be done by the time you get out of class. C'mon—I have to meet this guy and see the amazing, magical room where he works. Please?"

"Okay with me," Becca says. "Now that you've got all that cash, you can hang out with me all you want. But just so you know, you're buying the tea."

And what a story it is!

It takes several cups of tea and more than an hour, but after we tell him what we have already figured out about him, the Svindahls, and the mistaken Paul Werkman painting, Gus sighs and starts talking.

"Eight years ago, Cale Winokum was just another art school graduate, trying to find his way in the New York art world. But there was one big difference between me and most of the other struggling artists," he admits. "I was rich. Well, my parents were. After prep school and college, I vowed not to take any more of their money. I was determined to make it on my own. They agreed, except for one thing: they insisted on buying me an apartment. In fact, they bought the loft right above this gallery. That way, they knew I'd be safe, and I would at least have a place to paint until I got my big break. I think being over such a successful gallery seemed like a good omen to them—which is kind of ironic now, I suppose."

"Were you working for the Svindahls back then?" I ask.

"Not right away—that came later. I knew young Arthur a little from our school days. We went to Bramwell together. I ran into him one day, and ended up showing some of my work to him and his dad. My portfolio was a real mishmash back then; I was still trying to develop my own style. But the painting that caught Arthur senior's eye was a copy I had made of a Chardin still life. I can still hear his voice: 'If you can do this, you can do anything,' he said. A few months later, he invites me to a party at a friend's house; he promises me there will be lots of single girls, but the real reason he invites me is a little more complicated."

"Was that the birthday party where you met Debbie—Father Julian's cousin?" Becca asks.

Cale smiles, remembering. "That's right—Debbie. Sweet girl, and a very nice family. Except for her uncle Phillip. He was *not* a nice man. And that woman he—"

"Prunella," says Becca.

Gus shivers at the mention of her name. (I know exactly how he feels!) "Meanwhile, Arthur points out the real reason for my invitation—a painting hanging over the mantel. It's a Pommeroy, a very nice example of his work—and Arthur asks if I think I could make him a copy that would be impossible to tell from the original. I was honest with him; I told him that not only could I do it, I could finish it in a day. That made him very happy, and he brought Phillip over to tell him the news. Phillip didn't know much about art, but he knew that the Pommeroy was worth some money, and he wanted it for himself. He was willing to pay Arthur to make a copy and then pull a fast one on his own family."

"But you made two copies, didn't you?" I ask.

Gus nods sheepishly. "Yes. I'm afraid I did. Arthur asked me to, and I should have said no, but greed—and my ego—got in the way. I wanted to show off, so I took the job. And they were perfect except for one little thing. Just for fun, I switched the way two squares are overlapped, on purpose. I can't believe you noticed that! Arthur saw the two forgeries side by side, and right next to the original, and he didn't see it."

Becca smiles proudly. "So who figured out that you had painted over a Paul Werkman?"

"Oh, that," he says, looking nervously first at the door and then at the window. "*That* was the beginning of all my troubles. A nasty, nasty little man, he is."

"Who? Arthur?"

He leans toward us and whispers, "Paul Werkman." By the way he cringes at the sound, it's obvious he doesn't even like saying the name out loud. He's wearing a black turtleneck, and I swear his head starts disappearing down inside the collar. He starts mumbling incoherently and his eyes dart around the room; he even starts to sweat. "Can't talk about this anymore. You're going to have to go now."

I start to stir, thinking it's all over, but Becca holds her ground. "Let's take a break for a few minutes—have another cup of tea. What do you say?"

Gus relaxes immediately when she mentions the tea. He closes his eyes, collecting himself. Several deep breaths and half a cup of Earl Grey later, he returns to his story.

"It was Arthur junior—Artie, I call him—who noticed the missing painting. Anyone might have made the same mistake. It was leaning against the wall, right next to the blank canvases I had prepared for the Pommeroy forgeries. Maybe if the light in the hallway had been better, I would have seen it, but from where I was, it looked like a white canvas. I set it up on my easel and started laying out the basic composition. And that was that. In a few hours, I turned a Werkman into a Pommeroy."

"And then they handed over the two forgeries to Phillip, who never suspected a thing, I'm guessing," Becca says. "And Arthur Svindahl kept the original."

"Which has been hanging over *his* mantel for the past eight years," adds Gus.

"But then . . . ," I start.

"Right. But then, a few days later, Artie starts screaming that one of the Werkman paintings is missing. He's not the brightest guy in town, but it didn't take him long to figure out what had happened, and to start yelling at me. But that was *nothing* compared to what was coming. The Werkman show in the front room of the gallery was scheduled to start that night, and Werkman was on his way here with more paintings. Artie had no choice but to tell him what had happened—leaving out the part about me forging the Pommeroy, of course. That is *not* something an artist wants to hear from the gallery that's selling his work."

"Yeah, I guess I can see that," Becca agrees.

"Well, Werkman went absolutely crazy. He was screaming at Artie that the one that I painted over was just part of a work that was made up of four separate canvases—and that without *that* one, it was all worthless. It was the best work he'd ever done, he said, and we were all morons. But he saved his real venom for me. He called me a ninny. A nincompoop. A spineless, brainless invertebrate—"

"Golly," I say. "That seems a bit extreme." ("And redundant," Margaret noted when I told her the story. "I mean, *obviously* an invertebrate is spineless.")

"And then . . ." Gus pauses to collect himself once again. "Then he looked me square in the eyes and told me that he was going to make it his *mission* in life—that's how he put it—to see to it that every gallery, every art dealer, every artist, everyone with any connection to the art world would know what Cale Winokum had done. He actually said the words 'Cale Winokum will never work in this town again.' And then he spat on the floor in front of me. 'You're dead to me.'"

"Wow. Insanity much?" says Becca.

"*That's* why you changed your name!" I say. "But that was a long time ago. Surely he's not still after you—er, Cale, I guess."

Becca nods at him. "Sophie's right, Gus. It's time to move on with your life. Those paintings of yours out in the front room—do you even see any of the money from those? The Svindahls are totally taking advantage of you."

Gus immediately turns defensive. "No, that's not true. They pay me. And they take good care of me—they warn me whenever that nasty little Paul Werkman is in the neighborhood. He has a show at a gallery a few blocks from here, and Artie and Amelia saw him walk past one day. I had to hide upstairs for two days."

"Oh, Gus, they're *using* you," says Becca. "They know you're afraid and they use that fear to keep you trapped in here, painting for *them*."

But there's really no point in pushing him any further; his head is disappearing back inside his turtleneck, and I'm afraid that I'll explode if I drink any more tea.

As we get ready to climb out the window, Becca turns back to Gus one last time. "Just so you know, we're not giving up on you, *Cale*."

The look on his face when he hears her call him by his real name tells me that he is definitely *not* a lost cause.

Chapter 28

Let the great counterfeit canvas caper begin

"Well, this situation clearly deserves a plan of its own," Margaret announces after listening to Becca and me retell the story of how Cale Winokum became Gus Olienna and how he transformed a Paul Werkman painting into the Pommeroy knockoff that hung on Prunella Scroggins's wall for eight years. "I don't care how crazy this Werkman guy is—we have to help Cale Winokum get his life back."

"It sounds to me like he needs a psychiatrist," Leigh Ann says. "Anybody who basically locks himself in his apartment for eight years because some mean-spirited artist yelled at him needs some serious help."

"What are we supposed to do?" I ask. "He really still believes that Paul Werkman is after him. How do we make him believe that's not true?"

"How do we know it isn't?" Leigh Ann asks. "Maybe the Svindahls are telling him the truth."

Becca shakes her head vigorously. "No way is he still

holding a grudge for something like that. Eight years ago, his stuff just wasn't worth that much. I'll bet you he doesn't even remember the name Cale Winokum."

Leigh Ann is searching online for anything and everything on Werkman, and pulls up a magazine interview and some pictures of him. "He doesn't look so bad to me," she says. "In fact, he seems kind of nice. And look—he still lives with his mother in Brooklyn! How bad could he be?"

"There's one way to find out if he's after Cale," Margaret says. "We ask him."

"We're going to ask Paul Werkman if he's still mad at Cale?" I say. "It sounds like *they're* still in seventh grade. Are you going to pass him a note in gym class?"

That gets a smile out of Margaret. "Something like that. It's time to cash in a little favor, my dear. Werkman may live with his mother, but he's kind of a big deal now. He'll never talk to us. But a big movie star—that's different. Nobody can resist *that*. Nate even had me under his spell . . . for about half an hour."

"You really want me to ask Nate to do it?"

"Sure. You took care of his dog for three weeks. He owes you one."

"What about that twelve hundred bucks he paid her?" Becca asks.

"Totally different," explains Margaret. "That was strictly a *legal* matter—this is a *social* obligation. One has nothing to do with the other."

• • •

Luckily for us, rain is in the forecast for Monday, which means they won't be able to film the remaining scenes of *No Reflections,* which means that Nate will have nothing to do. And *that* means that he actually agrees to my strange request.

My phone rings a few minutes after I send him a long email explaining what we want him to do, without going into all the gory details. Guess what he wants to know?

The gory details.

Turns out that Nate's manager, Tia, is trying to get him interested in modern art, and when Nate said something to her about Werkman, she got very excited at the prospect of meeting the artist.

"I've never heard of the guy," Nate says, "but Tia says he's great. So we're going over there tomorrow. I'll give you a report when we get back."

"Oh, and don't forget—Elizabeth Harriman will be stopping by your hotel on Wednesday morning to pick up Tillie."

"Right. Elizabeth. Tillie. Wednesday. Got it."

"I think I'll send you a reminder on Wednesday anyway," I say, remembering Nate's past record for timeliness.

"Probably a good idea."

Phase one of Margaret's grand plan, code-named Operation STS (Swindle the Svindahls), gets under way immediately after the dismissal bell on Wednesday, which is an hour earlier than normal because of the monthly faculty meeting. Our objective: recover the original Pommeroy for Father Julian. By any means necessary.

Okay, that last part isn't actually true. We have our limits—honest!

Becca and Leigh Ann hop on the F train for Chelsea and the Svindahl Gallery, while Margaret and I run next door to the rectory to gather up Father Julian, Malcolm, and three packages—all the same size and shape, and all wrapped identically in brown kraft paper and twine.

"How did I do?" Malcolm asks. "I followed your directions exactly."

"They look perfect. Which one is the Werkman?" Margaret asks.

Malcolm points to the middle package. "See, there's a little red dot by every corner, so no matter which side is up, we'll be able to tell. The New York print you asked me to get has a yellow dot, and this other one—your big surprise—has no marks. Just like when you brought it in."

"And we resisted the urge to look at it, just as you requested," Father Julian adds. "You're not going to tell us what it is?"

"All in good time," says Margaret. "Let's go."

We totally luck out with the weather. It's a beautiful fall day, more like September than November; the temperature is pushing sixty degrees and the sun is shining.

"A great day for a caper," Malcolm says with a jaunty wink and a twirl of his walking stick. "We should have invited Elizabeth."

"Way ahead of you, Mal. She has Tillie, and they're

meeting us there," I say as we cross Park Avenue on our way to Central Park. "Maybe when we're all done, the two of you can go for a nice romantic walk. You know, holding hands, buying ice cream, sitting on a bench in the sun."

"Those sound like the words of someone with experience," he replies, and I feel myself blush.

"They are," Margaret says, nudging me. "Aren't they, Sophie?"

"La ferme, Marguerite."

Elizabeth and Tillie—Nate's Tillie, that is—are waiting for us at the outdoor café next to the Model Boat Pond. She has reserved two tables for us. With Margaret directing, we move them slightly closer together and arrange the chairs *just so.*

"Perfect," she says, finally. "Okay, Malcolm—you and Elizabeth here and here. Father Julian, you're going to be on this side. When the Svindahls come, make sure they sit in these two chairs—the ones closest to the other table. That's important. Rebecca called in with her update; the two Arthurs are coming. They left Amelia in charge of the gallery, just as we suspected. Sophie and I will be at that table. Now, everybody, remember: you don't know us. You've never seen us before. We're going to laugh and talk and make a lot of noise, so you might even want to look annoyed by us. Okay?"

"Got it," says Father Julian, who seems the most nervous.

Margaret turns her attention to me. "Okay, Sophie, time for you to make sure everything is all set for your big scene. Here you go." She hands me the mystery package—the one with no marks on the wrapping paper.

"C'mon, Tillie!" I say. "We have to hurry."

By the time Tillie and I get back to the table, the two Arthurs are seated at the table with Father Julian, Malcolm, and Elizabeth. Their package, wrapped in white paper with the Svindahl Gallery logo, rests on the ground next to Arthur junior's chair. If they can be trusted at all, it is the original Pommeroy.

A mighty big if.

Tillie and I approach the table from the side, avoiding Junior's line of vision, because I'm afraid he might recognize me from that fateful morning in the gallery. I get Tillie settled in under the table, next to the wrapped print of the Chrysler Building, and ask Margaret how things are going "next door."

"It's looking good so far here. I just got off the phone with Becca, and she says that Tillie's dad showed up on time, even. How's the other Tillie?"

I give her the okay sign and take a swig of the soda Margaret bought for me. "Thanks, Marg."

We start a stream of completely mindless chatter about movies we haven't seen and music we don't really listen to, while doing our best to catch every word from the next table. I type in a text message on my phone and keep my thumb near the send button. It reads: *On your mark. Get set . . .*

Malcolm, who is doing most of the talking for Father Julian, comes right to the point. "Here's my concern: you have all but admitted that seven years ago, you forged, or had someone who works for you forge, this painting—twice. Why should we believe that you're handing over the real thing and not another fake?"

"A fair question," says Senior. "I give you my word that it's the original."

"Would that be the same word you gave to my uncle Phillip when you handed him a forgery in place of the real painting?" Father Julian asks.

Ouch! Father Julian clearly draws first blood.

"We have concerns of our own," Junior says. "For instance, the *way* that you seem to have acquired the painting you want to exchange. Strange that it is *not* the same painting you brought to the gallery for an appraisal a few weeks ago. I wonder if your aunt is even aware that she has been the victim of a crime."

"Gentlemen, please," Elizabeth interrupts. "Since everyone at this table lives in a glass house, I think perhaps we *all* stop throwing stones. You each have something the other wants. I suggest you make the agreed-upon exchange. Now let's see both paintings—up here on the table. I am quite qualified to judge the authenticity of works of art."

Arthur junior sets the painting on the table and

carefully peels back the tape on one end so he can remove the paper it's wrapped in. He then hands the painting to Elizabeth, who uses a loupe to examine the signature, a few places on the painting itself, the bare canvas on the back, and the stretcher frame before passing it on to Father Julian.

Across the table, Malcolm carefully unwraps the painting from Prunella's wall—the painted-over Werkman—and hands it to Arthur senior. He ignores the painting itself, focusing instead on a series of pencil marks on the bottom of the stretcher frame. Junior leans in to look over his shoulder.

"That's it," he says. "The one we saw in the old woman's apartment. Amazing."

"Everybody satisfied?" Elizabeth asks.

"I'm happy," Father Julian says.

Arthur junior smiles. "We're good."

"Excellent." Elizabeth raises her glass in a toast. "One question, though. How did it happen? The Werkman, I mean. How does someone just paint over something like that?"

I realize that we haven't shared with Elizabeth what we learned from Gus on Saturday, and I strain my ears to hear how the Svindahls are going to answer her.

Junior leans back in his chair until he's almost touching our table. "Not as hard as you might think."

Senior tells the rest of their version of the story, which pretty much confirms what we already knew. "The young man we had hired to, um, well, to do some painting for us was—is—a gifted painter, but is completely clueless when it comes to anything abstract. Werkman sent us a grouping of four canvases, all with a white-on-white theme, something he's famous for. Very subtle, but quite profound in their own way. Well, our gifted young painter was looking for a canvas *this* size, and he found one. After we discovered what had happened, he said that to him it just looked like a prepared canvas."

"And by then it was gone," Junior adds. "We didn't know which one went to Phillip and which to the other house, so we were stuck. It definitely created some problems for us with Werkman. He was *not* happy."

He rewraps the painting in the brown kraft paper and sets it on the ground, next to his chair.

And that, my friends, is *my* cue.

Chapter 29

In which I share the stage and the glory with an up-and-coming actress

As soon as Arthur junior sets the package by his chair, I quietly slide *my* identically wrapped parcel next to his, hit the send button on my phone, and prepare for yet another inspired-but-certain-to-be-ignored-by-the-Academy performance.

"Well, I've gotta get going," I say to Margaret. "I've got a ton of homework tonight and my parents are gonna kill me if I don't get my grades up. Call me, okay? Give her a kiss, Tillie. Good girl!" I give Margaret a hug and make my grand exit. Instead of taking my package, though, absentminded little me "accidentally" picks up the one next to Arthur junior and walks off with it.

Oops.

As Tillie and I make our way out of the little café area and to the sidewalk around the edge of the pond, my phone vibrates in my hand. I grin when I read the new message: *GO!* Then I quickly call Margaret so I can hear what's going on at the table (and get a heads-up if something goes wrong at her end).

It's all going perfectly, though, and when I hit my mark, as we (ahem) *actors* like to say, Margaret interrupts the conversation at the other table.

"Hey, mister, I'm sorry, but I think my friend took your package by mistake." She shows him the little sticker from a frame shop on mine, and I can hear the panic in his voice over the phone.

"Where did she go? Which way? What is she wearing?" He and Arthur senior are on their feet immediately, scanning the park in all directions for a girl in a red blazer with a dog and a package wrapped in brown paper.

"There she is!" Junior shouts, pointing across the pond at me as I continue on my merry way.

"Junior's on his way," Margaret says quietly into her phone. "Hurry."

"No problem."

I step off the path as I hear Junior shouting at me; he's only a few seconds away from intercepting me when I step behind an enormous oak tree and stop.

"Hey, hold on a second!" Junior yells. "Wait! You've got my package!"

He puts his hand on the shoulder of a girl in a red blazer. She's blond, walking a black dog, *and* carrying a package wrapped in brown paper.

Livvy Klack spins around with her best how-dare-you-touch-me face. "What is your problem?" she says, sneering. (She was *born* to say that line.)

"I'm sorry, but you took my package," he says. "Yours is back at the café. We were sitting next to each other, and when you left, you must have picked up mine."

"Are you sure? This looks like mine."

"Open it up—you'll see."

With a dramatic roll of her eyes, she pulls away enough of the paper to reveal that it is definitely not her print of the Chrysler Building. Junior sighs with relief when he sees the bold colors of the Pommeroy peeking out from the paper.

"Sorry," he says. "I didn't mean to scare you, but this is pretty important to me. Come on, I'll buy you and your friend a couple of sodas. Your package is safe; my dad's watching it."

As they walk back to the café, I talk to Margaret by phone. "How did it look from there?"

"It was a thing of beauty. Seamless. Perfection. For a second, I actually thought Livvy didn't show. You should have seen the look on Malcolm's and Elizabeth's faces when he reached out and *Livvy* turned around. You'd better get out of there, just in case they take a closer look at things before they leave. I'm taking off right now."

"Okay, I'll see you at Perkatory at five."

Phase one of Operation STS is complete.

Perkatory is crowded for a Wednesday afternoon, so Margaret and I push two tables together and wait for everyone else to show up. It just about kills me that I missed what went down at the Svindahl Gallery while we were busy faking out the Arthurs in Central Park, but luckily, Becca and Leigh Ann were there to witness the whole crazy episode.

When they arrive, we pounce on them with questions.

"You're just going to have to wait," Becca says. "We promised not to tell the story until everyone was here."

Malcolm and Elizabeth are next, with Father Julian right on their heels. We're about to place our order for coffees and sodas and snacks when the door opens and Livvy comes in.

This is her first time officially meeting the grown-ups, so it's up to me to make proper introductions.

"This is Olivia Klack—but everybody calls her Livvy. She's the girl who broke my nose," I say with a grin at her. "We've been through a lot the past few weeks—a lot of ups and downs. But I think you'll all agree that she was brilliant today."

Father Julian scratches his head. "I'm sorry, but I'm really confused right now. I suppose it serves me right for not wanting to know the plan ahead of time, but *where* did she come from today? Sophie, I watched *you* walk away from the table carrying that package. But when you turned around, you weren't you anymore. You were . . . her."

"Smoke and mirrors," I say.

"Not quite," Margaret says. "Something a little more solid, like an oak tree. When Junior was chasing Sophie, she waited until he got pretty close, and then she turned off the path, taking a shortcut behind a big tree."

"Where Livvy and her Tillie were waiting," I add. "They stepped out the second I disappeared behind the tree. From Junior's point of view, there was no gap, no pause, nothing. It was perfect."

"But . . . why?" Father Julian asks. "What I mean is, he still got the painting, right?"

We all look at each other. "Do you really want us to answer that?"

"Oh no," he says. "What did you girls do? You might as well tell me now."

"It was all Rebecca's idea," Leigh Ann says. "She said that the Svindahls needed a taste of their own medicine. So we gave them one."

"Right about now, they're admiring my work," Becca says.

"And going bonkers trying to figure out how we scammed them," I say.

Father Julian lays his forehead on the table.

"Remember the third package?" Margaret asks. "Well, that was yet *another* copy of the Pommeroy, courtesy of our very own Rebecca Chen. And *that's* what the Svindahls took with them today."

"B-but I saw them identify Prunella's copy. They were positive."

"Oh, that's what they looked at, all right," Margaret says. "But Livvy was waiting behind the tree with Becca's copy."

"And he took only a very quick look inside the package," Father Julian says, finally understanding the whole scheme.

"Because he had absolutely no reason to suspect anything," says a thoroughly impressed Malcolm.

"And meanwhile, I walked away with *this*," I say, taking the painted-over Werkman from behind the bar and setting it on the table with a waggle of my eyebrows.

Meanwhile, Malcolm holds up the original Pommeroy for Father Julian to see.

"Do you really believe that's the original?" Father Julian asks.

"Unless the Svindahls did to us what we did to them," Margaret answers. "Which is always a possibility. We won't know until we have it X-rayed."

"I'm willing to bet it's the real thing," Elizabeth says. "It's definitely much older than the others."

Becca cackles mischievously. "Speaking of X-rays, boy, are they in for a surprise when they take a look at that thing."

"Oh no. Becca, what did you do?" I demand.

"A simple underpainting, kind of like *this*." She holds up a drawing of four blazer-wearing paper dolls.

"In red," she adds.

"So much for being *subtle*," Leigh Ann says.

I check my watch. "I wonder what happened to Nate—"

His name is still hanging in midair when the door bursts open and Nate makes his usual impressive entrance.

We cheer wildly, and he bows as deeply as if he's on a Broadway stage.

"*Now* can you tell us what happened down there?" I beg of Leigh Ann and Becca. "We're all here."

"Almost all of us," says Nate. "But that's okay. Tell the story, girls."

Becca starts: "Believe it or not, Nate was actually on time! And just like he promised, Paul Werkman shows up a few minutes later."

"He's a really funny guy," says Leigh Ann. "Not what I was expecting—at all."

"Yeah, well, when I first talked to him the other day, he was also very surprised to learn that he was 'after' some guy named Cale," Nate says. "Even after I reminded him about the painting, it still took him a while to remember that he had lost it on the guy who mistook his masterpiece for a blank canvas."

"He seemed really embarrassed," Becca adds. "He said he used to have some 'anger management issues,' but he's all better now. When we told him the rest—how the Svindahls were *still* using that whole screaming thing to keep poor Gus, er, Cale, painting away in their studio, totally for *their* benefit, he was like, 'I have to meet this guy.' "

"So we did!" Leigh Ann says.

"You mean you just walked in the front door of the gallery and said, 'Here we are'?" I say.

"Not exactly," says Becca. "I took them around to the back window, and I went in first, then Leigh Ann. Gus was in a pretty good mood—not too nervous—so I figured it was now or never, and I told him that we had talked to Paul Werkman."

"That freaked him out a little," says Leigh Ann. "Well, a *lot,* actually. He was worried that we told Werkman where to find him."

"And all this time, Werkman and Nate are right outside the window?" Margaret marvels.

"Yep. And Gus is pacing around the room, checking the lock on the door about ten times, until we finally calm him down," Becca says.

Leigh Ann continues: "And then we told him that Werkman wanted to see him, and to apologize for what happened eight years ago. It took a while, but we finally got him to believe us—that the Svindahls were playing him like a piano, totally taking advantage of the situation."

"So I go over and open the window," Becca says, smiling as she remembers it, "and it's like something from an old movie. First Nate climbs through, and then Paul Werkman. Luckily, he was wearing old jeans, because he tore them on a nail as he was crawling through the opening."

"What did Gus do then?" I ask. "When he first saw Werkman?"

"He looked kind of pale, and he was hiding behind his easel, but at least he didn't pass out or anything," says Leigh Ann. "After eight years, I think he had probably built the guy up in his mind into some lunatic monster, but when you see Werkman in the flesh, he's not exactly intimidating. He's just an average-looking guy—well, you'll get to see for yourself. When he gets inside, Werkman does most of the talking—"

The door opens and Paul Werkman looks around Perkatory, his eyes searching for a familiar face until they land on Nate.

"Hey, there's the man of the hour," Nate says, waving him over to our tables. "Where's Cale?"

Before Werkman can answer, the artist formerly known as Gus peers around the door.

Becca rushes over to greet him, and it's probably a good thing, because he looks like he might just turn and run. "Hey, Gus, er, Cale. Come on, there's a few more people you have to meet."

She introduces him all around and even brings him tea with milk and honey in a china cup, although where she found *that* in Perkatory, I can't imagine.

Not surprisingly, Cale is pretty quiet, but he does admit to looking forward to seeing some of the city's sights he's missed—especially the museums.

"I think I'll walk, though," he says quietly.

Werkman explains: "The poor guy gets in a car for the first time in eight years, and wouldn't you know it, we get a cabbie who is a complete maniac, weaving in and out of lanes, almost getting us run over by a bus."

"You don't need to go to museums," Becca says. "Your apartment is the most amazing place I have ever seen! You guys—everybody—you *have* to see it. He took us up there before we left, and it is *wild*. Every square inch of the place, walls, floors, ceilings, you name it, is painted to look like the rooms in the Met. There's everything from Egypt and ancient Greece all the way up to modern stuff—Impressionists, Picassos, Pollocks, everybody. When you walk in, you will *swear* there's a million paintings hanging on the walls, but it's all just—what did you call it?"

"Trompe l'oeil," Cale says.

"Ah, 'to trick the eye,'" I translate.

"There's been a lot of that going on today," Malcolm notes.

"Yeah, well, the whole thing oughta *be* a museum," says Becca.

"I'm glad you like it," says Cale. "It kept me busy at night. Kept my mind off . . ."

"Me?" Werkman asks.

Cale nods.

"I can't give you all that time back, but I can help you, Cale. I plan to talk to my agent and the owners of the gallery that shows my work tomorrow, and we're going to reintroduce Cale Winokum to the New York art world. How does that sound to you?"

"That sounds . . . really good," Cale admits.

"I just have one more question for you," Margaret says. "Did you go out the window, too? Or did you actually use the front door?"

"Oh, that was the best part," Becca says. "The five of us just walk out of Cale's studio and into the front room, where Amelia is sitting at her desk playing online solitaire. She had just taken a sip of coffee, and when she sees Cale and Werkman together, she spits it all over her computer."

"Her mouth is just hanging open as we walk past her to the front door," says Leigh Ann. "And then Mr. Werkman says, 'Don't worry, Amelia—we won't keep him out too late.' It was beautiful."

It's getting late, and as we're starting to say good night, Elizabeth brings up the original Pommeroy, which Father Julian is holding with both hands. "Father, I'm very interested in that Pommeroy, if you still want to sell it," Elizabeth says.

"Oh yes, but . . . what about the issue of its age? Don't we still have to prove that it was painted before 1961?" he asks.

"Oh, I took care of that a long time ago," I say proudly. "The proof was in the pictures all along—I just had to put it all together. Here, I'll show you." I take the

three pictures out of a notebook in my book bag and line
them up on the table.

"Okay, the one on the left shows the TV, but not the
painting. The game is from October 5, 1961. Those two
people on the bench are your aunt Cathy and her friend
Denny. The top right picture, with the birthday cake, is
important for what's in the background—the flowers in
that big floor vase. We can assume it was taken the same
day as the first one because Cathy and Denny are wearing the same clothes in both, and her birthday is October
5. But it's the one on the bottom that brings everything
together. You can see two important things in that picture: Cathy and Denny with a drink and a piece of cake,

about to sit on the bench, and that vase full of flowers. I used the magnifier to look at every single flower, and I am positive that they are the exact same flowers, in exactly the same position, as the ones in the top right picture, just from the other side. Put it all together and—ta-da!—you've got proof that the painting was on the wall on October 5, 1961. Before Pommeroy died."

"Good enough for me," Elizabeth says. "Father Julian, we'll be in touch."

Father Julian nods his agreement as his phone rings. He steps away from the table to take the call, wandering outside for a minute, before coming back with a strange look on his face.

Chapter 30

Life imitates art, take two

When we finally walk out of Perkatory, I feel a little let down, probably because I still have lots of questions:

What will happen to the Svindahls?

Will Cale really be able to just start his life over again? Will he and Debbie get back together?

Will I ever see Nate Etan again?

Mostly, though, I'm relieved that it's over—for now. I have some serious catching up to do on the rest of my life—something Livvy reminds me of when she reminds me that she'll see me at the pool at five-thirty in the morning. And now I have no cold dog nose to wake me, although Livvy does promise to let me borrow her Tillie when I'm in need of some dog time.

And then there's Saturday's mysterious two o'clock appointment in the park.

I throw the bowl, the book, and everything else into a canvas tote, pull on my new red Chuck Taylors (bought with my Tillie-sitting money), and set out for the Conservatory Garden and who knows what else. After passing through the Vanderbilt Gate (remember the skeleton key with the *V*?), I turn left, heading for the South Garden—the one that most people, I have learned, refer to as "the Secret Garden."

It's not called that because it's hard to find; it's because there is a lily pool and statue dedicated to Frances Hodgson Burnett, the author of *The Secret Garden*. When I come around the last corner, I spot Raf (just as I suspected!) and my heart, already beating fast, feels like it's trying to bust loose from my chest.

"Hey," I say, sitting next to him on the stone bench in front of the pool.

"I was starting to worry," he says.

"I'm sorry. I've been kind of a jerk lately. Sometimes I just—"

"Easy, Soph. That's not what I mean. You said to meet you here at two, and it's a little after. You're *usually* on time. Except when you're stuck in an elevator. Or out with a movie star."

"Wait. Back up a second. *I* told *you* to meet me here? Um, I don't think so. You're the one who sent me all this stuff. Aren't you?" Suddenly I'm not so sure.

"*What* stuff? What are you talking about?"

"This stuff. My copy of *The Secret Garden*. A big brass bowl. A bird."

Raf looks at me like I've lost my mind. "I've never seen any of this before. No, wait—the book. That's the one that I took from your desk a couple of years ago. It was one of those days when all us boys came over from

our school for some assembly at St. V's. I completely forgot that I had it, and then one day, Margaret said something that reminded me. But I gave it to her to give back
to you a long time ago."

"You stole my copy of *The Secret Garden*?"

"'Stole' is such an ugly word. I borrowed it. I got
tired of hearing how great it was from you all the time,
so I wanted to see for myself. I just didn't want anyone
to know I was reading such a girly book."

"A likely story," says a familiar voice from behind the
bushes.

"Margaret! What are you doing here?"

"The same thing we are," Leigh Ann says, pushing
Becca out in front of her.

"Spying on you two losers," says Becca.

"How did you . . . You mean, it was you guys all
along? What about all that 'Scout's honor' and 'I don't
know who could have been in our locker' stuff? And that
argument—you all . . ."

"All lies," Margaret admits with a shrug. "But sometimes the means do justify the end."

"Oh yeah? What is the 'end'? What are you up to?"

She points at the statue on a pedestal in the center
of the pool. I've seen it before, but had never really noticed how beautiful it is. A young girl is standing, holding
up a birdbath with both hands while birds rest in it and
on her shoulder. Next to her is a boy, his elbows resting
on a large stone as he plays the flute.

Mary and Dickon.

"Okay. I like it. What about it?"

"Anything seem familiar?" Leigh Ann asks.

"Wait a second. You want us to . . ." My eyes go from Raf to the statue and then back to Raf. The blank look on his face tells me he has no idea what's going on. *"Why?"*

"Because I have to do this 'living art' project for my class," Becca explains. "I'm supposed to re-create either a famous painting or a sculpture with real people. So, are you ready? I found the perfect spot, and the sun's shining on it right now. There's even a rock about the size of that one for the boy wonder to lean against."

"Is somebody gonna tell me what's going on?" Raf asks.

"Sure," says Margaret. "Basically, you and Sophie are going to use all the stuff in Sophie's bag—the bowl, the flute, and the bird—and you two are going to pose exactly like the two kids in the statue."

"And then I'm going to take a bunch of pictures," Becca announces. "And turn them into a painting."

"You're what?" Raf protests. "No. No way. Do you know what would happen to me if my friends found out about this? I can see it now: pictures of me posing like that guy in the statue—with that stupid flute—posted all over the Internet. No way."

"We thought you might say that," Leigh Ann says. "So we brought along something to convince you. Hey, Cam, come on out."

Cam Peterson comes around the bushes carrying a

large package wrapped in brown kraft paper. "Hi, Sophie. Hey, Raf. Good to see you again."

"Is anybody *else* back there?" I ask. "This is getting ridiculous."

"I'm the last one, I promise," Cam says.

"What's *that*?" I ask, pointing at the package. "Don't tell me it's a fake Pommeroy. If I never see another one of those, I'll be happy."

"Nope—not a Pommeroy, and this time, it's not for you, Sophie," Leigh Ann says. "We figured you would go along with the plan without putting up much of a fight, and Becca has promised to give you the painting she's going to do, but we had a feeling Raf might need a little extra convincing. And Cam has some interesting connections; it's amazing what he can get."

Cam hands the package to Raf. "I think you're going to like this. When I first saw it, I really wanted to keep it for myself. Open it up."

With the five of us standing there watching and waiting, he doesn't have much of a choice, so he tears off the paper.

"No way," he says when he realizes what he's looking at. "This is the real thing, isn't it?"

Cam nods. "And look—it's signed by Humphrey Bogart."

Raf turns to me and says, "Do you realize what this is? This is an *original* lobby card for *The Maltese Falcon.*"

"I thought we were getting him a poster," Becca says.

I nudge her. "A lobby card *is* a poster."

"I knew that."

"Leigh Ann told me you're really into the classics from the thirties and forties," Cam says. "I looked for one from the original *Frankenstein*—I heard you talking about going to see it with Sophie—but posters for that are *impossible* to find."

"Yeah, and they're worth, like, three hundred grand," Raf says.

The kid *knows* his movie memorabilia.

"Margaret remembered that you like this one, too," Leigh Ann says. "She said you quoted some line from it once."

"It's the stuff dreams are made of," says Raf, doing his Sam Spade imitation. "Trust me, this is *perfect*. It's amazing. You're serious—this is really for me?"

"Absolutely," says Cam.

"Told you," Becca says to Margaret. "I knew it would push him over the edge. He'd pose in a tutu if we asked him now."

"Don't push your luck, Becca," Raf says.

Five minutes later, I'm standing nice and tall, holding the bowl at eye level. I'm trying my hardest to look serene, but it's not easy with all those people shouting directions at me. Finally, I resort to my hasn't-failed-me-yet technique of taking several deep breaths. I gaze down at Raf's reclining figure as he plays a little tune on the flute.

"Beautiful," says Becca, snapping a picture.

"You guys are *perfect,*" Leigh Ann adds.

I couldn't agree more.

Chapter 31

Oh, you knew this was coming. There's always an epilogue

For exactly one week, my life is wonderfully, remarkably, surprisingly, boringly normal. Not that I'm complaining. It was actually . . . nice.

There were:

No new broken bones.

No dogs waking me in the middle of the night, howling at the moon.

No masterpieces dangling from open windows.

The good news is that I have time to work on some new songs for the Blazers, which is what I'm doing when Mom walks into my room with the day's mail. She flips an envelope onto my bed.

"This one's for you, Soph."

My name is printed in blocky letters that look like they were done by a first grader while riding in the back-seat of a car—on a bumpy road.

"Oh, great," I say. "*Now* what are those guys up to?"

"What guys?"

"Margaret and everybody. This looks a lot like the lettering on all those packages they sent me." I tear it open, and I almost drop my guitar. "No. Way."

"What? Something good?"

"No. Something *great*," I say. "It's from Nate. An invitation to a movie premiere next Thursday night. It's animated, and he did one of the voices in it. He says it's dumb."

"A school night?" Mom asks.

"Well, yeah, but, Mom . . . this is like a once-in-a-lifetime opportunity. Nate Etan wants us to go with him!" I hand her the note, printed in those same, barely legible letters.

> Sophie,
>   Looking for dates for this premiere—can you and your friends make it? I've got eight extra tickets, so invite whoever you want. Let me know.
>   Nate

Mom hands it back to me, unimpressed. "He's not going to make you watch his dog again, is he?"

"So I can go, right?"

"I'll talk to your dad."

Whew! I *know* Dad will let me go. When I remind him what a good customer of the restaurant Nate is, he'll have no choice.

• • •

The night of the premiere arrives at last. Margaret, Becca, Leigh Ann, and I leave our red blazers at home, because tonight we are the Red *Carpet* Girls. The limo doors swing open in front of the theater, and we do our best to look graceful as we crawl out. First to hit the carpet are Nate and Rebecca, who has declared herself to be his "official date" for the night. Next out is Cam Peterson, who takes Leigh Ann's arm in his, followed by *my* date, the dashing Rafael Arocho. He reaches into the limo and takes my hand, and suddenly I just can't stop smiling, smiling, smiling.

And finally, Margaret and Mbingu, whose fathers' attitudes about dating are strikingly (and tragically) similar, join us as we prepare for the long walk down the red carpet.

But wait! I forgot someone. My newest friend steps out of the limo and smiles at me.

"This is *so* cool," she says.

I take her by the hand and we start down the carpet. "Get used to it, Livvy. This is just a typical day in the life of a Red Blazer Girl."

Read an excerpt from the Red Blazer Girls' next mystery!

Available from
Alfred A. Knopf
Books for Young Readers

One does not argue with Fate, the Red Blazer Girls Code, or Andrew Jackson

I'm peeking through an opening in the threadbare velvet curtain that leads into the tiny storefront parlor of Madame Zurandot, who, according to the flashing neon sign in the window, is both PSYCHIC! *and* CLAIRVOYANT! Two of my fellow wearers-of-the-red-blazer, Rebecca Chen and Leigh Ann Jaimes, look over my shoulders and nudge me inside.

"I can't believe we're doing this. Maybe it's not such a good—" I say as four hands give me a final push. A combination of smells, none of them particularly pleasant, greets me: vanilla incense, mothballs, and, somewhere in the distance, slow-cooking cabbage. Before me is a small round table that looks exactly as I had imagined it would. Seriously, Madame Zurandot has a crystal ball.

"Can I help you?" a voice asks from behind another curtain.

Gulp.

• • •

Ten minutes earlier, the three of us had been enjoying a chilly December Saturday in Manhattan, doing
a little Christmas shopping and dreaming of the long
school vacation, just two weeks away. On most Sat-
urdays, Leigh Ann (the beautiful, graceful one) had
dance class, and Becca (talented, artistic) had art lessons, but they were both on break until January. Only
Margaret Wrobel (genius, absolute best friend in the
world) had plans; besides being the smartest person
I know, she's also a future violin superstar and takes
lessons from my mom every Saturday, rain or shine,
vacation or no vacation.

I spotted it first, a microsecond before Rebecca but
enough to beat her to it. Lying there on the sidewalk in
front of Madame Zurandot's, folded neatly in fourths,
was a twenty-dollar bill!

"Well, hello, Mr. Jackson," I said, unfolding it and
holding it up to make sure it was the genuine article.

"Sophie St. Pierre, you are the luckiest person I
know," said Leigh Ann. "I don't think I've ever found
a quarter."

"What should we do with it?" I asked. "I mean, it's
found money. We have to spend it."

"You could buy lunch," Rebecca suggested. "I'm
getting hungry."

Leigh Ann shook her head. "No, you should spend

it on something for yourself. Or for Raf."

Raf—as in Rafael Arocho—is my boyfriend-who-I'm-not-allowed-to-call-a-boyfriend-until-I'm-sixteen.

"No, no, no," protested Rebecca. "Absolutely not. The rules in this situation are clear: if you find money when you're with other Red Blazer Girls, the money must be shared."

"What rules?" Leigh Ann asked. "You're making that up."

"Actually, she's right," I admitted. "And it's even my rule. Last summer, before you started hanging out with us, I found a five in the park one day—"

"What! You found a five, and now a twenty! That is *so* not fair," said Leigh Ann.

I shrugged. "I can't help it. It just . . . happens. But I told Margaret and Becca that it was only right to share. The Red Blazer Girls Code, I guess."

"I have an idea," said Becca, pointing at the sign in Madame Zurandot's window. "First visit, twenty dollars. It's fate. We have to do it."

"A psychic? Are you crazy?" I said.

"What, you don't believe in them?" Becca asked.

"I, uh, no. Yeah, no. I mean, I'm not sure. Margaret says it's a bunch of hooey."

"Oh, jeez. I should have known," Becca scoffed. "So what if Miss Scientific Method doesn't believe. How often do you have a chance like this? Even Margaret would have to admit that having twenty bucks drop out of the sky the exact moment that you're standing in front of a sign that says FIRST CONSULTATION $20 is just . . . I mean, what are the odds?"

I had to admit, she had something there.

"Okay, but we don't tell Margaret. She'd be so disappointed."

"You have a serious problem," said Becca.

I didn't disagree.

A young woman—twenty at most, and dressed in jeans and a Lady Gaga T-shirt—appears from behind the curtain. Not at all what I'm expecting from a psychic. But then, maybe she knew that, and changed into those clothes just to catch me off guard. Pret-ty darn clever, these psychics.

"Hi," I say. "I, er, we were wondering if we could, you know, get a, um, reading. But if you're not . . . ready, we can come back later."

"Oh, yer lookin' for Ma," she says, laughing. "She's the psychic. Have a seat. I'll get her for ya." She goes back through the curtain. "Ma! Ya got cust-a-muhz!"

My eyes dart nervously from Becca to Leigh Ann to the ominous-looking crystal ball as we wait for Madame Zurandot.

"You should go first, Becca," I say. "It was your idea."

"Yeah, but *you* found the money," she says. "And I don't think she's going to tell all our fortunes for twenty bucks."

The curtain parts again and, following a dramatic pause, Madame Zurandot glides into the room as if she's on roller skates. (She's wearing a peasant skirt that drags on the floor, so, for all I know, she might actually be wearing skates.)

Without a word, she takes my fingers into her own cold, chapped hands and stares straight into my eyes for a full ten seconds without blinking. Then she closes her eyes and says, in an accent that I can't place, "I see a black dog running across an open field. You are trapped in a small room. And an old man with a cane, a man who is not who you thought he was, stands before a blue door with the number nine on it. And I see romance. . . . But wait! I see an enemy who becomes a friend, and a friend who becomes an enemy."

Okay, I'll admit it: I am freaking out as she finally breaks away from me and roughly grabs Leigh Ann's hands.

"Someone you love—someone who is far, far away—is waving to you from a boat. You are kneeling on a cold stone floor in the dark, searching for something that has been hidden away for many years. A girl in a red coat hands you a message. . . . I see the letters, but I'm afraid I cannot read the words; it is in a language I do not understand."

Rebecca's turn. Madame Zurandot takes her hands into her own and squeezes so hard that Becca opens her eyes wide. "You are standing alone in the midst of great beauty—a museum, perhaps. There is a single window on one wall, and when you look through it, you see a dead man, facedown at his desk, his pen still in his hand."

She drops Becca's hands and slumps down into a chair, her eyes closed and palms flat on the table.

The three of us stand there for a long time, waiting for her to say or do something. It's getting awkward, and just as I'm about to clear my throat to remind her that we're still in the room, she suddenly blurts out, "Others seek the same treasure you do, and though your quest may become dangerous, you must not give up. Trust no one."

She opens her eyes and looks up at us, her face expressionless. "And that is all I see."

"Ummm . . . yeah," Becca says. "About those things you saw. Are those all things from the past? Or are they things that haven't happened yet?"

One corner of Madame Zurandot's mouth turns up into a half smile. "That is a question I cannot answer. Perhaps you will find more money on the sidewalk another day and you will return."

I feel my mouth fall wide open. "Wait. How did you—"

"Duh. She's psychic," says Becca, earning herself a slug in the arm.

"Look to the stars," adds Madame Zurandot mysteriously. "The answers are in the stars."

• • •

Back in our neighborhood, the East Nineties, Margaret meets us at the pizza shop, where, sadly, Blue Eyes has the day off. Becca and Leigh Ann are determined to tell her about our Madame Zurandot experience, even though I beg them not to. I'm outvoted, though, so all I can do is listen, cringing at every cheesy detail, and wait for Margaret to scold us for wasting twenty bucks on a psychic.

But the new and improved, open-minded Margaret just listens and laughs. "I'm sorry I missed that," she says, and I think she even means it.

"So, wait a second," I say. "You believe in psychics?"

"I never said that. I just wish I'd been there to see the looks on your faces when she said all that stuff."

"But what about what she said?" Leigh Ann asks.

Margaret shrugs. "It's interesting, but it still doesn't make me believe that she's really psychic. There's always another explanation. She could have recognized you guys from one of the stories in the paper about us. Or it could all just be a coincidence."

From the pizza shop, we walk down to Eighty-First Street, where there's a used-book store that Margaret wants to check out. With Christmas just around the corner, we decided to pool our money to buy a small present for our English teacher, Mr. Eliot. After all, this whole Red Blazer Girls thing got started in his classroom the day I saw Elizabeth Harriman's face in the church window, and even Becca (who is certain that he doesn't like her) has to admit that he's been a huge help to us. Since he's kind of—no, he's seriously—obsessed with Charles Dickens, we're looking for an old copy of one of Dickens's books, something a little more interesting than your basic paperback.

Before I tell you about the bookstore, however, there's something I have to confess: I absolutely love Manhattan in December.

The bookstore is so tiny that we're almost past it when we see the sign painted on the door:

STURM & DRANG BOOKS
RARE EDITIONS BOUGHT AND SOLD
MARCUS KLINGER, PROPRIETOR

One of those old-fashioned bells jangles when we go inside. The shop is maybe ten or twelve feet wide, and it is crammed—floor to ceiling, front to back—with old books, giving it that distinctive dusty-old-book smell.

Standing on the third step of an antique brass and wood ladder is a middle-aged man, mostly bald, peering at us over a pair of reading glasses. Because he's up so high, it's hard to tell just how tall he is, but he seems to be well over six feet with long, birdlike arms and legs.

"May I help you?" he asks, shelving the book he was reading. Not exactly friendly (which is what I expect of a bookstore owner), but not obviously hostile, either.

Leigh Ann, Becca, and I are suddenly struck mute, and look to Margaret to take charge, which she acknowledges with a sad shake of her head.

"Hi, yes, I hope so," she says. "We're looking for a gift for our English teacher. He's a huge fan of Charles Dickens, so we were hoping to find a nice old copy of *Great Expectations* or maybe *A Tale of Two Cities*. But we're open to other ideas if you don't have either of those."

The man climbs down from the ladder without a word and moves to an eye-level shelf in the center stack, from which he removes a single book.

He opens the cover, beautifully bound in coffee-colored leather, and turns to us. "Do you have a budget in mind?"

We look at Margaret, and I'm sure we're all thinking the same thing: please don't say something crazy, like a hundred bucks. I mean, I do like Mr. Eliot, but let's be reasonable.

"Um . . . twenty or twenty-five dollars?" she says.

"Twenty would be good," I say.

The man sighs loudly and returns the book to its place on the shelf. "I see." He moves to another shelf and pulls down a thin volume. "I have this copy of *A Christmas Carol*—I assume you've heard of it. It's forty dollars, but I could let you have it for thirty-five. That's the best I can do."

"Can I see it?" Margaret asks.

Another sigh as he holds out the book. "Your hands are clean?"

Margaret glares at him, horrified, before snatching it from his hands.

He doesn't apologize; in fact, he seems completely oblivious. "Gilt edge. Calf binding. It's a reprint, an American edition, of course. A bargain at thirty-five dollars."

Margaret hands it back to him. "We'll think about it." She takes me by the arm and practically drags me out the door, with Becca and Leigh Ann on our heels.

"Man, what a loser," Becca announces as the door slams shut behind her.

"I was gonna call him something a lot worse than that," says Leigh Ann. "We have a word for people like him in Queens." She pauses, then continues, smiling to herself, "Actually, we have a lot of words for people like that."

"Tell me he didn't really ask you if your hands were clean," I say.

"Oh, he asked, all right," Margaret says. "And if that book is worth thirty-five dollars, I'm Cleopatra, queen of the Nile. It's a cheap knockoff that you can find anywhere for seven ninety-nine."

"Begging your paaaardon, miss," says Becca, mocking Mr. Klinger. "That's a genuine turtle-skin binding. The paper was made from leftover bits of wood from Noah's ark, and the ink was brewed from a baby bald eagle's blood."

"What kind of names are 'Sturm' and 'Drang,' anyway?" Leigh Ann asks, looking back at the door. "I wonder which one he was."

"They're not names," says Margaret. "It's German. It means 'storm and stress.' I think Goethe—he was a German writer—was involved somehow."

"Well, we can take a trip down to the Strand Book Store after school one day next week and look for Mr. Eliot's book there," I say. "They have everything, and they're not going to try to scam us. And besides, I have a list of books I want to buy, but can't afford them all if I get new ones."

"Or you could go to the library, like a normal person," says Margaret, who accuses me of having a compulsive book-buying disorder.

"You know, I don't think I've ever walked down this street before," I say. "Look at all those little shops on the other side. Let's go check them out—maybe I can find something for my dad."

"GW Antiques and Curiosities? Seriously? That's where you want to shop for your dad?" says Becca. "I'm not going in. Those places make me nervous."

"I know what you mean," Leigh Ann says. "I'm always afraid I'm going to knock over a stack of china plates that's worth a fortune."

I ignore their fears and run across the street, where I press my face against the front window and peek at the treasures inside. "Come on, you guys. It's not that crowded, and there's some cool old boat models and stuff."

As I step inside, I'm greeted by a woman who is probably in her thirties, but dressed like she's younger. Her hair is pulled back in a ponytail, and she's rocking a natural, almost-no-makeup look.

"Good morning, er, afternoon," she says, her eyes landing on the rock-star-cool jacket my parents surprised me with a few weeks back. "Wow. That is a great jacket."

She's right about that; it *is* pretty terrific. It's not really warm enough for mid-December, but I just can't bear to put it away until spring. If I have to suffer a little bit to look fashionable, so be it.

"Oh, thanks," I say. "It's my favorite."

The door opens and Margaret comes inside; a few seconds later, Leigh Ann and Becca follow reluctantly.

"Are you all together?" the woman asks. "Of course you are. I'm Lindsay. Is there anything in particular I can help you with today? Or are you just browsing— which is fine, too."

"I'm, um, kind of looking for a present for my dad," I say, eyeing an old wooden model boat hanging from the ceiling above me. "Wow. That is beautiful. He would love that."

"You have good taste," says Lindsay. "That's a Hacker model from 1935, with the original paint. It's twelve hundred dollars."

I hear Becca snickering behind me. "For twelve hundred bucks, I want a boat big enough to ride in, at least."

"That's a bit more than I want to spend," I say. "Maybe I'll look around a little."

I wander over to a display case containing an assortment of items: cuff links of every shape and size, a couple of gold pocket watches, wicked-looking straight razors, engraved cigarette lighters, money clips, and much more. And then I see the perfect gift for my dad.

"Margaret, come here," I whisper. "Do you see it?"

She leans over the case, her eyes scanning the contents until they land on an antique fountain pen. She grins at me. "You're right. It's perfect. Can you see the price?"

"Do you see something you like?" Lindsay asks, moving behind the case. When she realizes which case we're looking in, her face falls. "Oh, this case is . . . special. These are things from the estate of a gentleman who lived in the neighborhood, a Mr. Dedmann. Unfortunately, they're not for sale—not in the usual way, that is. They're all going to an auction next Tuesday afternoon. Which piece are you interested in, one of the Cartier watches?"

"No, the fountain pen," I say. "Can I see it?"

Lindsay unlocks the case and sets the pen on a felt pad on top of the glass. As I lift it, I smile at the heft of the thing: it is about as far from the cheap disposable pens I use as you can get. The rounded barrel is polished black, sleek and smooth, and the gold nib still looks new.

"It's a beauty," says Lindsay. "An old Reviens—made in France in the twenties. They've been out of business for years."

"How much is it worth?" I ask.

Lindsay smiles. "Well, that depends. If it were for sale here in the shop, Mr. W.—he's the owner, I just work for him—would probably ask two hundred dollars for it. But . . . if you were to buy it at the auction, you might get it for a lot less. Depends on who else wants it. And how badly, I suppose."

"Like, how much less?" I ask.

"With something like this, the auctioneer will probably start the bidding at twenty-five dollars. After that . . ."

Margaret and I share one of our are-you-thinking-what-I'm-thinking? looks and grin at each other.

"So, tell us more about this auction."

About the Author

Michael D. Beil's first Red Blazer Girls installment, *The Ring of Rocamadour,* was hailed as "a PG *Da Vinci Code* . . . with a fun mystery, great friends, and a bit of romance" (*School Library Journal*). The second Red Blazer Girls mystery, *The Vanishing Violin,* was similarly lauded, with *Kirkus Reviews* saying, "The red blazer gals feel and act like real tweens while tackling everything that comes their way with logic, humor and refreshing savoir faire."

Mr. Beil, who teaches English and helms the theater program at New York City high school, has, in his own words, "too many hobbies to count." When he's not teaching or writing, he loves reading, skiing, sailing, cooking, playing cello, and hiking—including climbing Mount Kilimanjaro. He finds literary inspiration in everything from classic films to Charles Dickens to that beloved barrister, Horace Rumpole.

In a starred review, *Booklist* called for "more Red Blazer Girls, please!" Mr. Beil, never one to disappoint, is pleased to continue the series with a fourth adventure in the works (this one Christmas-themed).

He and his wife, Laura Grimmer, share their Manhattan home with dogs Isabel and Maggie and cats Cyril and Emma.

YEARLING MYSTERY!

Looking for more great mystery books to read? Check these out!

- ❑ *The Case of the Cool-Itch Kid*
  by Patricia Reilly Giff

- ❑ ENCYCLOPEDIA BROWN SERIES
  by Donald J. Sobol

- ❑ *Harriet the Spy*
  by Louise Fitzhugh

- ❑ I SO DON'T DO . . . SERIES
  by Barrie Summy

- ❑ *Key to the Treasure*
  by Peggy Parish

- ❑ *Last Shot* by John Feinstein

- ❑ *Mudshark* by Gary Paulsen

- ❑ *The Mysteries of Spider Kane*
  by Mary Pope Osborne

- ❑ NATE THE GREAT SERIES
  by Marjorie Weinman Sharmat

- ❑ *Nightmare*
  by Joan Lowery Nixon

- ❑ OLIVIA SHARP:
  AGENT FOR SECRETS SERIES
  by Marjorie Weinman Sharmat

- ❑ THE RED BLAZER GIRLS SERIES
  by Michael D. Beil

- ❑ SAMMY KEYES SERIES
  by Wendelin Van Draanen

- ❑ *The Séance* by Iain Lawrence

- ❑ *The White Gates*
  by Bonnie Ramthun

Visit **www.randomhouse.com/kids** for additional reading suggestions
in fantasy, adventure, humor, and nonfiction!